A DARKENING OF THE HEART

MARGARET THOMSON
DAVIS

A DARKENING
of the HEART

B&W PUBLISHING

First published 2004
by B&W Publishing Ltd
99 Giles Street, Edinburgh EH6 6BZ

ISBN 1 903265 13 4

Copyright © Margaret Thomson Davis 2004

British Library Cataloguing in Publication Data:
A catalogue record for this book is available from
the British Library

Cover illustration:
Detail from *Robert Burns, 1796/98 (chalk)*
by Archibald Skirving *(1749-1819)*

Photograph courtesy of the
Scottish National Portrait Gallery, Edinburgh.

Printed and bound by ScandBook AB

I

Susanna's brother came over to stand beside her at the tiny, deep-set window.

'There he goes.' Half laughing, Alexander shook his head. 'Swaggering along as if he owned the village.'

'And look at his hair,' Susanna said eyeing the jet-black head in scorn. 'He's the only man in the parish who keeps his hair long and tied back like that.'

'They tell me he can be quite a danger to himself and others at times.'

Susanna looked round, startled. 'Really? In what way?'

'Working on the farm – with some of the sharp implements they use, I suppose. The other farm servants and his brother, Gilbert, have to keep an eye on him.'

'Well, I declare! What does he do?'

'He sometimes loses concentration, apparently. He goes about in a dream muttering and humming tunes to himself.'

'Gracious heavens! Is he mad then?'

'Actually, Robert Burns is the only intelligent man worth talking to for miles around. He'll just have been thinking about his Bachelors' Club and practising what he's going to say. He's the one who started the Club and makes up the subjects of debate. He'll be on his way there now. I'd better be going. If it wasn't for that Club, I'd die of boredom here.'

Boredom? Her brother didn't know the meaning of the word, Susanna thought bitterly. All she could do was to cling

1

to a desperate dream of escaping from the confines of her father's dark dungeon of a house. Her dream was of marrying one of the gentry who owned a spacious dwelling and a large estate around which she could stroll with freedom and leisure. She spent a great deal of time in her head imagining the house or even the castle she would live in. She saw the light of many chandeliers blazing in every room and corridor. She saw a long table sparkling with silverware and laden with delicious food. There would be many large vases of flowers. She smelled the sweet fragrance of the place. She would have many servants, of course, who would bow and curtsey to her.

Alexander had been educated in Paris and he'd done his medical training in Leydon. Even now he was able to get out and around far more than her. Like their doctor father, he regularly consulted with patients in the crowded taverns of Tarbolton, where he prescribed for them over a pint of ale or a glass of whisky. Or he sat alone in a corner of the tavern conscientiously working at his poetry. Susanna often thought that, for all his medical training, his heart was more in his poetry than in his doctoring. Alexander was a very clever and artistic man.

Unfortunately she had not been blessed with any literary talent that could help take her mind off her dreary situation. Most of the time she was stuck in the narrow, gloomy rooms of the house where candles needed to be kept lit for most of the day. Although they weren't always lit when needed, or never enough. Her mother was mean with candles and often they had to sit crushed up against the window to get enough light to do their embroidery.

As well as the depressing darkness, the air was heavy with the stench from the cupboard of a room where her father mixed his potions. No wonder they made such an abominable stink. The potions were made of ingredients which included excrement of horse, dog, pig and other animals. He also used bodies of frogs and juice of wood lice, not forgetting snails, worms, vipers, leeches, human blood, fat and urine.

2

Her brother and her father were always arguing about physicking. Alexander had lots of modern ideas. Her father pooh-poohed them and the patients were suspicious of them. They didn't trust Alexander's unfamiliar ways. His father's ideas and methods were still the most popular and accepted. As a result, most people preferred the older man to attend to them. It was terribly frustrating for Alexander but he had always his poetry writing to turn to and he frequently did. Often he lost himself in writing late into the night by the light of a candle. He was a very hard worker and a most conscientious man. His poetry alone gave him a more fulfilling life than his young sister's.

The only thing that kept her sane was her dreams. She kept trying to imagine a handsome young man of quality who would rescue her from her present predicament, someone as marvellously handsome as the ploughman – but a man of wealth and quality.

She had been quite shaken the first time she'd seen the farm worker close up. He had stepped aside to allow her to pass in the street. But not before she'd met his eyes, glowing darkly under black brows. It was only for a second or two, but she experienced such a strange sensation dart through her, a kind of sizzling that flew from his eyes to hers. Neither on that first encounter nor on the second had he smiled. She'd remarked to Alexander about what a serious fellow he was.

Her father had been there at the time, and he'd said, 'Och aye, the whole family's awful serious. Of course, it's hard grinding work on that farm. They've nothing tae smile aboot. Ah mind that young dominie that used to teach the older boys and some of the other farmers' sons. He telt me that even at meal times, that family always sat in solemn silence with a book in one hand and their spoon in the other. Especially the eldest boy. He even takes a book with him when he's working in the fields.'

Alexander said, 'I mentioned the Bachelors' Club to Lord Morton the other day and he said, "Oh, it was started by that staring kind of fellow, wasn't it?".'

'That sums him up quite well,' Susanna agreed. 'I've never seen such dark, piercing eyes.'

Alexander shrugged. 'But I can tell you he's also the life and soul of the Club.'

'Who's Lord Morton?' Susanna asked hopefully. 'Is he young like us?'

'He's from the other side of Ayr. I met his son in Leydon. He died of an infection. The best doctors in the world there couldn't save him. The old man likes to keep in touch with me because I knew his son.'

Susanna gave a deep sigh which her father and brother took to be in sympathy for either the deceased or the grieving father. Susanna, however, was sighing in sympathy with herself. The only gentry for miles around, it seemed, were elderly men. Most of them were patients of her father's, men with old-fashioned velvet coats, long, heavily-embroidered waistcoats and powdered, full-bottomed wigs.

The only glimmer of hope on the horizon was the fact that she had been promised another visit to Edinburgh in the not too distant future. At least there a cheerful bustle of all types of people, rich and poor, could be viewed from her grandmother's window. She would be seventeen by the time of her next visit and her grandmother had promised to take her to a dancing assembly. Perhaps her grandmother would find a suitable partner for her. Her mother wasn't much use. She suffered from a variety of indispositions that had to be treated with leeches. She needed to be near her husband most of the time to make sure of proper attention.

Alexander would accompany Susanna to Edinburgh. Through him she might have an even better chance of mixing with the 'quality'. Alexander knew his way around Edinburgh and was already acquainted with some of the literati.

Alexander enjoyed reading his verses to his grandmother and grandfather and some of their friends and they were all, including herself, most impressed. However, of the financial situation of the literati that Alexander knew, she wasn't sure.

She didn't want to put her life into the hands of a penniless poet either. She wanted and needed someone not only of quality, but of substance.

There must be plenty of that kind of person in the capital city. The thought of going there kept her spirits from sinking into an abyss of depression. It was a fascinating place where always something exciting was happening. Inside her grandparents' tenement flat in the High Street were six rooms, including the kitchen. The public rooms had signs of dignity and art with their elaborately stuccoed ceilings, finely carved massive marble mantelpiece and oak panelled walls. Grandfather Wallace had long since risen to the Bench and was now much respected (even feared by some) in the town.

He had a carriage but seldom used it, preferring the short walk to the court. He always put the carriage at the disposal of his wife, however, and she enjoyed going out to tea parties and card parties when she wasn't giving them herself. Susanna would have been quite happy to stay permanently in Edinburgh with her grandparents but her grandmother wouldn't hear of it.

'It's monstrous an' damnable of ye to even think of such a thing.'

Susanna had flown into a pretty passion of annoyance.

'Why should it be? Don't you want me? Is that it? I did not realise I was so unwelcome in Edinburgh.'

'Of course ye're welcome but it wud be insultin' an' disloyal to yer poor mither an' yer faither to tell them ye prefer ma hoose to theirs. Now stop yer silly clitter clatter. Compose yersel' an' tell wee Sissie to bring in the tea.'

Her grandmother was a formidable woman who punctuated her often caustic remarks with a big pinch of snuff. Sometimes she shocked Susanna by even voicing oaths. She had high-dressed hair, and a regal carriage. Her back was as stiff as her stomacher, and she always sat bolt upright, without ever touching the back of the chair. She had many friends who came to visit, despite being in constant danger of feeling the lash of her tongue. They could all give as good as they got, according to Alexander. Susanna agreed and was full of admiration for these elderly Edinburgh women.

Even to be occasionally shocked by them was exciting and far better than being in boring Tarbolton. The people of Tarbolton and the surrounding countryside were just plain coarse. They still spoke broad Scots, for instance, including her father and mother. Whereas everyone who wanted to be cultured and fashionable had learned to speak pure English.

Her mother said now, 'Come away frae the window, Anna. You're blockin' oot the light.'

Before she turned irritably back into the low-ceilinged coffin of a room (it always irritated her when her parents called her Anna), she saw Alexander making his way along the road, his three-cornered hat perched on top of his short, thick hair. His long coat flicked open in the breeze and his silver buckles glistened. In Edinburgh, he always wore a wig, but here he had just powdered his own hair. In Tarbolton it didn't matter. Nothing mattered here.

How she envied him and his Bachelors' Club. She wished she had somewhere interesting and stimulating to attend. She flopped into a chair near the fire and stared gloomily at it.

'Whit's up wi' ye noo?' her mother asked. 'Ye've been gey ill-humoured of late.'

Susanna gazed round at the pinched, hollow-cheeked face of her mother.

'Is it any wonder?'

'Aye, it is.'

'We never *do* anything or *go* anywhere.'

'It was only yesterday we went to tea with Mrs Douglas.'

Susanna rolled her eyes.

'Mrs Douglas!'

'An' whit's wrong wi' Mrs Douglas?'

'She talks about nothing but her jaundice. It makes me sick – never mind her.'

'Ye wicked girl! Ah hope for your sake folks'll be more

6

sympathetic to you when yer time comes.'

'What? My time for jaundice and all the other ailments Mrs Douglas complains of, you mean? God forbid!'

'Aye, well, God'll no' forbid. He'll no' forget either. Jist you wait till you're ages wi' me and poor Mistress Douglas.'

'Oh Mother, there's got to be more to life than that.'

'Och aye, of course.' Her mother's voice softened. 'Ye'll marry a nice laddie one day and settle in a wee house o' yer ain, an' have lots o' bairns. You'll see.'

'Mother, I'm nearly seventeen and I haven't met one decent man yet. Not one.'

'Ye've time enough, lassie. And there's plenty o' laddies around. Alexander's sure to ken some hard-working, decent laddie. Ah'll ask yer faither to have a word wi' him.'

The hard-working ploughman her mother meant, no doubt. Susanna experienced a frisson of panic. No thank you. Certainly, definitely not!

'Perhaps Grandmother or Grandfather may introduce me to someone in Edinburgh.'

'Aye, well, we'll see. But oor Alexander should be first. It's time he settled wi' a nice lassie.'

Oh yes, Susanna thought. Alexander always comes first. No doubt he'll find himself a young lady from the gentry and get an 'in' to proper society. She couldn't help being slightly cheered by the thought. If that happened, it might give her an 'in' as well. She was ready to cling to any hope – however small. Anything to get her out of the mouldy, stinking, narrow-minded, kirk-fearing village of Tarbolton.

2

Alexander picked his way carefully along the street. Unlike most of the men who would be at the Club, wearing boots of one kind or another, his slim feet were clad in silver-buckled shoes. He shrank from the everyday wearing of boots. They were so clod-like and clumsy – except for riding, of course, when they were part of the proper apparel. He was thankful that the Bachelors' Club was not far from his father's house. He rounded the corner of the street and there it was, next to the tavern. The tavern keeper lived in the bottom room of the thatched roofed cottage. The room above it was the meeting place of the Club and was reached by an outside stair.

There was excited conversation already buzzing around the room when he arrived, sparked off as usual by Burns. The man's excitement was infectious. The worst dullard could be stirred by it. Alexander's medical instincts occasionally whispered to him that the almost feverish excitement in Burns' glowing eyes and general demeanour was not quite normal. He wondered if it could be the symptom of some medical condition. He always succeeded in banishing such suspicions, however, and in enjoying the evening.

It was more than likely that the grim life Robert Burns had as a farm worker during and since childhood depressed the young man's spirits so much and he was so wildly glad to break free of this oppression, he soared to unusual heights of happiness and joy.

He certainly was afire with what looked like sheer unadulterated joy while he presided over his Bachelors' Club. The subject for debate this evening, he announced, was this:

Suppose a young man, bred a farmer but without any fortune, has it in his power to marry either of two women – the one a girl of large fortune, but neither handsome in person nor agreeable in conversation, but who can manage the household affairs of a farm well enough; the other of them a girl every way agreeable in person, conversation and behaviour, but without any fortune. Which of them should he choose?

Alexander argued strongly in favour of the girl with the large fortune. It was only prudent, and sensible, and indeed common practice, for a man of no fortune to acquire one in this way. Burns fought on the side of the imprudent. It was a lively debate which Alexander enjoyed. Then the subject of future debates was discussed. All of the subjects were proposed by Burns. A favourite and one of the most lively was: 'Whether do we deserve more happiness from love or friendship'.

In some Alexander could detect the influence of Rousseau:

'Whether is the savage man or the peasant in a civilised country in the most happy condition' or 'Whether is a young man of the lower ranks of life likeliest to be happy, when he has just got a good education and his mind well-informed, or he who has just the education and information of those around him'.

Alexander always suspected that many of the subjects revealed aspects of the problems in Burns' own life, a man whose knowledge, education and intelligence were far beyond his fellow farm workers and any of the young men of the village.

The rules of the Club were impossible in a way. They were so idealistic, Alexander doubted if many of the ordinary lads could live up to the ideals for long. The tenth and last paragraph of the list of rules and regulations summed them all up, especially when delivered with such joyous pride from the magnetic centre of the sparkling-eyed Burns.

> Every man proper for a member of this Society must have a frank, honest, open heart; above everything dirty or mean; and must be a professed lover of one or more of the female sex. No haughty or self-conceited person, who looks upon himself as superior to the rest of the Club; especially no mean-spirited, worldly mortal, whose only will is to heap up money, shall upon any pretext whatever be admitted. In short, the proper person for this society is a cheerful, honest-hearted lad, who, if he has a friend that is true and a mistress that is kind, and as much wealth as genteelly to make both ends meet, is just as happy as this world can make him.

It struck Alexander as showing a touching naivety of the world, even of this small corner of the world which was Tarbolton. Here fornication was an everyday occurrence and the resulting fire and abomination lectures in the kirk a delight in the otherwise dull lives of most of the congregation. The church was always packed when someone had to sit in the cutty stool or stand to be shamed – in great detail – by one of the elders or the minister. Other sins were ignored, Alexander noticed. Only acts of a sexual nature were picked on by the church and gone over with what looked like triumphant glee.

Excessive drinking was regarded as something to be proud of, rather than the reverse. Never in any other country had Alexander witnessed such regular scenes of total debauchery. Even his own father didn't feel he'd had a good evening with friends if he wasn't carried home unconscious by his servant. Men continued drinking until they slid under the table and there was always a servant whose special duty it was to loose the neckerchief in case the gentleman choked.

As far as the Bachelors' Club was concerned, when the business of the evening was exhausted, the members drank 'a common toast to the mistresses of the Club' before parting.

No debauchery there. Although Alexander suspected that after he and Burns left, some of the others may have returned to the tavern to continue toasting other ladies. Or anyone else they could think of.

Burns had quite a long trek home and then had to be up at some God-forsaken hour in the morning. As they strolled along for a few minutes together, they'd talk, usually about the Club. Burns said, 'I believe the Club should serve to promote mutual understanding, strengthen and expand the common intellectual interests of its members.'

Alexander agreed but not without a frisson of secret amusement when he thought of some of the members who were far less serious-minded than young Burns, couldn't even talk in the pure English that Burns could so easily adopt on formal occasions, and had far less lofty ideals. He kept thinking of his companion as 'young Burns' but in fact he was twenty-one, only a couple of years younger than Alexander himself. They parted with the usual firm handshake and Alexander turned, suddenly disconsolate, into the shadow of his father's house.

Robert's company was always so exhilarating that it tended to leave one exhausted afterwards. Right from the start he had made a rallying cry of holding fast to what were accepted as the highest ideals of Club life, which aimed at improving humanity, and to avoid 'all excesses, extravagances and follies, the end of which is guilt and misery'. It was interesting to observe how excessive and extravagant in mood and personality the man was who so eagerly proposed these ideals. Alexander knew he was thinking like a doctor and a student of human nature again but that, for better or for worse, was exactly what he was. And despite his comparative lack of experience in practising his art, he knew without a doubt that he was a much better doctor than his father.

He was a talented poet too. It was another reason he was glad of his friendship with Robert Burns. Robert had penned some verse. All of it he'd seen so far had been inspired by some maid or other that he'd either fallen in love with or felt slighted by.

Even as a child of fourteen, he'd been ruled by his emotions, it seemed.

Apparently he'd heard a song that a son of one of the local gentry had written to a girl he was in love with and Burns thought he could at least equal this effort.

Burns was touchy about the gentry. He had been infuriated by a rich girl sweeping past him with head in the air without deigning to cast him a glance. Alexander had smiled at one of the verses he'd penned as a result.

> There lives a lass beside yon park
> I'd rather hae her in her sark (*shirt or chemise*)
> Than you wi' a' your thousand marks
> That gars you look sae high –

Susanna was sitting by one of the candles trying to stitch something. She looked up and greeted him pertly.

'And how was your precious Bachelors' Club?'

'Very well indeed.'

'And your ploughman friend?'

'As entertaining as ever. I marvel at the man. He even writes poetry. How he finds the time and energy, I do not know.'

'He writes poetry?' Susanna echoed. 'Gracious heaven! What kind of poetry?'

Alexander shrugged. 'There was one about the sorrows of being a farmer but mostly his poems are inspired by women, as far as I can see. He strikes me as a very emotional man. Almost to an unhealthy degree.'

'Why don't you ply him with one of your magic potions?'

'Magic? God forbid! You've been in a very ill humour of late, Susanna. Perhaps it's you who needs a potion.'

'I feel cruelly confined, that's all. I can't wait for the day when we leave for the capital city.'

'We must be patient until the spring and the better weather. The roads are too dangerous at this time of year.'

'Fiddlesticks! I'm sure coaches are still managing to get through.'

'You know what Mother is like. She'd worry herself to death if we attempted the journey just now. Anyway, both Mother and Father are looking forward to us bringing in the New Year as a family. I've been away for so many years. Where are Mother and Father, by the way?'

'Mother is abed sound asleep after taking one of Father's potions. Father has not yet returned from the tavern.'

'And the servants?'

'If you want a dram, Alexander, you'll have to serve yourself. I think Mysie must have taken some of Mother's potion. And John will be waiting at the tavern to carry Father home.'

He could well understand his sister's impatience to be away from here. He felt depression weigh down on him with the fetid gloom of the place. He didn't know how he'd last out to the spring himself. More and more he was thinking of moving permanently to Edinburgh. There was no future for him in Tarbolton. Not while his father was alive and practising medicine. Even after his father's demise, he suspected the locals would still avoid him and prefer even old wives who meddled in herbs and spells to him and his different and more advanced methods and ideas.

No, Edinburgh was the place. While he was on this next visit with Susanna, he'd have a look around for lodgings and find out what his prospects might be in practising medicine in the city. It was time he was looking around for a suitable wife too. He and Robert had discussed this and Robert had agreed that it was time they both were married to a good woman.

Already, of course, he had an eye on what might prove a good prospect. Charlotte, her name was. Charlotte Guthrie. He had attended her grandfather, old Lord Guthrie – a cantankerous, overweight old widower much plagued with the gout. He still managed to go to church, though, helped by a cluster of sweating servants. He was a great admirer of one

13

particular minister who, he said, could 'dung the guts out o' five Bibles'.

His granddaughter, Charlotte – or Lottie as the old man called her – was an only child. Her father had died of smallpox and she was now the sole heir and beneficiary of the Guthrie estate. Old Guthrie was a sociable man (any excuse to drink to excess) and there was to be a big celebration at his home at New Year. The Wallace family had been invited. Alexander toyed with the idea of proposing to Charlotte on that occasion. Or should he wait until after his expedition to Edinburgh? There were several wealthy young ladies of his grandmother's acquaintance who had already been impressed by his poetry readings. One of these ladies might prove a more attractive alternative. He would look into the matter further before making up his mind.

It might be that he could also do something in the matrimonial way for his sister. It was obvious that she needed a husband to keep her unruly spirit in check.

Yes, he must think about that too. He felt slightly cheered as he lifted a candle and groped his way carefully to bed.

3

Susanna tried to feel some enthusiasm about the coming Hogmanay celebrations at the house of Lord Guthrie. In her imagination she saw herself meeting some handsome young man of fortune who was also a guest of the old lord. The word 'old' always succeeded in dissolving her dream. She had been at the Guthrie manor house before. Her mother and father had taken her to dinner there on more than one occasion.

The other dinner guests had always been of the same generation either of her parents or of the ancient lord. His grand-daughter, Charlotte, was in her twenties and even more uninteresting than Lord Guthrie. A quiet-spoken girl, she was obviously intimidated by her roaring bull of a grandfather – even though much of his roaring was good humoured. What a noisy, ill-mannered, coarse brute of a creature he was. Probably Charlotte was more embarrassed by him than anything else.

'Even I suffer agonies of embarrassment,' Susanna complained to her mother.

'Oh tuts, ye make such a drama out of everything, Anna. He's really a good-natured, generous soul and he adores Lottie.'

'Well, I'm much surprised to hear that, Mother. I pity the poor wretch.'

'Poor wretch indeed! What stuff an' nonsense ye talk!'

Susanna had nearly added, 'She's in an even worse situation than I am,' but thought better of it. For one thing, she wasn't totally convinced that it was true. At least Charlotte had many high-ceilinged rooms in which to escape from her tormentor, and beautiful gardens and grounds to wander in and take pleasure from. She had also obsequious and attentive servants at her beck and call.

Here Mysie and her husband John were good enough workers – John searched out and kept her father supplied with most of the requisites for his potions. Mysie did all the cooking and cleaning. But they could be very awkward, or 'thrawn' as her mother would say. At times, they were downright impertinent.

Susanna longed for a capable personal servant who could help her to dress and do her auburn hair, or powder her wig. More often than not, she had to struggle with everything herself or depend on her mother to help her.

At least Alexander was more knowledgeable and sophisticated. He knew about fashion, for instance, and had bought her several fashion dolls from France and Holland. She had managed to get an Edinburgh mantua maker to stitch up a couple of gowns. One was a copy of a French doll, the other of a Dutch doll. She was wearing the Dutch outfit for the Guthrie New Year celebration. Her powdered wig was decorated with small wax flowers. Around her neck was a pretty frill of the same material as the gown. The floral patterned gown had a low square neckline, tight elbow-length sleeves with a double lace frill, and a wide skirt that flounced out over ample panniers.

Susanna had ordered Mysie to bring as many candles into the bedroom as possible so that she could view herself in the long mirror. Mysie, however, had been in one of her moods and no extra candles had appeared. Susanna had to go herself to purloin a candelabra from her father's medicine room.

Now she viewed herself with some satisfaction. She was prettier than Charlotte. As well as even features and a pert, slightly turned-up nose, she had sparkling eyes and an aura of vivacity. Charlotte was so depressingly dull.

Susanna wasn't in the least looking forward to the evening. All that drinking and falling about and the bawling of 'Happy New Year' at the first peel of the church bells. What was going to be so happy about it, that's what she'd like to know. Except the proposed visit to Edinburgh, of course.

'Come away, come away.' Her mother fussed into the room and out again. 'Lord Guthrie has sent his carriage. We must not keep it waiting.'

'Why not?' Susanna felt like asking, but didn't. The whole thing was such a waste of time. At best it would be an ordeal that had to be endured with as much dignity as she could muster. Head held high, she swept out of the house and into the carriage beside her mother, father and brother.

Alexander said, 'You look charming, Susanna.'

'Thank you, Alexander.' She favoured him with a smile. 'And you look a picture of fashion.'

He raised a protesting hand. 'In Tarbolton, perhaps. But I had this outfit made in England earlier this year and no doubt it will already have been superseded by something far more à la mode.'

She couldn't imagine it. He looked so stylish in his silk stock, purple brocade coat with high collar trimmed with braid, long matching waistcoat, velvet knee breeches, silk stockings and shiny leather shoes. She wished with all her heart that the coach was taking them to some fashionable ball in Edinburgh or one of the estates in the countryside, not too distant from the capital.

But it was not to be. The coach tumbled them about on rough roads and muddy paths until it drew up with much clatter of horses' hooves and snorting and whinnying. A couple of liveried footmen helped them out of the carriage and led them through the open doors of the house.

Usually the hall was a dark, depressing place with creaky wooden floors, panelled walls hung with stuffed heads of stags and other animals and a huge empty fireplace of rough stone. An oak chest stood against another wall, along with a grandfather clock.

This evening, however, a fire crackled and sparked and sent orange light dancing, enfeebling even the light of two large candelabra.

They were shown into the big drawing room, where Lord Guthrie's rotund figure descended eagerly upon them. There was a noisy rabble behind him, not in the least intimidated by the rows of Guthrie ancestors in heavy gilt frames glowering down on them from all sides. Even the curtains that stretched from ceiling to floor did nothing to lighten the walls. Embroidered with all sorts of exotic birds and trees, the material had darkened and in places begun to disintegrate with centuries of dust.

It was as Susanna had feared. The room was full of elderly men and old-fashioned dames. The exception was the dutiful Charlotte in a pink open gown with a line of brown bows down the tight bodice. She wore no rouge, making her complexion merge into the paleness of her powdered wig.

Susanna patiently suffered the bear hug of a welcome by Lord Guthrie. She was thinking what an annoying creature he was, disturbing her clothing and wig, and nearly suffocating her with the fumes of whisky. Why couldn't he behave in a more civilised manner like a gentleman was supposed to and simply bow and brush her hand with a light kiss?

Thankfully he soon turned his enthusiastic attention to his other guests and Susanna was left to be looked after by Charlotte.

'Susanna,' Charlotte murmured with downcast eyes.

'Charlotte. And with what delights have you been passing the time since we last met?'

'Grandfather takes up much of my attention, as you know. But I have enjoyed a few little outings with my cousin, who has been visiting from Edinburgh.'

'Oh really? I had not heard there was a stranger among us.'

Charlotte gave a little smile that somehow made Susanna feel annoyed. All right, the Guthrie house was some miles from Tarbolton, but visitors to the house had made forays into the village on previous occasions and the news had easily got around. She didn't like to miss anything, or worse, be made to feel foolish or ignorant.

'A gentleman, is it?'

Charlotte gave another little smile that Susanna took to be an affirmative but couldn't be sure.

'A young gentleman?' she pressed on, regardless of Charlotte's reluctance to chat.

Then Susanna realised that Charlotte wasn't listening to her. Charlotte's eyes had fixed on some point beyond her. Susanna turned and saw a man, perhaps in his early thirties, moving towards them. She felt a twinge of disappointment. In the first few moments during which she had been in Charlotte's company and heard about the cousin, her vivid imagination had rapidly formed a picture of a handsome young man who, as soon as he saw the much more beautiful Susanna, would immediately forget about paying court to his plain cousin, and would sweep her more attractive friend off her feet. They would fall passionately in love, and live happily ever after.

But the man was not handsome – at least not like the man of her dreams. He had a rather cruel face with scant brows, pale eyes and an unusually thin, tight line of a mouth. But his manners were impeccable. He bowed. He kissed their hands. He offered them an arm each to lead them into the dining hall for supper.

Alexander came and sat at the other side of Charlotte and immediately engaged her in pleasant conversation. 'He is being gentle in his manner to her, even enquiring about her health,' Susanna thought with amusement. Poor Alexander, he can never get away from being a doctor. And a very good doctor, she hastily assured herself. She believed in him even if no-one else did.

Charlotte's cousin was called Neil Guthrie and was the only surviving son of Lord Guthrie's late brother. She had always believed, and suspected everyone else had too, that

Charlotte was Lord Guthrie's only heir, but now it surely must be this cousin. Property and fortunes always went down through the male line of any family, as far as she had always heard or seen.

For the first time, Susanna's lively imagination began to compose pictures of herself as mistress of the Guthrie manor house and estate. She would have the whole place redecorated, of course, in brighter, more fashionable colours. And she'd have those dreadful curtains torn down. She could just see, almost feel, the suffocating cloud of dirt and dust that would come down with them and fill the room. She'd order the servants to fling open all the doors and windows and to fly about shaking their aprons and brooms to clear the air. She smiled to herself at the merry picture.

'Something amuses you, madam?' She was startled out of her dream. 'May I share it?'

She suddenly realised that to make the dream come true must involve the man who had just addressed her. She flushed.

'I am a foolish dreamer, sir. It was nothing.'

'A dreamer perhaps, madam. But foolish? I do not believe it. I judge you to be a most intelligent young lady.'

She laughed. 'Thank you, kind sir.'

She tried to persuade herself that he was, after all, quite good-looking. He certainly was very charming and well-mannered. She liked that. Despite his calculating eyes and thin mouth, she began to feel quite warm towards him. Perhaps, of course, her melting emotions were helped on their way by the glasses of wine she was enjoying. Anyway, she was fast coming to the conclusion that Neil Guthrie might, after all, be quite a good catch. Her eyes began sparkling invitingly in his direction. She laughed and giggled appreciatively at his every bon mot or funny story about the antics of his servants or dullards of his acquaintance. She began to feel that there was a strength about him that she could admire. Even although at the same time it betrayed a streak of ruthlessness.

The midnight hour was almost upon them and, a merry

bunch now, they filled their glasses with whisky and hurried out into the hall where the large golden hand of the grandfather clock was clicking and jerking away the seconds.

Then on the stroke of twelve, everyone cried out 'Happy 1781' and raised their glasses. Susanna felt quite giddy with it all, with the alcohol and with her new-found interest and excitement. It was all mixed up with her wild imaginings. She could never quite remember if she'd fainted or if Neil Guthrie had kissed her, or if both events had taken place.

But in the end there was no doubt that it was her brother's strong arms that led her away and delivered her, after a horrendous coach ride home, into the not very tender care of Mysie.

'Drunk as an auld fishwife,' the servant bawled. 'An' Ah'll warrant yer auld mither'll be the same. Well, tae hell wi' her! Once Ah've got you put doon, Ah'm goin' tae ma bed.'

Then Susanna remembered no more.

4

Dawn's pale light slowly brought life to the farm. Robert heard the impatient crowing of the rooster alerting the farmyard to the break of day. His breath misted gently in the crisp cold. His feet crunched through a thin glaze of ice that rimmed the puddles dotted across the muddy farmyard.

His mind was far away from his bleak surroundings. He was thinking first of all of the book in his pocket that he had fallen asleep reading the night before. He was never without a book – night or day. Books were his closest companions. Digging his calloused hands deep into the hay bale, he grunted as he swung it up on to the rack in front of the stalls, pushing the eager heads away as he tried to spread the feed down to allow the beasts access. Watching them, he sighed. Come spring, they were usually so weak they had to be carried out.

He gave one of them a pat on the head before turning away. Soon he was lost in thought again, working automatically, even as he strained himself to his physical limits. He thought of his father, for whom he had a great deal of respect, as well as love. He could not look on his father's tall, gaunt figure and proud, stern face without his heart aching with tenderness. William Burns, his eldest son believed, was an excellent teacher of his children, although he never spoke to them as children, but discussed any subject with them, even as they worked side by side in the fields, as if they were men. Out of necessity, because they could afford no servants or labourers, they also had to work as men. As far back as Robert could remember, he had risen early and returned late.

His childhood had been one of unceasing and dreary toil in which he worked every day to the utmost of his strength and beyond. The only companions during most of the long days were his father and his brother, Gilbert. His father conversed with them both as if they were men and on all subjects that would increase their knowledge and confirm their virtuous habits.

As well as the physical difficulties and symptoms of fatigue he had suffered and still suffered, Robert experienced a terrible anguish of mind. He was worried about his father growing old and in increasing poverty, despite all his hard labour.

Yet, no matter how he showed his concern, his respect or his love, no matter how hard he worked and how diligently he listened to his father reading from the Bible, and studied his father's pamphlet, *The Manual of Religious Belief*, his open-hearted emotions were never returned. His father was an austere man, not given to showing emotions – except perhaps irascibility.

Then, after he'd gone against, indeed openly defied, his father's wishes and taken up dancing lessons, he had been saddened and distressed by the dislike his father seemed to harbour against him. It had been the only time he'd been disobedient. Desperation, however, had made him remain firm against the anger, the icy fury. He could not bear to look into the future and see nothing but the cheerless slavery that had always been his lot. His spirit refused to be defeated.

He needed to expand his social horizons and learn some of the polite manners of society. He thought his father would be pleased at any idea of improving himself. But no.

The only release from backbreaking toil was on the Sabbath. Only then, at the kirk, did they see any others of their fellow men. But for Robert, there was no release of the spirit in the kind of Sabbath that his father insisted on. Five or six hours in the kirk listening to a preacher telling them that they were all sinners destined to burn in Hell only made him feel bitter and harbour sarcastic thoughts against the minister and his pious elders.

These elders were among the minister's men who walked the streets on the Sabbath intent on catching people and reporting them for standing about in gardens or fields or – sin of sins – looking out of windows.

After the hours in church, people were supposed to spend the remaining hours of the day in becoming gloom, in hours of prayer and Bible study. Not even the comfort of a decent meal was allowed. No hot meal must be eaten until well into the evening.

As soon as Robert heard about the dancing lessons in a barn in Dalrymple, his heart skittered wildly with excitement and gratitude. He could have wept with relief at the mere idea of such an escape route. It was then, not for the first time, that Robert found he had a streak of the same pride and stubbornness as his father. At first he tried to reason with the old man. When that didn't work, he looked his father in the eye and announced in a strong, firm voice that he *was* going to Dalrymple to start weekly dancing lessons, and that was that. He regretted of course having to defy his father, but oh what joy he felt at the dancing lessons. How he loved the sight of the fiddler leaping and prancing about the room, his coat tails flying as he sawed wildly and energetically with his bow. How glorious it was to dance around the room with other young people, feverish eyed, laughing and sweating. There were other, more dignified dances too and Robert felt he was learning a very valuable social skill.

Now the Bachelors' Club in Tarbolton was a blessed exhilaration too. He walked on air even as he strode to the club. He came to thrilling life there. He discovered how wonderfully stimulating, how fascinating life could be. He revelled in it. It took him hours to calm down again and readjust himself to the drudgery of his existence on the farm with the deep depression and dull headaches that so often accompanied it.

The only other glimpse he'd had of light in the darkness of life was his love of the female sex. He'd been fifteen when he'd first discovered this joy. It was the custom to be coupled during the labours of the harvest, and he had to work that year with a female partner called Nell. For more than one reason, he would never forget her. Firstly she'd introduced him to what he now regarded, despite disappointments and heartaches, as the first of human joys, and dearest pleasure here below. At the time he didn't know why he liked so much to loiter with her when returning in the evenings from their labours. It was a mystery to him why her voice made his heart thrill and his pulse beat so furiously when he looked and fingered over her hand to pluck out nettle stings and thistles.

She was a sweet, sonsie lass and he remembered how he'd heard her sing a song that apparently had been composed by a local lord's son. A rush of pride had convinced him that he could do as well as any gentry. As a result, she had been the means of introducing him to poetry. In a wild enthusiasm of passion, he'd written his first song. His heart never failed to melt in remembrance of it.

> Oh once I loved a bonnie lass.
> An' aye I love her still
> And whilst that virtue warms my breast,
> I'll love my handsome Nell . . .

He'd written better poetry and songs and he'd fallen in love more than once since, but that first love and that first effort remained dear to him.

He had another joy. He loved to read. He had a passion for reading. He had been lucky in this respect. Books were very difficult – in many cases, especially in the country, impossible – to come by. But his father, despite the fact that he could little afford it, had subscribed to the private library housed in the burgh school in Ayr, which had been founded not so long ago. His father had also arranged for a young man by the name of John Murdoch to come and teach him and Gilbert and some of the other farm children. He had been six years of age at the time and had eagerly devoured all the books that Murdoch had supplied during the short time he had been their teacher. The first two books he'd ever read were *The Life of Hannibal* and *The History of Sir William Wallace*. Hannibal had stirred his young imagination so much, he used to strut up and down in raptures after the recruiting drum and bagpipes and wish he was old enough to be a soldier. The story of Wallace poured a Scottish prejudice into his veins that would, as he said, 'boil along there until the floodgates of life shut in eternal rest'.

Only one book had repulsed him. It was a play that Murdoch elected to read aloud to the family before leaving it as a parting gift. It had been the tragedy of *Titus Andronicus* and his childish mind and emotions reached an anguish of unbearable distress when a female in the play had her hands chopped off and her tongue cut out and was ravished. He had cried out for Murdoch to stop the reading at once and told him that if he didn't take the book away, he'd burn it.

Before his father had a chance to sternly reprimand him for his ingratitude and impertinence, Murdoch said, 'I like to see so much sensibility.' And he left *School for Love* instead.

He had been a good teacher and Robert remembered him with fondness despite the painful beltings he'd suffered. These punishments had been for not singing the hymns in tune like Gilbert. This was where his streak of stubbornness had shown itself, even at that early age. He did not like the mournful hymn tunes. He had more than enough of them on the Sabbath every week. Murdoch could thrash him as much as he wished. Let him praise Gilbert as much as he liked in comparison and insist that Gilbert was the brightest and had the best ear for music and he had no ear at all. He did not care. He hated the mournful, sanctimonious hymns.

Murdoch held no grudge against him however, nor he against Murdoch. Indeed, when he was fourteen and reunited with him for a brief few weeks in Ayr, to have tuition in English and French, it was like an oasis in a wilderness. His life all too often was the cheerless gloom of a hermit with the unceasing recently and during their friendly conversation, Tenant had remembered, 'Robert, your familiarity with the Bible never ceased to astonish me. And still does to this day. You had a better command of the New Testament even than our tutor.'

Thinking of the Bible Robert marvelled at how the minister and all his cronies could ignore so many of the texts in it.

'Do not be over-righteous', for instance and more importantly, 'God is love'. Their God was one of hatred who was determined to cast everyone into the fire of Hell. Everyone, according to them, was doomed from birth. But he'd studied the Bible, and quite a few books about it – Stockhomes *New History of the Holy Bible from the Beginning of the World to the Establishment of Christianity,* for instance – and come to a different conclusion. His favourite books however were still Hannibal and the life of William Wallace. He enjoyed fantasising about the characters and imagining himself escaping from his dreary life by going to be a soldier. It inspired him, comforted him even, and increased the stubborn, sturdy something in his nature. 'One day I'll be a soldier,' he kept thinking.

That visit to Ayr also gave him the opportunity to meet other youngsters who had better advantages than he had ever known. He came into contact with the young noblesse and gentry and saw to his intense interest and dismay the difference in attitude. Also the difference in dress between them. He became acutely conscious of his ragged ploughboy clothes. He saw their self-confidence and sense of superiority when mixing with ordinary village or country lads. It wasn't that they verbally insulted him or any of the others in his class. They simply had an unnoticing disregard for lads like himself, some of whom had been born in the same village as them.

He experienced boiling resentment and desperate pride in the face of these attitudes, and a detestation of the haughty class system that never left him. At the same time, he couldn't help being fascinated to observe his so-called superiors, and having to part with them was about as sore an affliction as having to part with Murdoch. He returned very reluctantly to life as a hermit and to the headaches and the now frightening palpitations that went with it.

The only other short respite he'd had in his youthful years was when his father sent him to Kirkoswald to learn Mensurating, Surveying and Dialling at Dominie Hugh Rodger's school. Knowing the sacrifice and effort in money it had cost his father, he applied himself as diligently as possible. Although he kept trying to concentrate his interest on geometry and trigonometry, he had to admit to himself that, even more than in Ayr, he made a greater progress in the knowledge of mankind.

In Kirkoswald smuggling was the interest of most of the inhabitants. It was a very rough place and he viewed drunken rabbles with as much, if not more, fascination as he had the gentry he'd met with at Ayr. Even on the Sabbath, there was so much drunkenness that the kirk session there ruled that no innkeeper should sell on that day more than two pints of ale to a company of three persons.

He'd had his first initiation into an ale house there because he'd been told that it was customary when enrolling at the school to take the dominie into the tavern for a liquid refreshment. The dominie, Hugh Rodger, unlike Robert's previous teacher Murdoch, had a limited grasp of any matters outside his field of specialisation. He was a very sarcastic man and he quickly tried to ridicule and demolish a habit Robert and a friend, Willie Niven, had formed. Instead of kicking a ball around or playing at other games in their two-hour midday break, they tried to improve their minds as they strolled to the outskirts of the village conversing on all kinds of subjects. Eventually they hit on a plan to have disputations or debates, one taking one side of the argument and the other the opposite, regardless of their personal opinions on the subject. Their whole object was to sharpen their intellect. They asked several of the sixty other pupils at the school to take a side in their debates but not one other person would do so. They only laughed at the serious young debaters.

It eventually came to the dominie's ear and one day in the classroom he set about ridiculing the two boys in front of all the other pupils. The class laughed uproariously at the master's sarcastic wit. Eventually Willie Niven spoke up. He said he was sorry if he and Robert had given offence. He was also surprised.

'I would have thought, sir, that you would have been pleased to know of our endeavours to improve our minds.'

Rodger sneered at this and asked what today's subject was for debate.

Niven said, 'Whether is a great general or a respectable merchant the most valuable member of society.'

Rodger laughed uproariously at the silliness of this question and said there would be no doubt of the correct answer.

'Well,' said Robert, 'if you think so, I will be glad if you take any side you please, and allow me to take the other, and let us discuss it before the whole school.'

Rodger immediately agreed and started the argument confidently on the side of the general.

Robert answered with points in favour of the merchant and very soon showed an obvious superiority over his teacher. Rodger tried to get back at him with reply after reply but without success. Soon, everyone could see the teacher's hands shaking, then his voice trembled until he became in such a pitiable state of vexation, he had to dissolve the school. It was too late to save his face or his reputation, however. He had been defeated and shamed by a sixteen-year-old.

Willie remarked to Robert afterwards, 'You were brilliant, Robert, but I'm afraid you've made an enemy for life there.'

Robert knew that Willie was right but he'd enjoyed the stimulating exercise of his mind far too intensely to care.

5

'Oh, I think they are splendid, Alexander.' His sister enthusiastically clapped her hands. 'I am proud of you. You must read your poems in as many drawing rooms in Edinburgh as possible. I'm sure the literati there will give you every praise and encouragement.'

Alexander gave a little bow. 'Thank you, my dear. My poetry means a great deal to me. More than my efforts at doctoring, I confess. And it seems that a few of the people in Tarbolton and the surrounding estates feel the same. I've given a reading in the ale house as well as in a few drawing rooms recently, and on each occasion, I was applauded. I believe I'm fast becoming recognised as the village bard.' He gave a rueful smile. 'As you know, my doctoring more often than not meets with the reverse of approbation. Even the minister refuses me in favour of my father. At least we can be thankful that the church, as well as representing the law, no longer acts as doctors as well.'

'That minister's a long-visaged, melancholy idiot!'

'My dear sister,' Alexander said with mock seriousness, 'I beg you to be more careful of how you speak of the minister or he'll damn you forever and a day.'

'What a bore he is. How he manages to be so boring for hours on end every Sabbath without fail truly amazes me.'

'Yes,' Alexander sighed. 'I suppose we can't be too surprised at the wild excesses of the inhabitants during the week after having to suffer the reverend gentleman every Sabbath. I'm beginning to indulge rather more than usual myself. The odd glass of wine with a meal was all I ever used to have when I was abroad. The people there were so much more civilised.'

'It will be different in Edinburgh. Oh, if only we lived permanently in the capital city.'

'I fear the customs there are no different, perhaps worse as far as bacchanalian excesses are concerned. However, I have been, I confess, thinking of some day taking up residence in Edinburgh. I cannot see a future and certainly not a fortune here as a doctor.'

'Oh, Alexander, I cannot see any future in Tarbolton for me either.'

'You will have plenty opportunities of marriage here. You must try not to be so impatient, sister.'

'What opportunities? There is no one of any consequence for miles around but men in their dotage or country yokels.'

'You seemed quite taken with Neil Guthrie. Not a man that I would recommend as a prospective suitor.' Alexander drummed long fingers on the arm of his chair. 'Such a pity about Charlotte. He will inherit everything.'

'Like you, he has been abroad, I believe.'

'Travelling, not studying. The grand tour, you know. Apparently his father left him enough fortune to indulge in such a whim.'

'You do not like him.'

Alexander hesitated. 'There's a coldness about the man that I find somewhat repellent. That is one reason I did not trust him with your care on Hogmanay, and for your sake I am glad he has returned to Edinburgh.'

She shrugged. 'I appreciate your care, brother, but surely a man of such good fortune cannot be so summarily dismissed as a bad suitor. And he seemed quite taken with me, did he not?'

'But for what reason? What fortune could you expect to offer him? Father lives and spends to the best of his abilities and beyond, despite Mother's efforts at good housekeeping. He enjoys life. As a result money keeps disappearing like snow on a sunny day in this household. And far too often, Father helps people who can only pay in eggs or meal or some animal they've procured illegally.'

'The reason could be love and admiration.'

'Oh ho, so you are still a dreamer. You have not lost your childish imagination.'

Susanna flushed. 'You insult me, sir.'

'Not at all, my dear. I am thinking of Neil Guthrie. I cannot imagine such a cold fish marrying for love, no matter how charming and otherwise desirable the young lady.'

'At least you have some diversion here with your poetry writing and your Bachelors' Club. Now you have the Masons. I envy you, Alexander.'

'Burns has become a member of the brotherhood as well.'

'Good gracious alive! Do they allow anyone in then?'

Alexander laughed. 'You are not taken with him?'

'Certainly not.'

'He is quite a ladies' man. He's frequently in love and I've seen for myself how agitated he becomes and how his passions blind him and make him endow the most ordinary servant girl with the most beautiful and angelic qualities.' Alexander laughed and shook his head. 'His brother Gilbert and I have both tried to bring him down to earth and talk some sense into him but all to no avail. Then if and when he's rejected, he sinks into a terrible abyss of humiliation and despair.'

'He sounds quite mad to me.'

'Mm. I do suspect he suffers from some sort of nervous imbalance but I find him very interesting.'

'As a doctor?'

'Yes, but in other ways too. Did I tell you about the first time I met him.'

She shook her head.

'Father was laid low with an attack of gout and couldn't answer the call to visit Robert's father, so I went in his place.'

Alexander's grey-green eyes became vague as he remembered. 'I found William Burns in very ill health. Consumption, I believe, not helped by the worry over the embarrassed state of his financial affairs. But he spoke very easily and clearly to me, as did his wife and his younger son, Gilbert. Gilbert struck me right away as being a very frank and modest young man. Robert, on the other hand, seemed distant and suspicious. He sat in a dark corner of the room by himself, a saturnine figure barely visible in the shadows. But I frequently detected him scrutinising me while I was conversing with his father and brother. Sitting there in the shadows, observing me with such a penetrating gaze, I found most disconcerting.'

'Was it any wonder?' Susanna gasped. 'That would have put me right out of countenance.'

Alexander smiled. 'At the same time, I couldn't help being intrigued by him. He was sizing me up, I think, before deigning to join me in conversation.'

'Well, I do declare! It should have been the other way around. You are an educated and a professional man. What is he that he should take such an attitude – a common ploughman?'

'Mm . . . A ploughman, yes, but not common, Susanna. No, I can't in all honesty say that of him. For one thing he converses as well as, if not better and more knowledgeably, than any educated gentleman I've known. But even more intriguing is his ability to observe and estimate character. It seems to be intuitive. And once he gets the measure of someone, he can, too often perhaps, make them the butt of an extremely sarcastic and satirical wit. Everyone laughs at the epigrams he makes up about people. He sets his rustic circle in a roar but at the same time it makes them suspicious and afraid of him. I've heard his neighbours observe that he has a great deal to say for himself and that they suspect his principles. I wouldn't be surprised if for every one friend he acquires, he makes ten enemies.'

'He sounds a very uncomfortable friend to have, to say the

least, Alexander. I think the quicker you get to Edinburgh and into more normal and genteel company, the better. Grandmother will no doubt introduce you to suitable young ladies.'

'I had been thinking of Charlotte, but . . . ' He shrugged.

'There will be plenty of ladies of great fortune in Edinburgh or some of the estates within travelling distance of the capital. Gentlemen too, I'm hoping. I too wanted to settle in Edinburgh but Grandmother wouldn't hear of it. I shall have to wait for marriage to rescue me. But for how long?' She rolled her eyes dramatically. 'For how long?'

Alexander laughed. 'Don't worry. I shall do what I can for you in Edinburgh. There should be no problem. You are very pretty. A little on the plump side, perhaps . . . '

'Oh!'

She flung her fan at him but he only laughed again and said, 'Come, let us take the air. You need something to cool your ardour and impatience.'

'Oh, very well.' She reached for her dark blue cloak and Alexander donned a green knee-length coat.

It was cold outside and Susanna put up her hood. It was quite a tight fit over her wig which she'd carefully powdered earlier with white flour. It was so annoying and frustrating not to have a maid to perform such tasks. She'd met women on her last visit to Edinburgh who had personal maids who even rouged their mistresses' faces as well as powdered their wigs and dressed them. She did not need rouge, of course. She had a fine complexion with a natural rosy flush to her cheeks; and long curly eyelashes. She remembered fluttering them at Neil Guthrie to some effect.

Susanna was suddenly jerked from her reverie by Alexander calling out, 'Burns! It's not often I see you here on an afternoon.'

Susanna gazed wide-eyed at the man in the top boots and tight breeches now striding across the street towards them. Every man of the peasant class had natural hair cut short. Gentlemen wore wigs, or at least had powdered their own short hair. This man had long, coal-black hair gathered in a beribboned queue at the back. Not content either with the hodden grey of his fellows, his plaid was the colour of autumn leaves and he wore it a different way round his shoulders from everyone else.

'Have you met my sister?' Alexander asked.

'I have not had that pleasure, sir,' Burns said in a deep, rich voice. His eyes probed into hers and she had to avoid his stare, it discomfited her so much. She felt annoyed and she would have liked to push past him with her head in the air. But good manners forbade such an action. She held out a hand. His big hand took her small one and he bowed over it. What a brawny figure he had. She felt quite dwarfed by it.

Alexander said, 'Robert, this is my sister, Susanna. Susanna, Robert Burns.'

'Madame,' he said.

'Sir,' she murmured.

Alexander had barely started a conversation with Burns when Susanna interrupted, 'It is very cold standing here, brother. May we move on?'

'Very well,' Alexander said. 'I'll see you at the Club, Robert.'

Robert gave another small bow.

Afterwards, Alexander said, 'Was it really necessary to be so abrupt, Susanna?'

'I'm sorry, Alexander. I just don't like the man.'

Alexander gazed curiously round at her.

'Are you sure about that?'

'What do you mean?'

Alexander shrugged. 'He seems to have some sort of animal magnetism as far as the female sex is concerned.'

'I do not like the man,' Susanna repeated, glad of her voluminous cloak now. It hid the fact that she was trembling. 'I've never been more sure of anything in my life.'

6

Robert believed that there were two main reasons why he wrote poetry and songs. One was to express his joy of being in love. The disappointments too. He'd treasured high hopes of winning over a lovely girl with a respectable job as a housekeeper. Looks on this occasion had not been the main attraction. Her intellect was far above that of any other woman he'd known. To have a wife like that would be a dream come true.

> But it's not her air, her form, her face,
> Tho matching beauty's fabled Queen,
> 'Tis the mind that shines in every grace,
> An' chiefly in her roguish e'en.

He had been in a spellbound anxiety to make her his wife and had expressed his feelings and his proposal in carefully constructed letters. She in turn wrote briefly, rejecting him. He was deeply disappointed and unhappy as a result. But also as a result, he wrote the best songs he'd so far produced. 'The Lass of Cessnock Banks' and 'I'll Kiss Thee Yet', 'Montgomerie's Peggy' and 'Mary Morison'. He admitted to a friend – 'She showed an education much beyond anything I have ever met in any woman I ever dared to approach and she made an impression on my heart that I do not think the world can ever efface.'

The other reason for writing poetry and songs was to

escape or to find release from melancholy and depression. The latter had been particularly necessary during his stay at Irvine. He had gone to the town to learn how to dress flax. He and Gilbert had leased a piece of land from their father a few years previously and had cultivated flax on it. Robert thought the flax-dressing would be a new profession for him that would give him more independence than he got from agriculture and he was anxious to complete his training. He was also looking around for the means to set up a household of his own. He had quickly come to realise that his dreams of having a wife of his own and his own fireside would remain only a dream so long as he was a penniless farmer with all his time taken up battling with the soil.

The manufacture and retailing of flax – that was the answer – and he set out with a hopeful heart and high expectations to the neighbouring town of Irvine. His high hopes were short-lived, however. He soon discovered that the work of dressing flax was carried out in heckling sheds where the smell and choking dust were unbearable. Nevertheless, because he had put what little money he had into the business in return for instruction of the proper techniques, and also because he did not easily give up on anything, he stuck manfully at it. It so affected his health and spirits however that he could barely drag himself each evening back to the Glasgow vennel where he had lodgings. It was a two-storey building with stairs on either side of the lobby. The right-hand stair was the one he had to wearily climb to reach his attic room at the back of the house. Once there, he sank into bed, struggling to cough the flax dust out of his lungs. Soon, the depressions which he had suffered on previous occasions returned to him as never before. He sank into an abyss, not only of aches and pains all over his body, but a deep, dark hopelessness of mind. Added to this distress was the growing suspicion that his partner in the flax business was dishonest. That he could not, would not, abide. 'Whatever my faults and weaknesses,' he told himself, 'I am an honest man.'

37

But it was his bodily weakness that became his most urgent concern. So much so that he had to send for a doctor. Doctor Fleeming called to see him five times in the space of eight days. At first he was given ipecacuanha which made him violently sick. Then a 'sacred elixir', as Fleeming called it, was prescribed. The elixir was a compound of rhubarb and aloes in powder form which had to be dissolved in fortified wine. It acted as a powerful laxative.

'I have always believed,' Fleeming said, 'that the best cure for severe depression is a good vomiting and purging.'

Continuously retching and sweating with the weakness of doing so and the pain and exhaustion of the purging of his bowels, he felt worse and far weaker after the treatment. On the next visit, the doctor plied him with opium as a painkiller. Subsequently, he was given massive doses of powdered cinchona. At one point he was so fevered and ill that his father had to make the journey to see him.

Despite his illness, Burns continued to struggle manfully with the flax dressing. In a half-conscious nightmare, he pushed himself to work in the heckling sheds. However, he had to cancel the visit to the family home on New Year's Day, as he'd promised his father. He wrote explaining that there was so much work to do and 'My health is much about what it was when you were here, only my sleep is rather sounder and on the whole I am rather better than otherwise tho' it is by very small degrees. The weakness of my nerves has so debilitated my mind that I dare not either review past events, or look forward into futurity; for the least anxiety, or perturbation in my breast produces most unhappy effects on my whole frame.'

He made it obvious in his letter that religion was now his only comfort and said he was looking forward to the thought that perhaps very soon 'I shall bid an eternal adieu to all the pains and uneasiness and disquietude of this weary life, for I assure you I am heartily tired of it, and, if I do not very much deceive myself, I could contentedly and gladly resign it . . . '

But his stubborn spirit would not allow him to 'resign it'

and he continued to drag himself every day to the heckling shed until only a few days later something terrible happened, owing to the drunken carelessness of his partner's wife.

As Robert wearily arrived for work, he was startled from his nightmare of fatigue by another nightmare. Choking smoke swirled around the bottom of the door of the heckling shed. Heat was already radiating through the flimsy panels. Then with a crackling roar, it ignited. Neighbours came clamouring to help and they quickly formed a chain. Bucket after bucket of water was hurled onto the flames, to no avail. The rosy glow lit the night sky as flames soared upwards. Sparks circled brilliantly high into the darkness.

Knowing by now it was a lost cause, everyone – including Robert – drew back, cheeks glowing red, rivulets of sweat making streaks on soot-caked faces. Robert's face acquired a strangely startled look caused by his eyebrows being singed from his frequent forays too close to the blaze. The heckling shed was burned to ashes and Robert thought, 'Now I'm like a true poet, not worth sixpence.'

Added to this disaster were worries about his father's health and financial situation. After the fire, he was left in his cheerless garret weighed down by the darkest melancholy, and he turned to his muse for consolation. He wrote 'A Prayer under the Pressure of Violent Anguish' and 'Under the Pressure of a Heavy Train of Misfortunes' and 'Raging Fortune' and 'A Prayer in the Prospect of Death'. Eventually, as his strength slowly returned, he was able to pen the defiant lines:

> Oh why the deuce should I repine,
> and be an ill foreboder?
> I'm twenty-three and five feet nine,
> I'll go and be a sodger!

He also wrote 'My Father was a Farmer', expressing how he 'courted Fortune's favour' but 'Some cause unseen still stept between, to frustrate each endeavour'. He concluded that he would now just live for the moment and that he'd rather be 'a cheerful, honest-hearted clown', than powerful and wealthy.

One good thing that had come out of his otherwise disastrous stay in Irvine was his friendship with a sea captain called Richard Brown. The captain had led an adventurous life but his career had been at a low ebb since an American privateer had set him ashore on the wild coast of Connaught stripped of everything. Burns felt they were companions in misfortune. He greatly admired his new friend. He had never before met a man so well-versed and knowledgeable in the ways of the world, and he was eager to learn from him. He thought him courageous and of an admirable, independent mind. In his eyes, Richard Brown was in fact full of manly virtues. He intensely loved and admired him. He tried his utmost to imitate him. It was only with women that Richard could be more foolish than himself. More than that, he talked lightly about whoring and thought nothing of relating his experiences in the stews and bordellos he'd visited in every port. Burns was horrified and repelled by these stories but even this side of his friend did not kill the admiration he had for Richard's other more noble qualities.

It was Richard Brown who first implanted the idea in Robert's mind that he should get his poetry published. It seemed an incredible and impossible idea at the time. Then other things came thick and fast to crowd out any such thoughts. As soon as the winter snow melted, he had to return from Irvine to lend what support he could to his father and the rest of the family. His father was in a desperate state and everyone was worried and distressed for him. He had become involved in litigation that could lose them the farm and everything they possessed. The dispute was with his landlord who had broken his word and behaved in a manner devoid of all honour. He claimed that William Burns owed him upwards of five hundred pounds besides the current year's rent. Burns senior denied this, and his eldest son held the ill man's pen, helping to write his replies

40

to the claims. Nonetheless, the family were humiliated and had to face the trauma of seeing the Sheriff's men prying over their goods and chattels. Then they had to suffer the Tarbolton town crier going through the parish at tuck of drum warning everyone against buying any of the sequestered property.

Robert suffered most of all for his father whose consumption was obviously killing him. He acutely admired the old man, who, despite his illness, was showing such indomitable spirit by resisting the bitter and unwarranted claims of an unscrupulous landlord.

I've notic'd, on our Laird's count-day
An' mony a time my heart's been wae, (vexed)
Poor tenant-bodies, scant o' cash,
How they maun thole a factor's snash; (sneers)
He'll stamp an' threaten, curse an' swear,
He'll apprehend them, poind their gear, (impound their stock)
While they maun stand, wi' aspect humble,
An' hear it a', an' fear an' tremble!

When their father's affairs grew near to crisis, the two brothers, Robert and Gilbert, secretly acquired the farm of Mossgiel from Robert's friend and lawyer, Gavin Hamilton, as an asylum for the family in case of the worst. All the family's savings were invested in stocking it and so it was a joint concern. The allowance of the two brothers was seven pounds per annum each and smaller wages were paid to the other members of the family.

Too soon their plan had to be put into practice. The consumption defeated William Burns' fight for life. Only Robert and his young sister Isabel were in the room at the time, and seeing the girl sobbing bitterly at the thought of parting with her father, William tried to murmur a few words of comfort and managed to add, 'Walk in virtue's path and shun every vice'. Then after a pause to gather enough strength again, he said, 'There's only one member of this family whose future conduct I fear.'

Robert, who had been hovering in silent anguish nearby came up to the bed and asked, 'Oh father, is it me you mean?'

The old man had no hesitation in saying it was and Robert turned away to the window, tears streaming down his cheeks, chest heaving as if it would burst in his efforts to restrain his distress.

Later he wrote the poem that was inscribed on his father's tombstone.

> Here lie the loving Husband's dear remains,
> The tender Father, and the gen'rous Friend.
> The pitying Heart that felt for human Woe,
> The dauntless Heart that fear's no human Pride,
> The Friend of Man, to vice alone a foe;
> For ev'n his failings lean'd to Virtue's side.

His father's death sent Robert's mind darting back to the past. He could not bear to dwell on any of the disappointment or worry he might have caused his father. Instead past scenes with his mother swam back to him and with his mother's old relative, Betty Davidson, who used to come and stay at the farm and help the family. His mother used to sing as she worked. Many of her songs reflected the coarse and robust attitudes of the peasantry – although he didn't believe his mother understood some of the bawdy songs she sang. He remembered one of her favourites, and his too, was an old ballad about sexual intercourse.

> Kissin' is the key o' love,
> An' clappin' is the lock
> An' makin' O's the best thing
> That e'er a young thing got.

The only times he remembered his mother being displeased to the point of anger with him was in his attitudes towards predestination. Most people like herself believed that they were damned and destined for Hell. On one occasion she'd been visiting a neighbour whose child was on the point of death. She's said to him when she'd returned, 'You should have been there, Robert. You never heard such a prayer as James Lee gave beside the poor child.'

Robert replied, 'Oh, Mother! Can you or Jamie Lee be so daft as to think that his prayer can be of any service to the dying bairn, or keep the devil at a distance? Would God send a child into the world to damn it?'

In a fury she lifted her fire tongs and tried to strike him but he dodged out of the way.

Betty Davidson, his mother's old relation, had filled his mind with the biggest collection in the country of tales and songs concerning devils, ghosts, fairies, brownies, witches, warlocks, spunkies, kelpies, elf-candles, dead-lights, wraiths, apparitions, cantraips, enchanted towers, giants, dragons and other trumpery. He never ceased to be amazed at the old woman's ignorance, credulity and superstition. Yet even to this day, her stories had such a strong effect on his imagination that if he was walking at night, he felt compelled to keep a sharp look-out in suspicious places.

After his father's death, Robert and the family moved to the farm at Mossgiel but before the move, Robert had started a Commonplace Book or journal, the writing of which gave him some relief or escape from the turbulent period he was living through and all the traumas going on around him. He expressed thoughts on people and life in general and also ' . . . how a farmer or farm labourer thinks, and feels, under the pressure of Love, Ambition, Anxiety and Grief, with the like cares and passions, which however diversified by the Modes and Manners of life, operate pretty much alike, I believe, in all Species'.

He was fascinated by people and liked nothing more than to keenly observe them and he wrote, 'I have often observed, in the course of my experience of human life, that every man, even the worst, have something good about them . . . ' He went into some detail about his reasons for this observation and ended with, '... I can say any man who can thus think, will scan the failings, nay the faults and crimes of mankind around him, with a brother's eye.'

He also expressed these sentiments in a poem called 'Address to the Unco Guid' or 'The Rigidly Righteous'.

> Then gently scan your brother Man
> Still gentler sister Woman;
> Tho' they may gang a kennin' wrang,
> To step aside is human;
> One point must still be greatly dark,
> The moving Why they do it;
> And just as lamely can ye mark,
> How far perhaps they rue it . . .

He found relief too in concocting in his imagination some verses headed 'The Death and Dying Words o' Poor Mailie – my ain pet ewe'. Mailie had not in fact died. He had rescued her from where she had been lying in a ditch in distress at becoming entangled in her tether. He comforted the animal, and set it to rights, and after returning home from the plough in the evening, he had recited the poem to Gilbert.

It wasn't long after the move to Mossgiel that Robert discovered that the new farm was little better than Lochlie in many respects. It lay very high and mostly on a cold, wet bottom. As he walked around Mossgiel, struggling not to feel too depressed, the rain battered down across the bleak landscape. Heavy droplets coursed down his face, pausing for a second on his heavy brows before pooling and trickling down over his eyes. He felt the rain slowly seep through his heavy jacket, insidious streams of it gradually finding their way down his spine. Mud coated and weighted his boots and he felt the water slosh around his toes and chaff against the pack of his boots.

There had previously been exceptionally long and hard frosts. Snow lay till April, followed in May by a piercing cold wind. Then there was continuous heavy rain. Ten days of hot weather in July preceded more torrential rain, making August as cold as February. In August a hurricane struck central Scotland and devastated standing wheat. There were then a few weeks of good weather, but too soon, more winds came, then hard frosts again. As a result any cereal crop which had survived could not be harvested until late November. However, severe frosts and deep snow were so intense that the mill-lades froze. All this caused the seed available for sowing to be of very poor quality, resulting in the terrible problems that he and Gilbert had to contend with.

Robert found some solace in an affair he was having with a young woman who had been a maid to his mother at Lochlie. She had not moved with them to Mossgiel but gone instead to work on another farm. He had not made any promises to Elizabeth, or Betsy Paton, and as she herself admitted, always treated her kindly. But when Betsy became pregnant, his mother was very keen that he should marry her. He might have done so because he admired the girl. She was an honest, independent creature and a great favourite of his mother's. Gilbert and his sisters, however, were very much against any idea of marriage. They said she was rude and uncivilised with a thorough contempt for any kind of refinement. They insisted that her faults of character would soon have disgusted him.

They could not stop Robert though from being fined a guinea by the Tarbolton Kirk Session and also made to do a penance for fornication. This gave Robert the inspiration for a poem called 'Fornication' in which he outrageously dismissed this fine as 'buttock hire' and also described the punishment in church as exposing him to further temptation.

> . . . Before the Congregation wide
> I pass'd the muster fairly,
> My handsome Betsy by my side,
> We gat our ditty rarely;

But my downcast eye by chance did spy
What made my lips to water,
Those limbs so clean where I, between,
Commenced a Fornicator.

He found himself composing more verses now than he'd ever done before. Even during threshing, his mind was feverishly occupied with his creative thoughts. Gilbert and the other workers complained that he worked so erratically, with such varied alternations from slow to quick, that he made it dangerous and even impossible for them to keep up with him. Then in an hour or two he was so exhausted, he gave in altogether.

Workers and friends alike had to be careful too about how they treated animals. Burns could not abide any form of cruelty to them. He had a soft spot for horses, dogs and sheep. Pet sheep, dogs and hens enjoyed perfect freedom to parade through the house whenever and as often as they wanted. One day he was walking with a friend, who had a whip in his hand and gave a slight touch of it to a sparrow, depriving it of some of its feathers. This immediately sparked Burns to anger and he accused his friend of committing an act of unnecessary barbarity.

Despite the heat of his creativity, Burns felt more and more driven by his physical labours to the point of exhaustion and depression. He began taking fainting turns at night and his aches and pains and palpitations returned. In an effort to deal with the fainting and the palpitations, he forced himself to brave the accepted cure of plunging into a barrel of icy water which he was instructed to keep near his bedside. He slowly slid down into the tub of glacial water. The cold burned his skin as it gradually enveloped his body. Firstly he burned from neck to toe, then the numbness set in. He gritted his teeth, struggling to endure the torture, muscles in his jaw clenched till they cramped, to still his chattering teeth. Finally, unable to take any more, he struggled out of the tub and flopped like some half dead creature dragged from the depths. The coarse woollen blanket that his clumsy fingers pulled around him felt like sinful luxury after his ordeal.

The whole procedure was enough to put anyone against doctors. One of these days, he vowed each time he had to gather courage to plunge into the icy water yet again, I'll write about them.

7

The carriage rattled and bumped and swayed as it sped along at a wild and dangerous pace. It jarred and shuddered as it struggled over potholes and boulders. The horses strained their muscles, their hooves and manes flying. The driver cracked his whip high in the air.

Susanna gripped the edge of the seat, stiff with excitement and terror. Beside her, Alexander, to all appearances completely relaxed, leaned back, making his three-cornered hat tip forward. One of his hands rested on his gold-topped cane, the other lay easily on his lap. Susanna marvelled at his elegant sang froid. It was all very thrilling, but she was thankful when the journey was over and they were at last in Edinburgh.

The sloping High Street where her grandmother lived extended from the Palace right up to the Castle in the air. It was the backbone of the city. Here, in the past, was the battlefield of Scotland where private feuds, jealousies between nobles and burghers, even between the Crown and the people, were settled at the point of a sword. Steep narrow closes and wynds diverged at each side of the street. Some lofty buildings, which in Edinburgh were called 'lands', were fifteen storeys high and were like vertical streets. Some had timber facades and projecting lofty gables. Tier after tier thrust out beyond the lower storey. Below were covered piazzas and darkened entrances to the secretive-looking shops. Alleys also had overhanging gables and projecting timbers, and were narrow and shadowy and steep, sometimes with flights of stairs to lessen the abruptness of the deep descent. These side streets were called closes, vennels and wynds and were so narrow you could lay a hand on either wall.

It was all so different and so much more exciting than the sprawl of low-roofed houses and cottages that was the village of Tarbolton. Edinburgh was densely populated. It was a terrific crush of humanity, of rich and poor, lords and ladies, divines, legal men, paupers and beggars, as well as crowds of idiots who leered and giggled at no-one in particular, and leaped gleefully about.

It was quite late when the carriage drew up at Grandmother Wallace's close and when they reached her upstairs house, they found she had a supper ready on the table and a couple of guests waiting to welcome them and share the meal. Soon glasses were clinking round the china punch bowl and the tapers were burning pale in the hot scarlet of the fire light. Susanna enjoyed the meal of roasted hens but found 'healths' and toasts a torment. Every glass of wine during dinner had to be dedicated to the health of someone. Then after the table was cleared, the after-dinner glasses were set down and it was necessary for each person to drink the health of every other person present. If there were ten persons present, therefore, it meant ninety 'healths' were drunk. Fortunately, Grandmother Wallace had only invited two people – a Mr and Mrs Logan. That was bad enough as far as Susanna's stomach was concerned. However, she managed to only take a few sips at each 'health'.

Afterwards the ladies retired to the drawing room and left the men to begin what they called 'rounds' of toasts when each gentleman named an absent lady.

'I warned you,' Alexander said when they were taking the air next day. 'Drinking habits are just as bad here as anywhere else in Scotland. In fact, in one way, Edinburgh is even worse than anywhere else because here even the judges drink at the bench while they are trying a case.'

'You are joking, Alexander.'

'Not at all. Lord Newton said, "Drinking is my occupation, law my amusement." It is the custom always to have wine and biscuits on the bench. In fact, I've seen it for myself when I went to view Grandfather at work. A black bottle of strong port was set down on the bench, along with a carafe of water, glasses and tumblers, and a plate of biscuits. Soon he was munching and quaffing and even when the bottle was nearly empty, you could hardly tell that he was intoxicated. Not from a distance at least. He was still crouched under his robes looking judicial enough.'

Susanna couldn't help laughing. 'One thing about the city – it's never dull or boring, is it? There's always something to fascinate me.'

As if to prove her words, there suddenly appeared before them no less a person than Neil Guthrie.

'My dear lady,' he said. 'What a pleasant surprise. And you, sir – have you business in the capital?'

'We are on one of our visits to our paternal grandparents,' Alexander replied in a polite if somewhat cool voice.

'May I know the address so that I can call and pay my respects?'

Before Alexander could reply, Susanna quickly furnished Guthrie with what he wanted, adding, 'I'm sure my grandmother will be delighted to receive you, sir.'

'I have to be out of town for a few days. Would a week today be convenient?'

'I'm sure it will.'

'Until next Thursday then.'

He bowed and moved away. Susanna was glad she was wearing her velvet cloak and a little brimmed hat trimmed with ribbons perched on top of her wig. She was sure she looked very fetching.

'I can hardly wait to tell Grandmother.' Her face was flushed and she was on tip toe with excitement.

'You are far too impulsive for your own good, Susanna. Remember Grandmother is taking you to the Dancing Assembly

50

in a couple of days. No doubt she will see that you meet plenty of interesting and suitable gentlemen there.'

Susanna had no doubt that Alexander's calmness stood him in good stead in medical emergencies but in other situations he only succeeded in dampening her enthusiasms. Although it would take more than anything her brother could say or do to spoil her enthusiasm for Edinburgh.

'I know, I know,' she told him, 'and I'm really looking forward to it.'

She continued strolling at Alexander's side in a dignified and ladylike manner. What she longed to do was give way to a burst of energy and happiness by skipping wildly along the street like a mad thing. However, decorum won and she proceeded down the High Street past the City Guard House from which a few guards had emerged resplendent in their red coats trimmed with blue, red waistcoats, red breeches, long black gaiters, white belts and large cocked hats bound with white worsted ribbon. They had muskets and bayonets but, according to Grandfather Wallace, they seldom used them. Their usual weapon was the old Lochaber axe. Most of the City Guard were old, hard-featured, red-nosed veterans of wars fought mostly in Highland regiments.

Apart from their duties of keeping the peace in the city, however, one of them always stood at each side of a prisoner at the bar of the Court of Judiciary, his huge hat on his head, his drawn bayonet in his large gnarled hand.

At last Alexander and Susanna reached Grandmother's close and, pushing roughly past some stinking beggars, they climbed the stairs. The smell was one thing Susanna found difficult to thole in Edinburgh. She understood very well why Grandmother's house was upstairs, and not on the ground floor. At ten o'clock every evening, the day's sewage was flung from every window on to the street below with only one warning cry to any pedestrian of 'Gardyloo'.

Pity the poor man or woman who was not quick enough to avoid the terrible downpour. At night every street stank to high heavens and was awash with disgusting effluence. Lower flats or homes were completely engulfed and overpowered with the stench. Even this did not put Susanna off Edinburgh, however. She counted her blessings that she was some way above the torrent and if she went out in the evening, she made sure she had the protection of her grandfather's carriage. She didn't believe that anything could spoil her love for and delight in the many pleasures and excitements of the city. They far outweighed any negative aspects.

Even after she married a wealthy gentleman with an estate in the country, she told herself, she would insist on spending much of the year in the capital. The winter probably. The country was always so dull and dreary in winter. A town house as well as a country estate. That was the answer. She took great pleasure in imagining such places. They became so real to her in her imagination, she became totally convinced that her dream would come true. It was only a matter of time. And not too long a time either. She wondered if Neil Guthrie would be at the Dancing Assembly. He had mentioned that he would be away for a few days. Still, there might be a chance that he'd be back in time and of course, everybody of quality attended these Assemblies.

Eventually they set out in the carriage down the long, narrow street with its crush of crowds and carts and dangerous jostle of sedan chairs. Susanna could hardly wait to find out if Neil Guthrie would be at the Assembly. She was distracted for a few minutes by one sedan chair which came ridiculously close to the carriage. Its occupant, a perky madame with a loop of amber beads swinging from her wig, wearing a low-cut gown and wielding a flirtatious fan, peered past Susanna into the coach to admire Alexander unashamedly. Her brother was admittedly looking very handsome in a high collared coat and breeches of russet velvet and a waistcoat of white silk with gold embroidery in a delicate floral design.

Susanna gripped the edge of her seat as the coach bumped along and the horses' hooves clattered and slithered alarmingly.

But at last they had arrived as near as the carriage could take them to their destination. They had then to use a sedan chair, because where the assembly was being held was through an unlit wynd. The sedans were carried by trotting Highlanders holding a torch aloft to light their way.

They all made a vivid splash of colour as they crowded into the lobby together. Grandmother rustled in striped silk in shades of pink and grey. Susanna blossomed in an open gown of apple green, which showed off her embroidered petticoat and flattered her bright green eyes. Grandfather, instead of his usual black, was resplendent in scarlet coat and white breeches.

They swept from the lobby directly into the dancing room. Above stairs, Grandmother said, was a tea room where later, if they wished, they could find refreshment. The room had a railed space in the centre for dancing and spectators sat round the outside, while at one end, the Lady Directress was enthroned on a high chair.

Grandmother and Grandfather danced a stately minuet under guttering sconces but they declined to join in any of the wild Scottish dances.

'Och, Ah've had my time of aw that. For years, naebody could keep up wi' me,' Grandmother said, energetically flapping her fan for air because the minuet had, as she said, 'nearly gone for her'. 'The spirit's still willin',' she insisted, 'but the damned flesh has gone sae weak an' Ah've that many aches an' pains, it takes me aw ma time tae walk these days. Geordie's the same.' She cocked her head towards her husband. 'He says he's just sittin' here tae keep me company but Ah'm no' daft. He's even mair ancient than me!'

Susanna flung herself joyously into the spirit of all the Scottish dances until she too was breathless. Nevertheless she was sorry to be dragged away home by the family before the evening was finished.

'Oh please, please, Grandmother, let me stay,' she pleaded.

'Stop being so foolish,' Alexander told her. 'You're getting over-excited.'

'Aye, lassie,' her grandmother said. 'It's time we were in our beds.' She dug an elbow into her husband who had dozed off despite all the noise around him. 'Come on, Geordie. Ye're no' on the bench the noo.'

Susanna was sorry that Neil Guthrie had not been at the Assembly. So many of the young men there were somewhat foppish and weak-looking in comparison. There was something strange, almost mysterious about Guthrie, she felt, and of course he was quite a few years older than her – which was what a husband should be if he was to prove a protector and supporter. All the same, she enjoyed the evening and hoped she would be allowed to stay in Edinburgh long enough to enjoy many more.

There were also times she had enjoyed being in the drawing rooms of the Edinburgh literati and proudly heard Alexander reading his poems and being applauded. It had even been suggested that he had his poetry published. Now Alexander was making enquiries about putting this venture into practice. It was all so thrilling she could have wept with happiness. Soon, however, she was weeping for a different cause. No sooner had Neil Guthrie begun visiting her, paying court to her, and had been on the point, she was sure, of declaring his love for her, than a letter had been delivered requesting her return to Tarbolton. Her mother was more poorly than usual and needed her home. Her father was also laid low with an attack of gout and needed Alexander's help.

A message was sent to Neil Guthrie explaining why they had to cut short their stay in Edinburgh. In reply he appeared in person and assured her that he was sorry to part with her. He requested permission to start a correspondence with her until such times as he also returned to the Tarbolton area.

'I have been concerned about my uncle's health for some months and I have been hoping to arrange a visit to see him in the not too distant future.'

Susanna felt cheered again. At least she still had something to look forward to. There could be no doubt now, despite what Alexander said, about the seriousness of Neil Guthrie's interest in her.

'Neil,' she savoured the name. Neil Guthrie. She felt like swooning with pleasurable anticipation as she imagined what it could be like to be his wife.

8

Tarbolton seemed as quiet and still as the grave after the noisy crush and bustle of Edinburgh. Alexander was glad to meet up with Robert Burns again and tell him all about his visit. The ploughman was completely fascinated, as Alexander knew he would be, especially when he spoke about the people.

He listened intently, his dark eyes glowing as if reflecting the picture and bringing it to life in his mind's eye as it was related to him. Alexander told him of the procession twice every day in which his grandfather walked to and from the court, fully tailed. Horns blew and torches were held aloft if it was dark.

Descriptions of the markets especially fascinated Robert. There was the fish market in Fish Market Close, a steep narrow stinking ravine where fish was sold unwashed because there wasn't a drop of water in the place, from old rickety, scaly wooden tables exposed to all the dust and filth and any abomination around.

Or the vegetables sold by old gin-drinking women who congregated with stools and tables round the Tron churchyard. Every table had its tallow candle and paper lanterns at night.

Robert was not nearly so fired up, if at all, by descriptions of the architecture of the old town, and the New Town that had started to be built over the other side of the Nor' Loch. The city had once been enclosed within the Flodden Wall on three sides and the loch on the other. As a result, most homes were built on the narrow rocky ridge on which stood the High Street. As the population increased, the only way to build was upwards.

'Next time you must come with me, Robert,' Alexander said. 'The place will interest you, I'm sure.'

Robert burst out wistfully, 'Oh Alexander, man, if only I could. If only I was not so burdened with worry and work at Mossgiel. It sorely depresses me.'

Alexander thought he perceived in Burns' cheeks the symptoms of an energy which had been pushed too far. He offered to make his friend a potion that might help to lift his spirits, but Robert was quick to refuse.

'I still have something your father gave me. But, my dear friend, I do appreciate your concern.'

Alexander felt a rush of genuine affection, as well as concern for his friend. He wasn't an emotional man as a rule, but there was something so genuinely loving about Robert Burns that it was difficult not to feel warmth in return. It was in the way he gazed at you so sincerely and intensely and gripped your hand in both of his when he shook it. Alexander admired his courage in taking on the church and making people laugh at its faults and hypocrisies. Yet Robert was a religious man who knew his Bible and believed in that of good or God in everyone. It was disturbing yet touching the way the flame, the joy of life, kept blazing up in his ardent soul.

Nevertheless, Robert – or Rob or Rab of Mossgiel as he was called now – was a complex human being who had many weaknesses, especially with the female sex. He was a strongly sexed man, and there was also a coarseness about him that could appreciate bawdry. This, it had to be admitted, was a common weakness among his fellow countrymen. Robert often collected bawdy songs and verses to send to a friend of his for the man's amusement. Indeed, he had also composed a few bawdy verses himself for the private entertainment of some of his other men friends. As usual, he'd horrified the elders by writing a poem called 'Address to the Deil' that seemed, to them, to even show a hint of sympathy for the devil.

And of course his poem 'Address to an Illegitimate Child', or 'Welcome to a Bastard Wean', as Robert preferred to call it, shocked many more. He made just as many, of course, laugh at his poems and his mock epitaphs. A brother Mason called Manson inspired,

> Here lies 'mang ither useless matters,
> A Manson wi' his endless clatters.

And of James Humphry, the senior warden who was always arguing with Robert,

> Below thir stanes lies Jamie's banes,
> O Death it's my opinion
> Thou ne'er took such a bleth'rin' bitch
> Into thy dark dominion.

Yet he could work himself up to a passionate state of mind that enabled him to write tender love poems. Poetry was something Burns and Alexander had in common. Robert Burns was the only man in Tarbolton to whom Alexander could talk about poetry and know he'd be understood. He could read his work to Robert without feeling nervous or embarrassed. His poetry was different from Robert's (better too, he thought). His work was more disciplined than Robert's and classical. But they encouraged one another. Robert Burns was like the brother Alexander had never had. One of the reasons Alexander did not believe Robert's poetry was as good as his own was that, although Robert spoke proper English, he tended to write in Scots, or in a mixture of both.

'Writing in Scots is a grave fault, Robert,' Alexander kept telling him. 'Surely you can do better than that.'

Alexander was also genuinely concerned to the point of anger about the desperately hard conditions Robert had to contend with on the farm at Mossgiel.

'If only,' he told Robert, 'you could make your fortune and be free of the land. It's disgusting having to suffer such hard work. If only I could make my fortune, I would gladly free you from it.'

Robert put a comforting hand on his shoulder. 'Och man, there's nothing disgusting about honest toil. If a man works hard and has an honest heart, he can be proud of himself and feel as good as any man on earth.'

'Have you had any amorous adventures while I've been away?' Alexander said, changing the subject.

'Of course,' Robert winked. 'I was at a dance not long ago and was taken notice of by a pretty girl called Jean. I confess, however, it was my dog who really was the means of her attention. The wee rascal would insist on keeping at my heels the whole time, even when I was dancing, and it annoyed her and got in her way.' He laughed. 'Then, would you believe it, a few days later she was laying her washing out on the green and the dog ran over it. She tried to aim a blow at it but I rescued it and said, "You can't think much of me if you'd try to harm my dog." "No, I don't think much of you," she said. But she's since proved differently, my friend. I've been seeing much of my bonnie Jean.'

His face and eyes became so lit up with pleasure and happiness that Alexander groaned.

'You are yet again enslaved by a woman, Robert. And now you will tell me that she's all but angelic and the most beautiful creature God ever created.'

'I am the luckiest of men, Alexander. Oh, wait until you see Jean Armour. You will understand, I promise you.'

He understood all right. He wasn't a doctor and a student of human nature for nothing. Jean Armour would be a buxom country girl like all the others, with a healthy complexion and the morals of an alley cat. Houghmagandy, as they called it locally, or fornication was the most common pastime for miles around. One of the few pleasures in a hard life, Alexander conceded, and so it was understandable. Not to the church, of course.

59

What made it a real problem for Robert, as far as he could see, was that his friend always fell in love. Others, he knew, enjoyed sex with a woman and that was all. Robert was always smitten by romantic love. This always inspired him to write a poem. Then, when things went wrong as they usually did, he'd sink into the most dreadful depression. But this mood produced poems as well. Then he'd swing from tremendous self-confidence and sexual boastfulness, expressed in lines like,

> O, leave novels, ye Mauchline belles
> Ye're safer at your spinning wheels!
> Such witching books are baited hooks
> For rakish rooks like Rab Mossgiel.

At other times, he'd be a nervous wreck with moods swinging wildly from foolish, reckless anger to equally reckless, despairing action.

The only good thing that resulted in all this was his poetry. He seemed to have written a great deal of late. 'A Cotter's Saturday Night', for instance, painted a moving picture of the lives of simple working folk. Gilbert had said of the fifth, sixth and eighteenth stanzas, 'They thrilled every ecstasy through my soul.'

Once again Alexander marvelled at the energy of the man, who also managed to write long letters to friends and included verses. Alexander had been both impressed and amused by the letters he'd received while in Edinburgh. Robert's letters were in pure English but not quite in the easy fashion in which Robert *spoke* English. Often speaking English while all around him in the countryside spoke broad Scots was unusual enough. In his letters, however, he seemed to have developed an ornate style influenced to some extent no doubt by his one-time tutor, John Murdoch. Murdoch had been, by all accounts, a terrible pedant who referred to the cottage or auld clay biggin' in which he'd visited the Burns family as an 'argillaceous fabric' or 'mud edifice' or 'tabernacle of clay'.

As it turned out, as far as Robert's new love was concerned, the problem lay with 'bonnie' Jean's family. He'd been told by a patient that Jean's father hated the sight of Robert and would rather have had the devil come to the house to court his daughter than Robert.

Alexander thought this spiteful and unfair. All right, Robert was known for having had many loves, but he had never hurt anyone. He'd had a child by some woman and, despite the fact that he'd never made any promises to her, he'd taken over all the responsibility of the child, including financial. It was now being brought up with him at the farm as one of the Burns family. Most young men that he knew would have left the girl with the worry, expense and responsibility and even denied being the father. Not Robert. He rejoiced in fatherhood and dearly loved the child, his 'dear bought Bess' as he called her.

But Mr Armour was a strictly religious man and a great friend of the minister and the elders who, it had to be said, had no love for Robert Burns either.

Alexander asked Robert what he planned to do and he said he wanted to make Jean his wife but couldn't take on a wife at the moment. The farm at Mossgiel was not doing well and it looked as if they couldn't even be able to afford to keep it on. His life was in a turmoil and he didn't know what to do. 'But I'll have to do something,' he said.

As he said the words, Alexander observed a cloud of dark melancholy dull Robert's eyes. But still his friend made an effort to be cheerful. 'And tell me, Alexander, what of your love life? Has any beautiful Edinburgh lady stolen your heart?'

Alexander sighed. 'I had been hoping to meet someone suitable but I'm afraid my stay in the city wasn't long enough.'

'Suitable?' Robert raised an eyebrow.

'Of course. I do not intend to fall in love like you, my friend, unless the lady is of good fortune.'

'Oh, Alexander!' It was Robert's turn to sigh. 'There's no greater pleasure in the world than loving a woman, even if she doesn't have a halfpenny to her name. You don't realise what you're missing.'

He could see very well what he was missing – if Robert's experience was anything to go by. A great deal of suspense and heartache. He shied away from that. Robert, it seemed, enjoyed the challenge and the suspense of the chase, and in his letters he often wrote of courtships as if they were a military operation. It was Alexander's opinion that this revealed a view, that even Robert was unaware of, of a woman being a target or a quarry to be stormed and captured. In many ways, Alexander found his friend a most interesting subject for study.

That was about the only subject of interest he could find in Tarbolton. His thoughts soon turned to Edinburgh again. It was his only chance of any future. Interest had been shown in his poems and a plan was afoot to publish a slim volume. As soon as he received a letter confirming this, he announced the good news to his father and mother and sister.

'It means, of course, that I must go back to Edinburgh and this time I believe it will be best if I think in terms of a more permanent move.'

They had all been delighted and excited at the prospect of a published author in the family. Susanna especially was practically dancing with delight and clapping her hands with excitement, her auburn curls flying about.

'You will become famous, Alexander. You will be sought after and welcomed and feted in every mansion and noble estate in the country.'

He laughed.

'How you always exaggerate, Susanna.'

But secretly he hoped, indeed believed, that her words would come true. After all, he had a special talent for versifying. Many people in Edinburgh had paid him this compliment and no one would have agreed to print his verses or buy them, had this not been true. He was a very happy man.

His father, although as delighted as the rest of the family, added to his congratulations, 'but we'll miss ye, son. Especially

Ah'll miss ye. Ye've been a guid help tae me.'

Of course his father broadcast the good news to all and sundry and before Alexander had the opportunity to tell his friend, Robert, the news had already reached him. He appeared unexpectedly on the doorstep to personally offer his congratulations. Alexander invited him into the house, thinking how it showed the generosity of spirit of the man. After all, Robert wrote verses himself but here he was, to all intents and purposes perfectly genuine in his delight at his friend's success and good fortune.

Old Doctor Wallace was at the ale house seeing a patient but Alexander introduced Robert to his mother, then said, 'You've met my sister, Robert.'

'I have had that pleasure.' Robert gave a polite little bow and Alexander marvelled, not for the first time, at Robert's apparent good breeding and calm composure in polite company. He was, after all, a common farm worker.

But no – Alexander mentally corrected himself – not common.

9

Susanna was in a flutter, and angry at herself at the same time. Everything had been proceeding very nicely and smoothly. Neil Guthrie was definitely paying court to her. She had seen him several times in Edinburgh. He had taken her to a play and also to a musical evening. They'd gone for walks in the countryside on the outskirts of Edinburgh. They'd even climbed the hill called Arthur's Seat together. His letters were full of pretty compliments and promises. He'd be arriving for his eagerly awaited visit to Tarbolton very soon now, and she felt sure that during this visit, he would propose to her. He'd hinted at such in his last letter. Already she'd imagined herself married to him and the subject of his adoration and generosity. She'd thought of nothing else until now. Her mind had been one beautiful calm pool until now. She had been enjoying pleasant, dreamy anticipation of being with Neil again. Until now.

Now, all at once, she was plunged into an acute turmoil at the mere sight of this man, Robert Burns. She couldn't understand it. She thought he looked almost obscene in the small dark confines of the room. He was not a gentleman and did not belong in polite company. He was a man of the earth with brown skin, black brows and a heavy-looking, muscular body. He was too near to her.

He was chatting amiably enough to her brother and her mother but she imagined he was casting dark, suggestive glances towards her. She was so agitated she hardly knew what he said when he spoke to her, or what she said to him.

Alexander of course was in ecstasy about having a book of his poems published. His thin, colourless face was quite flushed with laughing and joking and eventually, much to Susanna's relief, he invited Burns to accompany him to the ale house to celebrate. She was asked by Burns (impertinent man!) to join them, but she politely declined.

After they left, she had to flop down on to the nearest chair. There she fanned herself energetically.

'Whit's up wi' you?' her mother asked. 'Ah hope ye're no' comin' doon wi' anythin' just when Neil's due tae arrive at any time noo. It wid jist be like ye tae be sae awkward.'

'No, no,' Susanna snapped. 'I'm perfectly all right and I'm greatly looking forward to Neil's arrival.'

'Ah didnae get a chance tae tell ye with aw the excitement aboot Alexander and then Rab Mossgiel arrivin'. But one o' Lord Guthrie's servants came wi' a message sayin' we're tae go tae his place for our supper tomorrow. He's expectin' Neil to be there by then. He'd sent word tae Neil that his auld uncle was keeping' poorly and felt he hadnae long for this world. Sly auld devil. He's no' that poorly but he knew that would bring Neil home tae him. He's grown that fond o' his nephew.'

'Well, I declare! Oh splendid! I did expect him but not quite so soon. I shall wear my French outfit. When I wore it at the musical evening Neil said he felt proud to have me on his arm. He turns a pretty compliment.'

The French outfit she had in mind was an open robe in champagne-coloured taffeta with matching flounced petticoat. There were ribbon bows on the stomacher and elbow-length sleeves, finished with soft ruffles. She'd wear a matching ruffle round her neck and pearls above it and pearls in her hair too.

She would astonish and delight Neil with the beautiful picture she'd make. Neil didn't like the mountainous hair styles and wigs and terribly ornate hair decorations he'd seen women wearing in some cities. He said he believed such excesses would soon pass. Meantime he preferred natural hair and so that is what she'd have. Fortunately her hair was long and had a natural curl. All she needed to do was give it a dusting of white powder.

She wondered if there would be other lords and ladies at the supper but sadly doubted it. Lord Guthrie didn't do much entertaining at home, preferring – as most people did – to socialise in taverns and ale houses. But then, most people had no choice. Their houses were so ill-suited for company. Lord Guthrie had plenty of space in his mansion and enough servants to attend to any size of gathering. He had no excuse. Except perhaps, she grudgingly admitted to herself, ill health. Even her mother couldn't deny his health had been getting somewhat worse of late. Thoughts of the supper and meeting Neil again banished all thoughts of Alexander's poetry from her mind.

But next day, when entering the Guthrie house, she was somewhat taken aback when Neil greeted Alexander first and complimented him on his achievement.

'I am,' he said, offering Alexander his soft hand, 'very proud of you, sir.'

Susanna wanted him to have greeted her first, to have had no eyes for anyone else, or even compliments for anyone else but her. He eventually did pay her a pretty compliment on her appearance, however, and she had to be content with that. It occurred to her, observing the others round the supper table, that Neil and Alexander were not unlike one another. They were both gentlemen, of course, with an easy, confident manner. They were both about the same height and slim with lean, pale faces and long-fingered hands. They both had grey-green eyes, only Neil's were paler and rather cooler perhaps? And Neil's mouth was thinner – not so full-lipped as Alexander's. She was glad that her brother seemed to have become more used to Neil and to be accepting him with good grace (good humour even), as a potential member of the family.

This state of affairs was confirmed that very evening when

Neil made the opportunity of speaking to her privately in the library room. Once in the room he shut the door, then turned towards her. She guessed what was coming and felt a flutter of excitement. Neil, however, appeared as cool and controlled as ever.

'Miss Wallace,' he said. 'Would you do me the honour of agreeing to become my wife?'

She could have danced all round the room with excitement. She was going to be mistress of this large mansion and huge estate. Cheeks pink and hot, she smiled happily at him.

'Yes, I will indeed, Sir.'

'Very well.' He took her hand and raised it briefly to his lips before leading her from the room. 'Let us go and announce the news of our engagement.'

It had been a very polite, formal kind of proposal, not the passionate, romantic one of her dreams, but it was a proposal. She was going to be the lady of the Guthrie mansion. The evening became a celebration not only of Neil's homecoming to the Guthrie estate and Alexander's poetry, but of the official engagement of Susanna Wallace and Neil Guthrie.

Glasses were raised and even Alexander raised a 'hurrah' along with his father and old Guthrie. Charlotte, Susanna noticed, did not join in but kept her eyes lowered and said very little for most of the evening. Surely she had not had any serious expectations of romance with her cousin, Susanna thought. She was such a plain girl, and so dull. She could not even play an instrument or sing. It was Susanna who entertained the company, small though it was, with a song or two. Charlotte had clapped politely enough but she looked very unhappy. Susanna began to feel sorry for her. She must be feeling very insecure, apart from anything else. If anything happened to her grandfather, Neil would inherit the estate. Old Lord Guthrie had now made this quite plain. Poor Charlotte would be wondering what would happen to her then. Would she become homeless after her cousin and his wife moved in? Susanna was tempted to give the girl a few words of comfort and reassurance.

She wanted to tell her that she had no need to worry. She would be welcome to remain where she was for as long as she wished.

However, by this time it was very late and her father and mother – especially her mother – had begun to feel 'the worse for wear', as her mother said, and needed to be quickly transported back home to bed.

Some other time, Susanna thought, I must remember to have a talk with Charlotte.

Lying in bed that night, Susanna couldn't sleep. Her mind kept going over the momentous evening. She kept thinking, 'I'm going to escape this awful stinking house. I *really* am. I'm going to live in a beautiful big house with lovely gardens where I can stroll at my leisure.' Only occasionally did Neil come into the picture. It suddenly occurred to her with a little start of unease, that she hardly knew the man – not in any depth. He had been gentlemanly company in Edinburgh, escorted her to most interesting places, and paid her some pretty compliments, but that was all. No, that was not all, she tried to reassure herself. She knew (although it was her grandmother who had told her, not Neil) that his father had made money in shipping and had various monetary interests abroad. What these were exactly, her grandmother hadn't been too sure. Anyway, both Neil's parents were now dead and he had no brothers or sisters. Old Guthrie in fact, and of course Charlotte, were his only living relatives, apart from a great aunt on his mother's side who lived up north in Aberdeen.

Like Alexander, he'd had most of his education abroad after being attended to by a private tutor at home in his childish years. Like Alexander, he was a sophisticated and worldly-wise man. She liked that, and he had such gentlemanly restraint. He had certainly not taken advantage of her youth or innocence. He had never even kissed her on the lips. Unexpectedly, Robert Burns returned to her mind and she felt herself blush. She knew about him, all right. He had a very bad reputation with women. Already the church had shamed him on the cutty stool and on more than one occasion had severely reprimanded him. He had done more than kiss girls. She felt her cheeks flame at the very idea (damn his eyes!).

She tossed and turned in bed, appalled at herself at the intrusion of shameful thoughts into her mind. What would it feel like, for instance, to be kissed on the lips by such a man. Her whole body flamed and pulsed at the mere idea. She could have wept at the shame of it and eventually had to rise and fumble for a candle, light it at the dying embers of the fire and go and purloin some of her mother's sleeping potion.

Damn his wicked, suggestive, sarcastic eyes!

Next day, Neil came to call and they had a long talk in which they made practical plans for the future. Neil, it appeared, was a very practical man. Charlotte, he said, would go to Aberdeen to live with their relation there. When Susanna protested that there was no need for Charlotte to move from the Guthrie estate, Neil had assured her that Charlotte was more than happy to do so. The day after that, she and Neil went out riding. She wore a cream outfit and a hat with a long, curled feather. Neil too looked most elegant and she felt proud to be seen with him. Especially while they were riding along a bridle path and they passed the big, plodding figure of Robert Burns. He was in his work clothes, which Susanna thought showed him in his true colours. He was a coarse peasant in corduroy breeches, dark blue stockings, gaiters, a long tailed coat and broad blue bonnet.

He made to smile and raise a hand in greeting (the impertinence of the man!), but she kept her back straight and her head held high.

As he moved on, she caught a glimpse of his face and was taken aback at the black fury she saw in it. Of course, neighbours had spoken about Burns in terms of suspicion about what he'd been reading on the subject of religion and some even avoided him, as a heretical and dangerous companion.

Susanna determined to have another word with Alexander about the suitability of having such a man as a friend.

At one point, Neil said that as soon as his uncle died – and his death shouldn't be far off by the look of him – the marriage would take place and they would immediately move into the Guthrie mansion. It occurred to Susanna that this sounded rather cold and unfeeling. After all, the old Lord was family to Neil. But no doubt it would just be Neil's way of talking. He was definitely a very practical man and liked to plan everything in advance. After they were married she could be very well looked after, she was sure. He was a gentleman and she would be proud to be his wife.

And after all, Lord Guthrie was very old. It occurred to her then that her grandparents were very old too and she felt a pang of fear and distress. She loved her grandmother and grandfather and couldn't bear the thought of losing them. Come what may, she'd return to Edinburgh at the earliest possible date to see them again and treasure whatever time she had left with them. She'd plead with Alexander to take her with him on his next visit. Apart from the pleasure of being reunited with her grandparents, she could then share in all the excitement of Alexander's book and the appreciation of it by all the quality of the town.

What a stir the book would cause in the capital city and in all the noble estates for miles around. Susanna dreamed of basking in her brother's fame and reflected glory.

First of all, though, she had to plead with her mother to allow her another visit to Edinburgh.

'You should be thinkin' an' plannin' for yer wedding, no' stravaigin' awa' tae Edinburgh. Think o' aw the sewin' ye have tae dae,' her mother scolded.

'It's all planned already, mother. I've started my sewing too and I can continue it at Grandmother's house. They're too old to travel to my wedding and I feel it's important to see them while they're still in the land of the living. Oh, please, Mother. Come with us, why don't you? Father too. We could all go. Grandmother and Grandfather would be so delighted.'

'Dinnae be daft. Yer faither cannae leave aw his ill folk an'

Ah'm no' fit tae set foot in a carriage. The thought o' bein' rattled aboot for hours in one o' them contraptions makes me feel as if Ah'm dyin' already. No, no. Ah'm no' a well woman. It's as much as Ah can dae tae keep on ma feet in the hoose,' she sighed. 'You go if ye must. Ye'll no' gie me a minute's peace if ye dinnae. An' the auld folks'll be glad tae see ye, Ah suppose.'

Susanna was delighted.

'But here,' her mother suddenly added, 'whit aboot yer man? He's stayin' wi' his uncle. What'll he say aboot ye stayin' awa' in Edinburgh before yer weddin'?'

'As long as I'm happy, Mother, that's all Neil cares about. He'll understand why I need to spend some time with Grandmother and Grandfather. He's a very understanding man.'

And I'm a very lucky girl, she thought to herself. First the visit to the capital city to look forward to. Then the excitement of her wedding and her wonderful new life as the lady of the manor.

Oh, how lucky she was!

10

Bonnie Jean Armour was his jewel. She was six years younger than him, the eldest daughter of Mauchline's stone-mason and the oldest in a family of eleven. She was a lovely girl with brown curls peeping out from under her bonnet and calm, thoughtful eyes. Underneath the calm exterior, however, there was a passion that continued to surprise and delight Robert. She loved him and was not afraid to show it and allow him to physically demonstrate his love for her. The courtship was not easy, because of her father's bitter opposition, but 'love will find a way'. One of the ways they made contact was verbally by way of Jean's bedroom window. A window at the rear of the Whitefoord Arms looked on to Jean's bedroom with only a very narrow lane intervening. The courtship, both verbally and otherwise, made steady progress until, as a result, Jean found out she was pregnant. She well understood that Robert and his family were in desperate financial straits but something needed to be done. Jean was his responsibility.

Eventually Robert came up with the idea of going to Jamaica to make some money. A friend had promised to use his influence with his brother in Jamaica to get Robert a job as a book-keeper there. Many young men in the past had solved their problems by going to the West Indies.

At the same time Robert was mulling over advice given by other friends to get his poems into 'guid black print'. He had for some time now been circulating epistles, epitaphs, elegies, songs and poems among friends and acquaintances.

Now he was in such a desperate predicament that necessity forced him to think of himself as anything other than a farmer. Meantime, for Jean's protection, he wrote a paper in which he and Jean accepted each other as man and wife, making them legally, though irregularly, *per verba de presenti* – man and wife; for by Scots law a promise to marry, sealed by anticipatory consummation, constituted a true and valid marriage. This way she could stay respectably with her father until her lover could improve his situation enough to support her and their child.

His depressing worries with the farm had been making him suffer a recurrence of dull headaches, joint pains and palpitations of the heart. Now that Jean was his wife, however, Robert felt euphoric. He overflowed with gratitude. He was a lucky man. He only needed to look at Jean for his heart to lighten and his blood-warm through his veins, banishing every ache and pain.

His euphoria fed his muse and, crouched in front of the fire at home struggling to see by the small flicker of light from the fire and the crusie lamp hanging from the lintel, with the squeaking of the rats in the rafters above, he penned a long poem. It was called 'The Holy Tulzie' (or brawl), satirising a quarrel that had been going on between two ministers of the Auld Lichts – two Reverend Calvinists who had lost all command of temper and abused each other with terrible rages and fiery virulence.

The poem met with an immediate roar of applause from every friend and neighbour who read it. It was passed around the taverns to the immense entertainment of everyone, as far as Kilmarnock and beyond. He produced another long satire poem, even more savage than 'The Holy Tulzie'. It was called 'Holy Willie's Prayer'. It alarmed the kirk session so much they held several meetings to see if they could find any way of punishing the 'profane rhymer'.

Soon Mr Armour was on the warpath again and not only because of the satirical poetry. Jean had confessed that she was

73

pregnant and shown her father the paper they'd signed, making her the wife of Rab of Mossgiel. Mr Armour had vowed to get it annulled. Robert began to worry again. Could the man legally do such a thing? Soon he had worked himself into a state of complete wretchedness.

During the day, while he was straining over the plough, he turned up a mouse in her nest and was deeply moved by the predicament of the wee thing. Before he'd returned home after his hard day's work, he had composed a poem in his head to the mouse. The last two verses expressed a sympathetic comparison with his own predicament.

> But mousie, thou art no thy lane
> In proving foresight may be vain;
> The best laid schemes o' mice and men,
> Gang aft agley,
> An' lea'e us nought but grief and pain,
> For promised joy!
>
> Still, thou art blest, compar'd wi' me!
> The present only toucheth thee;
> But och, I backward cast my e'e,
> On prospects drear!
> An' forward, tho' I canna see,
> I guess an' fear!

Then he discovered that Jean had agreed to their names being cut out of the paper by the lawyer, Robert Aiken. Aiken was a friend – although now Robert was not even sure of that – and had done the mutilation of the paper which proved that Robert Burns and Jean Armour were no longer joined in matrimony. He had sent Aiken one of the poems he was hoping to gather for eventual publication. Now he wrote in an anguished, confused and almost hysterical state to another friend, Gavin Hamilton, to whom he'd also sent various poems.

'Old Mr Armour prevailed with Mr Aiken to mutilate that

unlucky paper, yesterday – would you believe it? – tho' I had not a hope, nor even a wish, to make her mine after her conduct; yet when he told me, the names were all cut out of the paper, my heart died within me, and he cut my very veins with the news. I am indeed a fool, but a *knave* is an infinitely worse character than any body, I hope, will dare to give the unfortunate Robert Burns.'

He felt feverish, delirious with unhappiness and despair. 'Never a man loved,' he wrote, 'or rather admired a woman than I did her and to confess a truth between you and me, I do still love her to distraction.' He felt nine-tenths mad.

He found desperate expression and release in writing – even just in letter writing. In one sad, rash, bawdy letter full of sexual braggadocios, he used military metaphors about how he had successfully besieged and captured Jean but had been outflanked by James Armour. He wildly expressed intimate feelings in letters to total strangers. 'Sad and grievous of late, Sir, has been my tribulation, and many and piercing, my sorrows . . . I have lost, Sir, that dearest earthly Treasure, that last best gift which complicated Adam's happiness in the garden of bliss . . . I have lost a wife . . .

'But this is not all – Already the holy beagles, the houghmagandy pack, begin to sniff the scent; and I expect every moment to see them cast off, and hear them after me in full cry; but as I am an old fox, I shall give them dodging and doubling for it; and by and by, I intend to earth among the mountains of Jamaica.'

By April the 'holy beagles' had made an entry into the kirk session book: 'April 1786. The Session being informed that Jean Armour, an unmarried woman, is said to be with child, and that she has gone off from the place of late, to reside elsewhere, the Session think it their duty to enquire . . . But appoint James Laurie and William Fisher to speak to the parents. April 9th 1786. James Laurie reports that he spoke to Mary Smith, mother to Jean Armour, who told him that she did not suspect her daughter to be with child, that she was

75

gone to Paisley to see her friends and would return soon.'

It was the talk of the parish and no doubt was left in everybody's mind that James Armour's fury was intensifying by the day. Two things were most urgently concerning him: the scandal affecting his good name and his pathological hatred of the young blackguard who had violated his daughter.

Jean had gone. Robert, in his highly emotional state, thought of her going as her total desertion and rejection of him. It hit him hard. He desperately turned to his poetry and his earlier thoughts of going to Jamaica. He needed money for a ticket, however, and thought he might earn enough from the publication of his poems to cover all of his expenses for the journey. He was coming under more and more enthusiastic pressure from friends to gather names of subscribers. Over and over again, they assured him that there would be plenty of people ready and willing to subscribe. Everyone was confident of the outcome, except his good friend Alexander Wallace. Robert could understand Alexander's attitude. Poor man, his book of poems had sunk without trace. The book had not even merited one single review. The distress caused by this terrible blow still showed on Alexander's pale, sad face.

'I don't want you to suffer the disappointment and humiliation that I have suffered, Robert,' he said. 'Indeed you may come off even more badly. So many of your poems are in Scots and the vernacular is not fashionable.'

Robert appreciated his friend's concern but could not take his advice too seriously. He knew that his poetry – vernacular or not – was better than Alexander's. Not that he'd dream of saying that to the man. Poor Alexander had suffered enough and had now made up his mind to go and try his luck at doctoring in Edinburgh.

'Although I will not give up my poetry writing. I will never do that,' he assured Robert. 'I believe that with perseverance and hard work, I will succeed. That is always the best recipe for success. But alas, my poetry has not yet made me the fortune I'd hoped for and so, until it does, it's more doctoring for me, Robert.'

'You are a good doctor,' Robert assured him. 'You will do well in the city and be much happier there.'

'Yes,' Alexander agreed. 'You are right, Robert. I don't take easily to country living. I doubt if I'd have stayed this long had it not been for your intelligent and entertaining company.'

Robert had been genuinely, indeed desperately, sorry to see him go. In the midst of all his other losses, to lose a friend was the last thing he wanted. Near to tears, he gave Alexander a bear hug of a goodbye.

'Calm down, Robert. You will come to Edinburgh to visit me one day. I'll write to you as soon as I find lodgings.'

Robert grabbed Alexander's hand and, not daring to say anything, he silently pumped the hand up and down. Then he released his friend and allowed him to climb into the waiting carriage.

Not long afterwards, Jean returned to Mauchline and was 'called, compeared not' which meant that Mr Auld, the minister, was planning to cry out for her to come forward from the body of the kirk to be severely rebuked for her shameful conduct.

Instead, however, Jean wrote a letter of confession and apology. Robert himself had been chastised before the kirk session where he acknowledged his guilt. Three fortnightly acts of public penance were to be his punishment. Having been told of Jean's return and her letter, Robert decided to call and see her before his first ordeal. Afterwards he wrote to a friend who'd endured a similar experience of kirk vengeance.

'I have waited on Armour since her return home; not from any view of reconciliation, but merely to ask for her health, and – to you I will confess it, from a foolish hankering fondness – very ill-plac'd indeed. The Mother forbade me the house, nor did Jean show that penitence that might have been expected. Now, the Priest, I am informed, will give me a certificate as a single man, if I comply with the rules of the church . . . '

Robert flung himself into the business, despite Alexander's warnings, of collecting subscribers for the publication of a book of his poems. Also he made enquiries about a passage to Jamaica.

Then something happened to save him from sinking into total despair. He met a most beautiful and enchanting Highland girl called Margaret Campbell. Alexander tried to discourage his sudden, wild devotion to this serving wench, or light-skirts as Alexander called her. He insisted that, as usual, Robert had blinded himself to the true character of the object of his love. Margaret Campbell, he told him, was loose in the extreme and even had been *kept* for some time by a brother of Lord Eglinton's. Nothing produced a change in Robert's sentiments. Fortunately, in Alexander's view at least, Robert's association with the girl was short-lived. Margaret Campbell had gone home like most servant girls to spend the time with her family between her resignation from one situation and her entrance into another.

After a time, she had obtained a post with a Colonel McIvor in Glasgow. First she travelled with her brother to Greenock where they visited relatives in a tenement house in Charles Street. There, her brother took ill and Margaret nursed him until eventually she too fell ill with a malignant fever and died.

Alexander didn't know for certain who wrote the letter informing Robert of Margaret's death but he guessed it was from her father. This man had much the same attitude to Robert as James Armour had had. As a result, he could imagine the cruel words the letter to Robert must have contained. It was obvious that whatever the words were, they had found their mark. Robert was strangely quiet, refused indeed to talk about Margaret. But his painful grieving was there for all to see.

Everyone hoped that the publication of his book of poems would raise his spirits, would make his mood swing from the pit of despair to the heights of euphoria. Alexander expected that Robert would find inspiration from this latest bout of love fever for a new poem or song. That is exactly what happened, of course. But he noticed Robert had changed the name from Margaret to Mary.

He had used the name in a previous poem. It had been about a girl who had turned down his proposal of marriage. Her name had been Elizabeth Gebbie, or Begbie, but Robert could not cope with the rhyme required for a name like that, and so for the purposes of the song, she became Mary Morison.

> Tho' this was fair, an' that was braw
> And yon the toast o' a' the town
> I sighed and said among them a'
> Ye are na Mary Morison.

In this more recent case, Mary obviously made for a smoother and better metre than Margaret!

Alexander believed the Highland girl had caught Robert on the rebound from his mad anguish at losing his 'bonnie Jean', and Margaret's death was yet another blow to his already devastated romantic spirit. But Alexander had no doubt that Robert would be smitten by yet another love fever that would cure him of his present one. As far as he could see, every time Robert wanted to write a song or poem, he had to look for or think of a woman to write it to.

And then he worked himself into this madness he called love.

II

The tiny church was bursting at the seams. It was a tight, jostling, bustling riot of colour. The dazzling shades of the women's dresses and the elegant apparel of the men made a startling contrast to the usual dark and dirty state of the church. The bride wore sapphire blue taffeta with much silver ribbon and lace flouncing. Earlier Susanna had thought, 'How beautiful I look' when she had gazed in delight at the vision of herself in the bedroom mirror. She had spent hours dressing and doing her hair into the long curls that now draped over one shoulder and had been carefully powdered.

Even Mysie shared in her excitement and helped her as much as she could. 'Fancy,' Mysie enthused, 'ye'll soon be the mistress o' that big hoose. Ma wee fat Anna.'

For a moment, despite her happy excitement, Susanna felt outraged. 'I am not fat! How dare you try to spoil my wedding day by saying such a thing.'

'Och, Ah was just rememberin' ye as a wee bairn. Ah know ye're no' fat noo. Ye look just grand. Just grand.'

'I was never fat,' Susanna muttered, mollified now and her happiness fast returning. 'Should I take my fan, Mysie?'

'Ye shouldnae need it to cool yersel' in that kirk. It's aye as cauld as the tomb. But I see yer cheeks are burnin' that much, maybe ye'll need a few flaps tae cool doon yer excitement.'

Eventually, the bride's party, led by old Doctor Wallace, set out, praying that they'd avoid meeting a funeral on the way because that was bad luck. The bride had to approach the church from right to left and it was sometimes the custom to walk three times around the church sun-wise before entering. Susanna chose not to do this, so impatient was she to 'tie the knot', as a marriage was sometimes called because both bride and groom had to have all knots on their person removed before the ceremony to ensure there would be no barrier to fertility. As soon as the ceremony was over, they were retied. The groom had already arrived, resplendent in a maroon silk coat with a gold embroidered waistcoat, followed by the bridesmaids, all led by a piper. Susanna thrilled to the sound of the pipes and the chatter and the squeals of laughter filling the streets outside.

Now she was actually in the packed kirk. The minister had performed the ceremony. Now pistols were firing and church bells ringing, and everyone was stamping energetically to keep the evil spirits away. There was the custom to kiss the bride. The minister got to her first and then she was nearly knocked over in the rush. Now they had reached the tavern where a room had been provided for the dinner.

After the dinner, the bride's mother broke a cake of shortbread over Susanna's head. If it broke into small pieces the marriage would be fruitful. Unmarried girls in the company scrambled to grab a piece so that they could put it under their pillow to dream on. Then the bride's cog or bowl was passed around from lip to lip, filled with hot ale, whisky, cream, beaten eggs, sugar and spices, and everyone drank Susanna's health.

By the time Susanna reached Guthrie House, her head was in a swirl and she was exhausted with all the noise of talking, of laughter, and of the dazzle of colour. The house made a shocking comparison. Had it ever seemed so shadowy, so silent, so gloomy, when old Lord Guthrie had been alive? She had no recollection of it being so. He had been a coarse but jolly, noisy old fellow who seemed to fill the whole place with his rude good cheer.

On reflection, she thought it rather insensitive of Neil, the way he'd told her of his uncle's death, insensitive to her feelings as well as to the suddenness of the old man's demise. He'd dropped dead in the middle of enjoying an evening in the ale house with friends. It was the casual tone of Neil's voice even more than his words that had taken her aback.

'My uncle has died and so we can now begin planning our marriage.'

She did not detect one note of sadness or regret in his expression or demeanour.

'Oh, Neil, poor Lord Guthrie,' she'd cried out. 'Everyone had a high regard for him and I'm sure everyone will be as sorry as I am.'

Neil shrugged. 'He was an old man. He'd had his day.'

Susanna's mind tightened with worry and apprehension. It suddenly occurred to her that her father and mother were old. She fervently hoped and prayed that they both would be spared many, many days yet. She suddenly felt lonely without them, and her brother, and the old familiar servants Mysie and John. She even felt a pang for the familiar old house and its dreadful stinks.

Neil said, 'Why are you standing there dreaming? The servants are waiting with candelabra to light our way to the bedchamber.'

She had not heard or even noticed the servants entering the hallway holding the candelabra in front of them. The yellow pools seemed to make the surrounding darkness even darker.

She tried to smile as she walked beside her new husband across the hall, up the creaking stairway and along a corridor. Eventually they stopped at a door, the servants flung it open, entered and put one of the candelabras down on to a high chest of drawers. A flickering fire did little to dispel the chill in the room. The woman servant gave a little curtsy, the man a slight bow.

Susanna's euphoria frittered away, leaving her confused. She felt embarrassed too. She'd known of course that married couples slept together. Her mother and father, and her grandmother and grandfather slept together. Now that she came to think of it, that must mean they undressed in front of each other as well. The trouble was, she'd never really thought of it before. Not really. Not in any detail. Vague thoughts of such embarrassing intimacies had only occasionally fluttered across the surface of her mind. There had been so many other more exciting and pleasurable thoughts and dreams to busy herself with.

Now details crowded in on her. She was thankful her dress had front fastenings so that she could manage unaided. But if she took off her dress standing here in the light of the fire and the candelabra, she would be naked. The thought was an agony of embarrassment. It was bad enough to witness Neil divesting himself of his clothes. Closing her eyes, she fumbled to unhook herself. If she did so quickly, then immediately plunged under the covers of the bed, perhaps her modesty could be protected.

She did this as best she could but she had no sooner cowered under the bedclothes when Neil came into bed beside her and immediately flung back the covers. Appalled, she struggled to clutch at them for protection again but Neil tore them completely from the bed and began to roughly knead at her breasts. In pain now as well as panic, she managed in a tremulous voice,

'Please, Sir, let me be. I am exhausted and wish to compose myself to sleep.'

He gave a coarse laugh. 'You're not going to get any sleep tonight.'

'But Neil . . . '

'Be quiet. You belong to me now and you'll do as you're told.'

No words could express the shock, the confusion, the suicidal despair she felt. Not even to herself. She could not believe what was happening to her. Neil had always behaved to her as a perfect gentleman. He had never even ventured to put an arm around her waist.

Now his hands were fumbling all over her body. He was staring at her, examining her in a kind of mad intensity that seemed to go on for an eternity. Then suddenly his body was on top of hers, crushing her and making it difficult for her to breathe. She felt a stabbing agony between her legs and deep inside her, making her cry out in pain. He was grunting like an animal, making her burst into tears of terror. Eventually he rolled away from her, pulled the bedcovers back on to the bed and in a few minutes, he was snoring.

She lay rigid with shock and horror, as well as pain. Was this what marriage meant? Why didn't someone – her mother, or her grandmother, or even Mysie – warn her? How could they happily allow her to get into such a terrible trap? Was this dreadful behaviour supposed to go on for a lifetime? Surely that was not possible. Perhaps it was something – some kind of ritual – that was only performed on the wedding night. She gratefully clung to this hopeful thought but didn't really believe it. Surely there should have been at least one word of love or affection from her husband. Surely he could have been more gentle. He had not said one word of any kind to her after commanding her to be quiet. He had hurt her cruelly both mentally and physically.

Nothing was as she'd hoped. Her dreams were shattered. She was broken-hearted.

12

Alexander didn't know what to make of it, didn't know what to think or feel. Never for a moment had he thought . . . well, there had been the occasional moment when he had thought Robert's poems were good. At least the few that were expressed in decent English. He'd liked:

> . . . Tho' mountains rise, and deserts howl,
> and oceans roar between;
> Yet, dearer to my deathless soul,
> I still would love my Jean.

The vernacular of others of his poems was scarcely understandable to educated people. Some of his lines were destined to get him into one kind of trouble or another. But Robert's head had always been full to overflowing with rhymes of all sorts. He even scratched lines on window panes that had suddenly come into his mind. He never stopped to think of the consequences that might arise.

On the window pane of one inn he had inscribed the Jacobite sentiment,

> The injur'd Stewart line are gone,
> A race outlandish fills their throne;
> An idiot race, to honour lost;
> Who know them best despise them most.

85

Realising the danger of this in the political climate of the day, and with a job in the Excise at the back of his mind, Robert had returned and kicked in the pane, but it was too late. The verse had already been copied and passed around.

On another occasion, he had been passing a church, and found that inside a thanksgiving service was taking place to celebrate a naval victory. He'd immediately composed,

> Ye hypocrites! Are these your pranks?
> To murder men, and gie God thanks!
> For shame! Gie o'er – proceed no further –
> God won't accept your thanks for murder!

Alexander had persuaded Robert not to circulate these lines around friends and acquaintances as he had long since got into the habit of doing with so many other poems. It seemed he couldn't send a letter without enclosing poems or songs, and breaking into rhyme in the middle of a letter, or even writing the whole letter in rhyme. It was ridiculous to go to such extremes.

It couldn't be denied of course that even his scurrilous satirical poems could be amusing – especially if Robert recited them. The memory of his friend performing – because that what it amounted to, a performance – 'Holy Willie's Prayer' could still make him laugh.

It was the way Robert had rolled his dark eyes heavenwards as he delivered some verses and the way his face could take on a wickedly hypocritical smirk when reciting others. No wonder the church had been furious and had tried their best to get revenge on him.

'You'll get yourself into really serious trouble yet,' Alexander kept warning him.

The last Alexander had heard, Robert had been planning to escape from all the troubles and woes that beset him by sailing to the West Indies. Apparently, somebody had promised him a job as a book-keeper there. As far as Alexander understood, he'd even purchased a ticket. A single ticket costing about nine pounds, he remembered. He'd written to Robert from his lodgings in Edinburgh (he was lodging with Professor Purdie from the Infirmary) saying he'd be sorry to lose him but perhaps, in the circumstances, it was the only way.

That Robert had also been giving thought to a job as a gauger was surprising, to say the least. Robert of all people! A King's man was a ridiculous idea. The Customs and Excise might – indeed *did* – pay very well but they were universally hated. Anyway, with Robert's reputation, it would be even more surprising if they accepted him. No, he'd reckoned Robert would be much happier and much better served as a book-keeper in Jamaica. He certainly wasn't happy in Mossgiel or Mauchline, or anywhere in Ayrshire.

There was the serious business of Jean Armour and what her father had done. First of all, Robert had been outraged at Mr Armour's insult to his honour, and also wounded at the faithlessness of the girl. He had admitted to Alexander that he went 'stark staring mad' and felt himself 'nine-tenths ripe for Bedlam'.

'I have run into all kinds of dissipation and riot, Mason meetings, drinking matches and other mischief to drive her out of my head but all in vain. So now for the grand cure – the ship is on her way home that is to take me out to Jamaica and then farewell, dear old Scotland, and farewell dear ungrateful Jean, for never, never will I see you more!'

The arrangements Burns made for leaving the country, which he set on paper and had been publicly proclaimed, was that he duly appointed his brother Gilbert as his chief heir, and bequeathed him not only his share of Mossgiel but also whatever profit there might be from the publication of his poems. This was on condition that Gilbert undertook to clothe and educate Burns' natural daughter, Elizabeth.

The absence of any settlement in favour of Jean Armour's expected issue made old Armour take out a warrant of arrest against Burns. Burns, learning of the impending danger, fled from one friend's house to another. Eventually, a wretched and embittered figure, he'd found shelter in the vicinity of Kilmarnock with a relation of his mother's. It was under these circumstances that his volume of poems called *Poems Chiefly in the Scottish Dialect* left the press.

The immediate and incredible reception the book had met truly astonished Alexander. All over the countryside, old and young, learned and ignorant people were delighted, absolutely transported by the book. Alexander had been told that ploughboys and maid servants were willing to give up hard-earned wages, which they needed to purchase clothing, for a copy of the book. One country friend had confessed to him in a letter that he'd opened the book late one evening, meaning just to give the first page a glance before laying it aside until morning. He'd kept on reading, however, and couldn't stop until he'd finished the whole book.

Alexander couldn't understand it. Well, perhaps naive country folk who were not used to books could be forgiven for being so excited and impressed. What he really couldn't fathom, and what shocked and confused him, was the reaction of the quality, the literati, the book reviewers and even the nobility. Robert's work was actually receiving adulation from people outside his own class. Yet most of the poems were in Scots. How could this have happened? After all, people were paying large sums of money to be taught and speak pure English, and lose their Scots language. Even judges and professors and others of note were attending classes run by English teachers and earnestly studying and repeating like school children English words and proper English pronunciations.

Only very old people like his late grandmother and grandfather – God rest their souls, they had recently died within weeks of each other - had still clung to the unfashionable Scots tongue that they had used all their lives. They had been too old and set in their ways to change. But Robert was only twenty-seven and should know better. Didn't he *speak* perfectly well? So why did he not write properly? And why on earth were educated people praising his poems? Perhaps, he thought, they were just favouring the ones in English. But no, he'd heard 'The Twa Dogs' called brilliant. Brilliant! Such a long poem in such broad Scots! And about dogs expressing their thoughts on different classes of people!

Alexander had read the poem long ago and knew that the dog called Luath in it was inspired by Robert's own dog, that someone, according to Robert, had 'cruelly killed'. Robert had been terribly upset by this incident. He was so ridiculously over-sensitive about animals.

Then there was 'The Holy Fair' which, right from the time he'd first written it, caused a terrible stir among the clergy. Admittedly it gave a startlingly accurate picture of everybody for miles around flocking to see a sacrament and hear all the outdoor preachers. In the process, there was always much dreadful drunkenness and all sorts of disgusting indecencies and follies. He'd witnessed himself that at the time of the administration of the Lord's Supper on the Thursday, Saturday and Monday, as well as on the preaching in the fields near the church, there had been a great number of men and women lying together in the grass.

Robert had made the point to him that his satire in this long poem was focused on the people in the kirk yard and surrounds. The sacrament itself and the building in which it was held, formed no part of the picture. It was a long poem which ended with:

> There's some are fou o' love divine;
> There's some are fou o' brandy;
> An monie jobs that day begin,
> May end in houghmagandy
> Some ither day.

Perhaps if all of the poem had been written in English, he could have understood it, but so much of it was not.

This poem had actually been referred to as a masterpiece! A *masterpiece*! He'd heard the very words with his own ears.

He'd read the words with his own eyes. Otherwise he would not have believed it.

His emotions were more and more confused. He tried to be firm with himself. He was glad for Robert's sake, of course. *Of course* he was! Robert was his friend. His good friend. If he, Doctor Alexander Wallace, had ever come near to loving another human being, it was Robert Burns. How could he not be glad to hear of the success of Robert's work? He must write and congratulate him post haste.

The quill hesitated, hovered aimlessly over the page. How to sound sincere? But he *was* sincere. The tiny seed of displeasure that had begun to take root in his heart was not aimed at Robert. It was at the stupidity of others in not appreciating his own poems. Robert had appreciated them. It was the unfairness of life he had to face and struggle with. He must get a grip of himself for his own sake, as well as Robert's.

Determinedly, he began to write.

'My dear friend,

'How wonderful it is to hear of the success of your book. You have become famous overnight, and my congratulations to you. Are you planning to come to Edinburgh in the foreseeable future? If so, I look forward to shaking you by the hand and expressing in person my heartfelt delight at your success.'

He went on to give some news of his work in the Infirmary and ended the letter by repeating his congratulations.

He thought he'd feel better after consigning the letter to the post. But sadly, he did not. He was still being pulled one way and another inside himself. He was still confused, upset, insulted. He began to feel angry. Trying to get a grip of one's unruly emotions, he discovered, was a very difficult task.

A doctor, of all people, must never allow emotion to take charge. Never before had he allowed such a thing to happen. He had never even realised that he was capable of much emotion. Now he was surprised and disturbed at how powerful his feelings were, and what a strange, dark core they came from.

13

'What on earth are you doing, Murn?' Susanna asked.

The cook was sitting on one of the wicker chairs in the stone-flagged kitchen, reading a book. Two of the other younger servants were leaning over the cook's broad shoulders and joining in the laughter at whatever it was on the printed page.

The cook was a fat woman with a mop of frizzy grey hair and a badly pocked face. She struggled to her feet, still heaving with merriment, and making the wicker chair creak.

'Och, it's this book, Mistress. Ye'll ken Rab Mossgiel. Ah've heard he's a guid freen' o' yer brother's. Well, he's come oot wi' this book. It's had us aw laughin', an' weepin' tae. Huv ye no' managed tae get a copy yersel?'

Astonished beyond words, Susanna shook her head.

'Och,' Murn clutched the book against her monstrous bosom, 'ye'll be able tae get one, Ah'm sure.'

She had obviously no intention of being parted from her own copy.

Susanna found her voice at last. 'You mean Robert Burns? Robert Burns, the farm labourer? He has written a book?'

'Well, he's no' actually a labourer, is he? Tho' he labours gey hard. But by rights he an' his brother Gilbert are tenant farmers, are they no'?'

Susanna shrugged. Somehow she managed to make her way back to the oak-panelled drawing room. She sat down on a chair nearest to the warmth of the fire. She must write to

Alexander and ask if he could send her a copy of the book. She wondered apprehensively, fearfully, if Neil already had a copy. When she thought of her husband, it was always apprehensively, fearfully.

She was long past the stage of even thinking of confiding in her mother and asking for help. She was far too ashamed at what had been happening. Anyway her mother (like most people) believed that 'once ye mak yer bed, ye huv tae lie on it'. As things had gone from bad to worse, from shocking to despicable to sadistic, it was unthinkable to mention anything about Neil's behaviour. She felt certain now that her mother, or any other woman, could not have any knowledge or experience of what she was suffering.

Neil was mad. She had convinced herself of this. But who would believe her? What could be done. 'Till death do us part,' they'd vowed in church. And the church was the law.

She knew now why Neil had given the servants cottages on the estate. They only came to work in the 'big hoose' from morning until evening. No one, not even the servants, could suspect what was going on. Every evening after they left had become her waking nightmare. It was then that Neil forced her to submit to shameful and sadistic behaviour. For hours she suffered physical and mental torture. Or he needed only any small excuse, or none at all, to beat her.

He had used his horse whip on her until she bled and was forced to scream for mercy. He had tied her splay-legged to the bed posts and subjected her to acts of obscene and agonising brutality. Her only peace was when he disappeared for most of the day to attend to the business of the estate, or to visit taverns, or to have gambling sessions with people on other estates.

She had never known what real fear or real hatred was until she'd married Neil Guthrie. She could not go on for the rest of her life like this, she kept telling herself. It was mentally and physically impossible. Any kind of life, anywhere, would be better than this. She had thought of running away to Edinburgh and turning up at her brother's lodgings. But her brother was a proud man. He could not and would not, she felt sure, have either the desire or the ability to cope with such a scandal as a runaway wife.

Anyway, she had not enough money even to pay for a coach journey to Edinburgh. She knew where Neil kept some money though. She could steal it. Her face burned with shame at the thought. But the thought remained.

Sometimes she felt she was going mad. Both she and Neil lived double lives. During the day or some evenings, they had guests. Then Neil would be the polite, charming, elegant man she'd thought she knew before they married. He had always been elegant in his posture and dress. Now, when they had company, they both appeared beautifully turned out, the perfect host and hostess.

Her mother was delighted that she'd made 'such a guid match'. She'd also remarked, 'Marriage suits ye, Anna. It's made ye settle doon. Ye even look more sensible an' mature. Ye were aye such a reckless an' excitable wee lassie.'

Indeed, she had been tragically reckless in rushing into marriage with Neil Guthrie. Her quiet composure was not due to the maturity that her mother so fondly imagined. She now had nothing to be gay and reckless and excited about. She felt she'd aged ten years or more. She was certainly no longer her plump, bouncy self. She had lost weight.

The housekeeper, Mrs McIntyre, enjoyed sewing and was very handy with her needle. She had volunteered to take in the dresses that hung loose on her and make them fit properly again. When her mother and others came to tea, she – the lady of the manor – could sit in the drawing room smiling vaguely at whoever happened to be there. Mrs McIntyre, a long leek of a woman in a white cap and dangling lappets, and Matty the maid, would fuss over the tea equipage which they'd set on a low table in front of the glowing fire.

Delicate rose-patterned china chinked on to an embroidered tea cloth, and polished silver reflected the dancing flames.

And her mother would say, 'Isn't this lovely? What a lucky lassie ye are.'

Or some of Neil's gentlemen friends and their wives would come of an evening. The men would play cards at the green-topped card table while the ladies discussed recipes or the latest scandal.

Only the day after Susanna's discovery about the publication by Robert Burns, there was such an evening. This time the ladies launched into an immediate discussion of the book.

'You haven't read it, my dear?' Alice Wilson cried out. 'Oh, you must. It's the talk of the whole country. Edinburgh is buzzing with it. There's even been reviews of it in London magazines and papers. "This Heaven-taught ploughman", one of the reviewers called him.'

Euphemia Mackie, in a bright yellow gown, twittered with excitement. 'My husband subscribed for several copies. I'll give you one, Susanna. I'll send a servant over with it the moment I return home.'

'Thank you, Euphemia.' Susanna managed a tight smile. 'How very kind of you.'

The book came as promised and Susanna read it in amazement and also with a strange sadness. The poems showed not only keen observation of character, not only much tenderness, but in verses like 'Despondency – An Ode', they reflected her own feelings.

> Oppress'd with grief and care
> A burden more than I can bear . . .

Suddenly it was all too much for her and she dissolved into broken-hearted weeping. She was obviously no judge of character. She had seen the man and judged him only by his social status. She had dismissed him as a common peasant and no more. She'd always thought of nothing and no-one else except people of what she regarded as 'the quality'. Her own ambition had been to marry someone with a good fortune and a large house.

Well, she had achieved her ambition and she was being punished for her stupidity. She tried to tell herself that she had been no different from anyone else she knew. Ladies needed to marry gentlemen who could provide for them, give them a decent place in society. She had been unlucky, that was all. But what did anything matter now in her secret hell?

All the wives of Neil's friends thought he was wonderful, of course, a proper gentleman. This was understandable from their point of view. Neil was quiet-spoken, slim and elegant, with a pale complexion and eyes. The husbands of most of these ladies had robust limbs, fat faces and red noses and spent much of their time dressed for the hunt in red jackets and thick yellow ancestral buckskins with brown tops to their boots. And they were so noisy, especially at the hunt. Such a clatter and chatter. Such a hallooing and horn-blowing and dogs in full-throated chorus.

'What a charming man,' they often said of Neil. Sometimes she even believed they were jealous of her. What a joke, she thought. If only they knew. But her thoughts always came back to the bitter question — who would believe her?

Instead of it being a relief to be in company, it had become yet another torture, especially if Neil was present. She preferred to escape outside on her own if she could, after the coaches of the guests had lurched and rumbled away. She'd put on her shawl and slip outside. Even when winter had closed in, even when it was pitch black and the paths around the house were like quagmires, she'd still venture out. The wind screaming through the branches of the trees, the overgrown bushes angrily shaking themselves, nothing was as frightening as being alone in the house with her husband.

This large old house that she'd once admired and coveted so much had become a brooding monster with long silent corridors and dark panelled walls — her prison, her place of misery and terror.

More and more, she was thinking and dreaming of escape. In the crowded mass of humanity of Edinburgh, for instance, she could disappear, never to be found by anyone, not even her brother. She remembered Edinburgh very well from her visits to the capital in previous years. She remembered its warren of side streets and high tenements or 'lands', like perpendicular streets. She remembered the dark entries giving glimpses of confusing obscurities, or leading steeply down a narrow tunnel with an unexpected vista of the New Town at the end of it. She could get lost in Edinburgh. She could be free to melt into another world. She didn't care what that world would be like. Nothing could be worse than, or even as bad as, the world she was in now. Perhaps from Edinburgh she could eventually travel farther afield, away from Scotland altogether.

The desperate dream sustained her. All she needed was enough money to get to the city and to pay for lodgings so that she could feel safe until she decided what her next move would be. She began to make a plan. She began to watch where Neil kept money in the house, and how much. If he had a successful evening gambling he could return with a considerable amount.

She began to feel some of her old reckless excitement returning.

14

His heavy scythe over his shoulder, Robert strode in an easy gait along the rough, muddy track to the high field. The cold air cut sharply into his lungs as he trudged along and a dry, bitter wind hummed eerily through the hedges.

Then with an even rhythm from his waist, he swung the scythe in clean sweeps, slice and step, slice and step. Slowly he cut his way across the rough terrain, the sweet, damp smell of the cut grass redolent in his nostrils. He had been up and working since the crack of dawn. He laboured automatically, ignoring his usual aches and pains and growing fatigue, concentrating all of his mind on his poetry or his songs.

More and more, he was becoming drawn to sing and he often found himself humming a tune to himself.

Today, after his day's work, he escaped for a short time to enjoy the luxury of a walk alone, and to read, or rather to re-read, McKenzie's novel, *The Man of Feeling*. It was one of his favourite books. He always carried it around with him on the farm. Before he realised where he was, he had strayed on to the Ballochmyle Estate. He stopped under the shadows of a tree and, leaning against it, he continued reading his book. After a few minutes, he became aware of someone approaching along the path. It was a young woman.

He watched her with dark observing eyes as she passed with her head disdainfully in the air. She would be the lady of the estate. That fact alone, however, was not a good enough reason

97

– or any reason at all – to be so proud and haughty. Robert bristled with resentment as he always did when he thought of the way the so-called 'quality' gave themselves airs and regarded themselves better than anyone else just because they had more money, or by accident of birth, had been born into the aristocracy.

He had had to work hard to deserve anything he'd acquired in life. However, he still couldn't believe the success he'd acquired with his book of poetry. It certainly meant working hard at distributing the poems and making so many journeys in order to do so. He also had to travel around collecting money from subscribers. There was much business in the course of publication and marketing of a volume. At the same time, he'd been making his preparations for leaving the country. As soon as he'd had the nine guineas, he had booked a ticket on the first ship that was to sail.

With this in mind, he wrote several poems of goodbye to family and friends. What took up a surprising amount of his time was the unexpected number of letters he received from complete strangers. He received letters from well-wishers who wrote to congratulate him. What was most surprising of all was the number of letters he received from professional men and the landed gentry. This, it had to be admitted, proved quite an expense because, of course, it was the custom that the recipient of letters paid the postage. Nevertheless, he couldn't help feeling some excitement at the amount of post he was receiving, especially from the nobility, even though at the same time, he kept a grain of his normal cynicism about such people and was ever ready to suspect any hint of snobbishness.

However, he not only politely responded but enclosed verse epistles and songs with his letters of reply.

He also took time to write to, and enclose a song to, the young lady he'd seen at Ballochmyle. By the time he'd reached home from his walk, his resentment had melted away and he'd penned 'The Bonnie Lass o' Ballochmyle'. He'd sent it to the subject of the song along with a letter in his best ornate style in which he'd asked her permission to publish the song.

(Although he did not in fact need the lady's permission, because he had not specified her name.)

The lady did not acknowledge the song or the letter. He'd learned afterwards that she'd made enquiries about his character. She had been immediately suspicious of him because, for one thing, she knew very well, as she'd told a friend, that she was anything but bonnie and she was a mature woman in her thirties. Then she found he had a reputation as a well-known fornicator. This infuriated Robert, when he considered the amount of houghmagandy that abounded in the area. At the time, however, he had felt hurt and bitter at having his song and his letter – especially his song – ignored. She had not even sent one polite word of acknowledgement.

It wasn't until years later it was found that she had made a bower of the place where she had seen Burns, and her friends said she'd treasured his letter so much and had shown it to so many people, it had begun to disintegrate.

Robert had a surprising and different experience with another aristocrat. It was a most unexpected one, while on a visit to the home of the philosopher, Professor Dugald Stewart.

Professor Stewart lived in a house only a few miles from the farm and he'd invited Robert to his home, along with the Mauchline surgeon, Mr McKenzie. It turned out another man joined them by chance. A lord, no less, Lord Daer, son of the Earl of Selkirk, and an exceptionally tall man. Apparently he had been a pupil of the professor.

Robert had barely returned home from this visit before enthusiastically dashing off seven verses to mark the occasion. He was especially pleased with one of the verses:

> Then from his Lordship I shall learn,
> Henceforth to meet with unconcern,
> One rank as weel's another;
> Nae honest, worthy man need care,
> To meet with noble youthful Daer,
> For he but meets a brother.

It was during this period when he'd been on business to Kilmarnock that a letter from another of the landed gentry was delivered to the farm. It was, he discovered, from a Mrs Dunlop.

'What is it this time?' Gilbert asked.

Robert looked up from reading the pages. 'It's from a Mrs Dunlop, of Dunlop House.'

'I know it. It's that big place about fifteen or sixteen miles from here. You'll have seen it yourself.'

Robert looked vague, trying to remember. He had so much on his mind these days.

His mother joined in the conversation. 'I mind her. She's a widow buddy. Her faither was Sir Thomas Wallace o' Craigie. She married John Dunlop of Dunlop, och, years ago. She must be gey auld by noo. I heard that the puir buddy has never been the same since her man died. Awfu' depressed, puir soul.'

'She hints at that,' Robert said, 'and apparently a daughter of the laird of Craigengillen gave her a copy of 'The Cotter's Saturday Night' to read. It must have done her some sort of good. It's cheered her enough anyway to want half a dozen copies of my poems. She's also invited me to call at Dunlop House.'

Gilbert sighed as he edged a path across the kitchen, between a couple of Robert's pet hens, Mailie the sheep and a collie dog.

'You'll find that house a lot different from this, I warrant.'

His mother immediately piped up, 'There's nothin' wrong wi' this hoose, Gilbert Burns.'

'I didn't say that, Mother.'

'I've only got five copies but I'll send them to the lady right away,' Robert said, and then added, 'I'm thinking of going to Edinburgh in a week or two to try for a second edition. I'll tell her I'll call at Dunlop House as soon as I return.'

Before he had the opportunity to do this, however, he received another long letter, first of all acknowledging the books he'd sent and then going on to suggest that he should appoint her as his literary critic, adding, 'I have been told that Voltaire read all his manuscripts to an old woman and printed nothing but what she would have approved. I wish you would name me to her office.'

Robert very much doubted the truth of this and had no hesitation in ignoring her suggestion. Despite this, however, the lady enthusiastically took the role upon herself. Meantime, Robert prepared for his journey to Edinburgh with high hopes and a great sense of adventure. He sincerely hoped for a second edition to take place but he still had his sailing ticket to Jamaica. There was also the possibility of gaining security and a long-term solution to his financial and other problems with farming. At the back of his mind, there still lurked the possibility of the Excise.

But now it was Edinburgh and he set off on a pony loaned to him by George Reid of Barquharie, and headed east. He had to make a detour on the journey because George Reid had also arranged for him to break his journey and spend the night with someone Reid knew – a farmer called Archibald Prentice, or 'Bauldy' Prentice as he was nicknamed – a huge man of at least six feet three.

What Robert didn't realise was that Prentice and every farmer for miles around had not only read his book, but were desperate to meet him.

Bauldy Prentice's farm was situated in the middle of several combined parishes that formed a kind of amphitheatre. The signal of Burns' arrival was to be a white sheet attached to a pitchfork placed on top of the cornstack in the centre of the barnyard. The moment the flag was seen, and it was seen by every house in the parish, there was a stampede of farmers from their houses to converge at the point of meeting.

Robert, already somewhat exhausted by his long ride over rough and difficult terrain, was flattered but a bit overcome by the admiration and enthusiastic hospitality thrust upon him. However, the dinner, late though it was, and the liquid refreshment pressed upon him made him forget his fatigue. A glorious night it turned out to be, with much conversation and laughter with one man saying, 'God man, you talk even better than your book.'

Next morning, he breakfasted with a large crowd of admirers at the next farmhouse, tenanted by John Stodart, and had lunch with another crowd of men. It was just as he was leaving the house to make for his pony, which was tethered at the gate, and resume his ride to Edinburgh, that Bauldy Prentice strode out in front of him and called at two or three young lads who were obviously hurrying on their way to school,

'Stop here, lads, an' haud the stirrup for this man who's going to mount this pony.'

One of the boys said worriedly, 'We'll be late, an' we're feart o' the maister.'

'Stop an' haud the stirrup,' Bauldy roared from his great height. 'Ah'll settle it wi' the maister. Ye haud this stirrup an' ye'll boast o' it to yer dyin' day!'

Robert was touched by this and by Prentice's warm and generous hospitality. The hospitality had perhaps been over-generous because Robert set off on the rest of his journey not feeling one hundred per cent fit.

However, he arrived in the city in the evening and was interested to find that his arrival had coincided with a historic day – the advent of the first of John Palmer's mail coaches from London. It was on everyone's lips that this mail coach had accelerated the mail between the capital cities to a mere sixty hours.

He had arranged to share a room with an old friend, John Richmond, who lodged with a Mrs Carfrae in Baxters Close. Tired and weary, Robert struggled to encourage his pony to finish the last few yards of the journey to where the stabling was situated in the Grassmarket. He was finding his first view of Edinburgh at night a traumatic experience. He was a country boy whose only experience of urban life had been Ayr and Kilmarnock.

It appeared to his tired eyes a bustling human ant heap of humanity of the worst kind. He saw pickpockets and street robbers at work and hordes of women obviously abandoned to vice.

He had always had a horror of prostitution – the profession itself, and how it degraded women. Here a multitude of women were jostling, and crowding, screaming, plying their trade unashamedly, and pestering all and sundry.

He was glad to reach Baxters Close. Here in the dark stairwell he had to squeeze past elegant ladies with their hooped skirts, as well as coarsely garbed artisans. Despite his fatigue, Robert was interested in the incongruous mix of different sorts and classes of people.

At the lodgings, he was warmly welcomed by John Richmond who introduced him to the landlady, Mrs Carfrae. She looked a very staid and pious widow in her forties.

'This is a respectable hoose, Mr Burns, I'll have you know,' she informed Robert. 'Please dinnae judge my hoose by that awfu' hoose wi' awfu' folk up the stairs.'

'Who is in the house upstairs?' Robert enquired politely.

'Wicked women, that's who. Wi' their wicked singin' an' drinkin' and screechin' and laughin' an' aw their wicked carry on wi' men.' She worked herself to such a pitch of agitation, her cheeks burned bright scarlet. 'I toss an' turn in that bed every night somethin' terrible. I look for rest, Mr Burns, an' fin' none.'

Robert said afterwards to Richmond, 'Poor woman, I fear she is coming on her grand climacterick and is jealous of her laughter-loving, night-rejoicing neighbours.'

The next day, as if she had read his mind, she engaged him in heated conversation again, saying, 'We shouldnae be uneasy an' envious because the wicked enjoy the good things in life, Mr Burns, for those base jades who lie up gandy going with their filthy fellows, drinkin' the best o' wines an' singin' abominable songs, shall one day lie in Hell, weepin' an' wailin' and gnashin' their teeth over a cup o' God's wrath!'

Mrs Carfrae, he discovered during the many conversations she pressed on him, was a very flesh-disciplining, godly matron who firmly believed her husband was in heaven and, having been very happy with him on earth, now vigorously and perseveringly practised some of the most distinguishing Christian virtues, such as attending church, railing against vice, and so on, so that she would be qualified to meet her late bedfellow again in heaven.

She seemed to find some release in talking to Robert, despite the fact that she said he was 'but a rough an' roun' Christian'.

15

'You're a friend of the ploughman poet, aren't you, Alexander?' Professor Purdie said. He was a bulky man with short legs, a huge purple face and a capacity for claret drinking that made him universally admired.

'Yes,' Alexander replied, putting down his quill. He'd been working on a poem and was not pleased at being interrupted. 'We come from the same area.'

'We must make him welcome in the city when he arrives, and introduce him to as many people of influence as possible.'

'Of course.' Alexander cleared his throat and struggled to appear enthusiastic. In a loud voice, the professor then began to recite a list of the most prominent members of the literati – professors, medical men, philosophers, the most brilliant brains in Edinburgh.

'None of the quality or nobility must miss him.'

'Yes, I suppose . . . ' Alexander stumbled over the words. 'Some of them may wish to meet him.'

'Everybody will want to meet him, man. Isn't that obvious by what we've heard and read? You must let me know the moment he arrives. No doubt he will contact you first.'

In fact, Robert had already contacted Alexander by messenger and explained that he'd had to stay a full day in bed after he'd arrived because he felt so exhausted and unwell. He still did not feel fit. He had a stomach upset, apparently, as well as his usual nervous headaches that always dragged him down into depression. Alexander suspected the cause on this occasion was the liberal hospitality that had been forced on him en route, especially whisky. Strong drink never agreed with Robert. For the most part, he managed to avoid it, something very difficult to do in such a hard-drinking country. He'd seen for himself how drunkenness could even be used as an excuse and justification for crime.

'He'd had a *good* drink' was common parlance in defence proceedings in court. Certainly in his grandfather's court. And to say a fellow could take a good drink was to admire his manliness.

Alexander felt annoyed at the professor. After all, for all he knew, who he was calling 'the ploughman poet' would suffer agonies of embarrassment and feel completely out of place and inferior among any gathering of such luminaries. Of course, this was not the only subject about which he felt annoyance with the professor. It was the practice, and had been for years, for all the members of the College of Physicians and Surgeons to attend the hospital by monthly rotations. That meant the patients could have an opposite treatment according to the whim of the doctor every thirty days.

Alexander was one of those supporting Doctor Gregory, who attacked this absurdity and believed that the medical officials should be appointed permanently. Professor Purdie, quite an amiable man in most ways, vehemently and loudly opposed this idea and was all for holding on to their right, as they called it, which was really the power of annoying patients in their turn.

Power was the key word, it occurred to Alexander. Now the professor was all for being the power behind getting Robert Burns organised. No doubt he visualised all the social evenings Robert's visit would engender and the many bottles of claret he would have an excuse for consuming. Not that he needed an excuse. Alexander was constantly amazed at the amount of drink Professor Purdie could down. It made him feel sick even to think of it.

106

Robert couldn't cope with that. He would be doing his friend a favour to try to keep him away from such company. He must try to make sure Robert was kept out of the public eye as much as possible. Robert had a bad reputation for womanising in Ayrshire. Alexander wondered whether, if this were made known to the quality in Edinburgh, it would dampen their eagerness to pursue a meeting with Robert, or to talk so highly of him.

It was one thing admiring his poetry. Quite another surely to allow a man who had a reputation for fornicating into your drawing room to meet the ladies of your family. Alexander had begun to believe that it wasn't so much the poetry per se that was proving the biggest attraction. It was the novelty of a common, uneducated ploughman being able to write anything at all. It was all a myth. Robert probably had a better knowledge of English writers and poets than the literati and all the others who were so entranced by the romantic idea of the 'heaven-taught ploughman'.

Admittedly, Robert had only had about two years' formal education in his life, but they had been with an excellent tutor. He'd also had a father who had been unusually well-read himself and determined in the extreme to make sure he supplied his family with books and with as much education as he personally could give them. Robert in fact, despite having to work on the farm since he was a young child, was steeped in literature of all kinds. He had also an amazingly retentive memory. There was nothing 'heaven-taught' about him.

As it turned out, Professor Purdie did not get the chance to introduce Robert to anyone. Robert had already been invited to all the drawing rooms of the quality and nobility, or noblesse as Robert called them, before the Professor had even met him.

Alexander had been on duty at the hospital and kept so busy that he didn't see Robert for over two weeks. Apparently, James Dalrymple of Orange Field had been the one who had opened doors for Robert. Before their meeting, Robert had sent Alexander a letter saying, 'I have met very warm friends in the Literati, Professors Stewart, Blair, Grenfield and also Henry MacKenzie, author of *The Man of Feeling*. I am likewise kindly and most generously patronised by the Earl of Glencairn, the Duchess of Gordon, the Countess of Glencairn, with my Lord and Lady Belting; Sir John Whiteford, the Dean of Faculty, the Honourable Henry Erskine, and several others. Our worthy friend, Mr Stewart, with that goodness truly like himself, got me into the periodical paper, *The Lounger*.'

He wrote home on a typically sardonic note, 'I'm in a fair way to becoming as eminent as Thomas à Kempis or John Bunyan; and you may expect henceforth to see my birthday inserted among the wonderful events, in the Poor Robin's and Aberdeen Almanacs along with the Black Monday, and the Battle of Bothwell Bridge. My Lord Glencairn and the Dean of Faculty, Mr H. Erskine, have taken me under their wing, and by all probability, I shall soon be the tenth Worthy, and the eighth Wise Man of the world . . . '

Of course, Alexander told himself, the whole thing was just a novelty, a bit of excitement to amuse people who had time on their hands. It wouldn't last. Every year, Edinburgh had to have some diversion, some novelty. It just so happened that this year it was the novelty of a ploughman poet.

He wondered if all the adulation would turn Robert's head. After being taken up by the Earl of Glencairn especially, every door in polite society would be open to him. Glencairn had even introduced Robert to the best publisher in Edinburgh. Not only that, he'd written letters to every one of his friends ordering them to subscribe to the second edition. He'd also persuaded every one of the Caledonian Hunt to do the same.

Robert had become very emotional and completely carried away with enthusiasm about Glencairn. His dark eyes glowed with excitement. 'Alexander! The providential care of a good God has placed me under the patronage of one of his noblest creatures, the Earl of Glencairn: Oublie moi, Grand Dieu, si jamais je l'oublie!'

Alexander became sick to his soul with Robert's emotional

ravings about the Earl. The Earl daren't pay even polite attention to anyone else without Robert being devastated. The last time they'd supped together, Robert was in such an emotional state.

'The noble Glencairn has wounded me to the soul, Alexander, because I dearly esteem, respect and love him.'

'Why?' Alexander picked at his food, unable to look up and meet Robert's eyes. 'What crime has the noble lord committed against you?'

'Yesterday he showed so much attention – engrossing attention – to a member of the aristocracy, an absolute blockhead, a dunderpate. I was within half a point of throwing down my gage of contemptuous defiance. But he shook my hand and looked so benevolently good at parting.' Robert sighed. 'God bless him, I thought. And if I should never see him again, I shall love him until my dying day!'

Alexander could not bear it. 'You'll have more to worry you than that incident if some of the gossip I've heard reaches the noble lord's ears. He will not be so benevolently good then, I fear.'

The light went out of Robert's eyes. 'I know I have enemies who have been circulating unfavourable gossip about me. Probably it's in connection with the Armour affair. Probably it originally stems from old Armour. That man hates me so much. I can only hope that my Lord Glencairn would defend me as stoutly as Sir John Whitefoord did.'

'He defended your conduct?'

'So I'm told by MacKenzie. I wrote to Sir John immediately to thank him. I acknowledged that too frequently I'm the sport of whim, caprice and passion – but reverence to God, and integrity to my fellow creatures, I hope I shall ever preserve.' Robert pushed his plate of half-eaten food away. 'It's all very humiliating and depressing though. I did love Jean – I think I still love her – and we did go through a form of marriage. It hurt me beyond words when she allowed that to be annulled.'

Alexander stole another look at Robert's weather-browned

face, with its black brows and black frame of hair. Despite his well-cut coat and buckskin breeches, he still had the brawny, rough look of a farmer. Alexander couldn't fathom what women saw in him. Country wenches could be attracted by some sort of animal sexuality he exuded. But even ladies of the aristocracy like the Duchess of Gordon had become enamoured with him. This was despite his, at times, sarcastic and sardonic tongue. His wit was ready but not the most pleasing or to everyone's taste.

He was glad to note however that although high-born ladies made a great fuss of Robert, he was allowed no liberties. If Robert wanted or needed sexual favours, it looked as if he'd have to seek wenches of the lower orders, more of his own class.

Perhaps the discreet warnings that he'd managed to circulate had paid off in that respect. Whisperings about Robert's drinking habits had not been so successful.

Dugald Stewart had said, 'Yes, I too have heard reports of Burns' predilection for convivial and not very select society. But from my own observation, I have concluded in favour of his habits of sobriety.'

Alexander managed a smile. 'It seems that Edinburgh is having a good effect on my friend. I'm extremely relieved about that. I was afraid that all the excessive attention he's been having would spoil him.'

'No.' Professor Stewart shook his head. 'On the contrary, he is showing much good sense and behaving wonderfully well.' He fixed Alexander with a curious look. 'Don't you think so yourself?'

'Yes indeed,' Alexander hastily assured him. 'As I say, I'm extremely relieved now that I find my anxieties about him have proved quite unnecessary.'

It was true. It was all true, Alexander kept telling himself in an effort to quell the strange demons that kept clawing up inside him. If he hadn't had his work and the comfort of his poetry, he didn't know how he'd cope with them. But in the hospital, when he was amputating a man's leg for instance, he needed a clear head, steady nerves and a cool determination. This was not easy while the patient was screaming and violently struggling. It also needed quite strong helpers to fight to hold the patient down, and a strong arm to wield the saw. He stifled his wayward thoughts about his friend and concentrated on the operation. He'd acquired the ability to keep any emotion in check, and carry out his duties efficiently. He had always been a good, conscientious doctor and surgeon.

It was only with Robert that he tended to lose control of his inner self. Sometimes he wondered if Robert's extreme emotionalism could be infectious. Only recently, he'd gone with Robert, at Professor Stewart's invitation, to one of the weekly conversazione among the most brilliant literary society in Edinburgh. At first Robert had seemed little inclined to mingle easily in the company. He strolled round the room looking at the pictures on the walls. He stopped at a picture representing a soldier lying dead on the snow, his dog sitting in misery on the one side, on the other side his widow with a child in her arms. Robert read aloud the lines written underneath. To everyone's shock and to Alexander's acute embarrassment, Robert's voice broke and tears filled his eyes. The room turned silent as Robert looked around and asked who had written the lines. Not one philosopher could remember. Then, after a decent interval, a pale, lame boy — Walter Scott, Alexander believed his name was — ventured a reply.

'They were written by one Langhorn.'

Robert rewarded him with a look and said, 'You'll be a man yet, Sir.'

But not like Robert Burns, Alexander hoped. What kind of man would be moved to shed tears at a painting? He was quite unbalanced. He'd once expressed to him that he'd felt near to Bedlam, and Alexander was beginning to think Robert Burns was on the verge of a nervous breakdown most of the time. That was despite other people's observations and opinions that Robert behaved with nothing more than simple manliness. Simple manliness indeed! What about his extremism? His moods of alternating elation and depression. His foolish tears. His powers of exaggeration. Even Professor Stewart had noticed that.

'But Professor,' Alexander had said mildly, 'what you have observed about my friend's sobriety may be a true picture of him. I hope it is. However, he himself has, in the past, written to me about fits of debauchery and licentiousness.'

The professor had actually laughed. 'Man, man, you of all people should know that part of the genius of Burns is his powers of exaggeration. He loves to make vivid word pictures of folk, including himself. What an imagination he has! What emotion he is capable of expressing! It completely carries him away at times.'

Alexander experienced a state of pure hatred. Immediately he smoothed it over, cooled the heat of it. He smiled at the professor. 'Yes,' he said. 'Doesn't it?'

16

The clock beat a ruthless tattoo and the wind every now and again pounced on the window frames and angrily agitated them. Susanna was waiting. She had everything arranged. Nothing could go wrong. Yet her stomach churned in terror in case it did.

Neil had joined a group of friends at someone's house for a game of hazard. On this occasion, the ladies had not been invited. She had waited for such a night. It had happened before. Neil had come home very late and very drunk. But still his glass of whisky had to be laid ready on the bedside table. He never missed his nightcap. Once he had nearly killed her for forgetting it.

Tonight she made doubly sure that it was there. Into it she had stirred the sleeping potion her father kept ready for her mother. She had secured twice her mother's normal dose. Plus the whisky, it should render Neil unconscious for the whole night and, hopefully, most of the next day.

Early next morning, before the servants arrived, she would hide all his clothes to delay him further. Then she would saddle up one of the horses, secure the saddle bags containing as many of her clothes and possessions as possible, and gallop away. Her whole body pulsed with fear and excitement. She felt light headed. Beads of sweat trickled down over her eyes and between her breasts.

'Oh please God, let me get safely away,' she kept whispering.

'Oh please God.'

She sat at the bedroom window, the moonlight ghosting her white nightgown and flicking silver on to her shawl and the long auburn tresses that hung over it. She was watching and listening for the sound of Neil's horse. So intense was her concentration on the dark distance outside, she was unaware of the iciness of the inside of the room, until the dawn chorus startled her. She began shivering uncontrollably. What if he had decided to sleep overnight at his friend's house? Gambling sessions could go on for hours but he'd never been this late before.

She was on the point of weeping in despair when she caught the sound of a horse's hooves. The clatter became louder and she shrank quickly back from the window in case she could be seen. Her bare feet pattered across to the bed.

She burrowed underneath the covers, closed her eyes and prayed that he would be too drunk to notice her trembling. Her straining ears heard the first bang of the outside door, the stumbling feet along the corridor and up the stairs. The muffled oaths as he staggered and fell. Her skin crept with the draught of the bedroom door opening. The creak of the floorboards. She felt him near. Then there was a faint scraping sound, a gulp, and a smacking of lips.

Oh, hallelujah! He'd taken the whisky laced with sleeping potion.

She waited. Soon he was snoring loudly. Carefully – very, very carefully – she eased herself out of bed. Not daring to light a candle, she crossed the room with only the grey mist of the moon guiding her way. On the landing outside, a candelabra guttered low. It had been left to light Neil's way up the stairs. Still in her nightdress and bare feet, she tiptoed to the room in which her outdoor clothes lay ready. She had chosen a black riding outfit with a calesh hood tied with ribbons under her chin. When she'd worn the outfit before, she'd been out riding with some of the local gentry. The ladies in the party had remarked on her 'modest' appearance. She hadn't been sure at the time whether the remark had been a compliment or an insult.

Now she didn't care how she looked, or what anyone would think, as long as she could get away safely and as quickly as possible.

She held her breath until she was out of the house, on the horse and, quietly at first, was guiding the animal along the rough path in the direction of Tarbolton. Once away from what she imagined was the earshot of the house, she urged the horse into a wild gallop. Suddenly it reared high in the air and she was tossed from the saddle to jar painfully onto the hard ground. For a moment, she was too shocked to move. Then to her horror she caught sight of a man's top boots striding towards her and then the man towering above her.

'Please, please.' Sobbing in terror she cowered away. 'Don't hurt me. Oh please . . . '

'You've nothing to fear from me, lassie. Here, let me help you up.'

The voice was gentle and concerned, and vaguely familiar. She dared to look up and recognised the big solid figure of the ploughman, Robert Burns. Still trembling, she allowed him to grasp her hands and ease her to a standing position. Her legs were too weak to support her, however, and she had to lean against him. She felt the roughness of his work clothes against her cheek and the warm sweaty smell of his body in her nostrils. She was still sobbing.

'Please don't tell my husband. Please don't tell him you've seen me. Oh please.'

'Sh, sh . . . ' Burns soothed. 'I'm not going to tell a soul. I promise you.'

'I'm afraid of him, you see. Terrified. I must get away . . . ' She couldn't stop a torrent of words escaping. 'I'm going to leave a note at my mother and father's house explaining and pleading with them not to try to find me. But you see, they won't believe me. They think Neil Guthrie is a gentleman and a good husband, but he's neither. No-one will ever believe me.'

Her companion's face darkened with anger.

115

'I believe you, lass. You wouldn't be in such a state if it wasn't true. By God, I'd like to get my hands on Guthrie. Any man who gets his wife into such a state deserves a good thrashing.'

'No, no, please!' Susanna cried out. 'I appreciate your concern but I just want to get away. I don't want any more trouble. He will be angry enough as it is. Just forget you ever saw me or spoke to me.'

'At least allow me to ride along with you to Tarbolton.' Burns was obviously struggling with his anger. 'And see you safely on your way again after you've delivered your note.'

'Oh, would you?' Susanna made an effort to regain some vestige of polite composure. 'I'd be most obliged.'

Her horse had wandered some yards away and Burns retrieved it, then lifted her into the saddle as if she was as light as thistledown. In a few moments, they were galloping away side by side through the windswept darkness. Neither spoke until Burns said, 'Have you some place to stay? Where exactly are you aiming for?'

She had no idea *exactly* where she was going.

'I have good friends in the capital city,' she lied. 'They will keep me hidden and safe.'

'Are you sure you will be all right on the journey? It's a very long ride to Edinburgh.'

'I will put up at an inn en route. I have travelled to Edinburgh before and know all the best places.'

'I could accompany you further.'

'No, no.' Her voice quickened with agitation as the dark outlines of the village of Tarbolton came into view. 'Wait here.'

She dismounted some way from her parents' house and crept silently towards it.

The note for her mother and father, briefly stated that her life might appear normal and happy, but in fact she was suffering a secret life of hell, physical and mental torture at the hands of her husband. She'd come to the conclusion that he was both mad and cunning, and she could not live her life of terror with him any more. She had run away to make a new start for herself, somewhere she could feel safe.

'Please try not to worry about me,' she wrote. 'Please, PLEASE, do not try to find me. I'll be all right as long as I'm as far away as possible and free of Neil Guthrie.'

Slowly, painfully, she turned her key in the lock of the front door. Like a shadow, she slipped into the house, propped the note on her father's desk and, hardly daring to breathe, slipped away again.

Burns was waiting for her, the reins of her horse dangling in one of his big hands.

'I don't like the idea of you riding all the way to Edinburgh alone and in such a state.'

'I'm perfectly capable of making the journey on my own, I do assure you.'

Reluctantly, he assisted her back onto her horse.

She straightened her back and raised her chin in a desperate effort to regain some of her normal, ladylike composure.

'Thank you for your help, Mr Burns, and I will trust you to completely forget about this incident.'

'Oh, I cannot promise to forget our meeting, Mrs Guthrie. But rest assured, it will remain a secret between us.'

'Thank you,' she repeated before suddenly urging her horse on. Within moments it was flying away as if the devil was on its tail. All the time Susanna was thinking tearfully, if only she'd never left her parents' house in the first place. At least she'd felt perfectly safe there. Now she realised how much she'd been loved and how well she'd been treated. How could she have been so stupid as to give that life up?

The sad and frightening thing was that because she'd been so reckless and stupid before, her parents – especially her mother – would think she was just being even more reckless and stupid now.

She didn't want to risk stopping until she got to Edinburgh. It was too long a distance to travel without a stop, however, especially for the horse. Even when they'd visited the capital on previous occasions, the coach they'd used, pulled by several horses, had to stop and everyone stayed overnight at an inn while the horses were stabled, fed and watered.

Purposely, she avoided the inn that had been used before in case anyone remembered her. She chose another smaller and less reputable-looking place. None of the inns she'd ever frequented, either with Neil or previously with her brother, Alexander or, earlier still, when she'd been a child and made an occasional journey with her parents, none of the inns she remembered were very admirable places. Few had clean beds, most were bug-ridden. Servants were without shoes and stockings, coarse meal was served without a knife and fork and butter was thick with cow hair.

She remembered her mother had refused to drink anything when one glass or tin can was handed round the company, which included grubby-looking strangers, from mouth to mouth.

The small hostelry where fatigue forced Susanna to stop had not progressed one whit from the early days of the worst hostelries that she remembered.

The landlord's wife was a loose-bosomed, filthy-looking woman with tousled hair, a short bed gown and no corsets. Susanna was shown by the light of one small candle into an attic room with a low sloping ceiling. The unmade bed had obviously been slept in and even by the flickering light of the candle, Susanna could see that it was moving with bugs.

She decided not to undress and just to try to get some rest sitting upright in a wooden chair, the only other furniture in the room. She had wisely brought her saddle bags in with her. The landlady and her equally disreputable-looking husband, she suspected, would not think twice about trying to steal some of her belongings. As well as money, she had brought every piece of jewellery she possessed.

Stuffing the saddle bags against the wall, she jammed the chair up against them. She slept fitfully, jerking awake at the slightest sound, and was glad when daylight came and she was able to be on her way once more.

After a short time in the saddle, she felt more exhausted than ever. She now ached in every bone as a result of sitting all night in such a painfully hard chair. She found herself nodding off to sleep as the horse plodded along. Until suddenly, looking around, she was startled to realise she was in the midst of a thickly wooded area. She had no recollection of seeing this place before on any of her journeys to Edinburgh.

Panic, so intense, almost caused her to faint. Gripping the reins, she fought to take deep breaths as she turned the horse around. She could see its hoof prints on the muddy ground between the overhanging trees and prayed that if she followed them back, she might get herself into the right direction for Edinburgh again.

Sometimes the prints disappeared and she floundered about in rising panic again. But eventually she came to a clearing where to her blessed relief, there was a wooden signpost bearing the faded word 'Edinburgh'.

Now, wide awake with anxiety, she flicked at the horse's rump with her whip and quickened its pace. She must reach the city before darkness enveloped it. She must find a caddie to lead her to respectable lodgings. The Edinburgh caddies were a bedraggled-looking bunch of men who slept in closes or stood all day long and most of the night in the High Street waiting for employment. They were known for their honesty and their ability to perform any task, and faithfully execute all commands at a very reasonable price. They had formed themselves into a society with strict rules.

Her grandmother had once told her, 'Trust them with any sum of money no matter how large and know that it will be perfectly safe. The rules of their order oblige them to make good everything they lose.' She'd given an example of one man who'd once sent a caddie with a letter enclosing bills worth a hundred pounds. The caddie lost it, and the society restored the sum in full to the man.

Impudent, ragged, alert and swift, they darted about during the day and at night and they lighted their way in the dark streets with paper lanterns. They carried messages and parcels to any part of the town for a penny. They knew every lodging, who stayed there, and who had vacancies.

Susanna desperately needed the help of a caddie and must seek one out the moment she reached Edinburgh.

Once in Edinburgh, however, she could not see any of them. Fog had come down suddenly, thickened and darkened by hundreds of smoking chimneys. Coach lamps swayed from side to side. Torches flashed eerily on peering faces. In the distance, the torches looked like smouldering flames trying in vain to penetrate through the dense mass of smoke. Susanna put her handkerchief to her mouth and tried to control a bout of coughing. It was as if all the smoke that had ever gone up from Edinburgh's chimneys had been kept somewhere above the clouds to rot, then had fallen down, thick and foul smelling, to catch at the throat and make the chest wheeze.

Eventually, seeing a tavern's lights and hearing the sound of voices, she made her way towards the place. Once inside, however, she was dismayed to see it was crowded with at least twenty Scottish drovers regaling themselves with whisky and potatoes. Susanna felt even more shocked at the sight of a girl coming towards her dressed only in an indecently short linsey-woolsey petticoat, and with no shoes or stockings.

The girl informed her that this was the best inn in the metropolis and, although Susanna did not believe this, she was too fatigued to look any further. In daylight, she would feel more confident to search for a better place. She allowed the girl to lead her up a rickety stair to a room hardly better than the one in which she'd spent the previous night. It was a relief, however, to find that there was a bolt on the door.

It made a loud scraping noise as Susanna locked herself in.

17

Instead of Professor Purdie and Alexander taking Burns to meet the literati and people of quality, it became the other way around. Alexander, at Burns' invitation, was accompanying him into exalted places where he, even as a doctor, had never dreamed of entering. He, Doctor Alexander Wallace, who had been educated in Paris and Leyden, was the one who, although he managed to retain a cool and dignified front, felt nervous and more than a little ill at ease. In the castles and sumptuous dining rooms and drawing rooms of the noble lords and earls, the wealthiest upper crust of society to which Burns was given such an enthusiastic welcome, Alexander felt out of place. It was Robert Burns who had never been educated in any university, who had never been anywhere, who appeared perfectly calm and quietly self confident in every social scene in which they found themselves. He also behaved, as Professor Dugald Stewart had already observed, 'with total sobriety'.

The only criticism, if it could be called criticism, of his behaviour Alexander had heard was that Burns' attitude appeared somewhat hard, as if he was always at the ready to squash any appearance of the haughty class snobbery that he so detested. But on the contrary, he was treated as if he was some sort of god that had favoured the nobility with his presence.

Even the celebrated Duchess of Gordon and every other noble lady was agog with curiosity and excitement and fluttered around him, flattering him and plying him with questions.

In between these invitations, he was forever engaged in business in connection with his original book and the second edition. There were innumerable letters to write about subscriptions and of course, there were visits to the printers to correct proofs. Edinburgh was full of stories about Burns which constantly buzzed around the town. Even his visits to the printers were excitedly reported and discussed. The printer's name was Willie Smellie and Robert had written of him:

(Shrewd Willie Smellie to) Crochallan came;
The old cock'd hat, the brown surtout, the same;
His grisly beard just bristling in its might,
'Twas four long nights and days from shaving-night;
His uncombed, hoary locks, wild-staring thatch'd,
A head for thought profound and clear unmatch'd;
Yet, tho' his caustic wit was biting rude,
His heart was warm, benevolent and good.

Apparently, it was Robert's habit to walk about the printing room three or four times cracking a whip he carried, much to the surprise and fascination of the men who worked there. He paid no attention to his own copy. Instead he looked at any other that he saw lying in the cases. One day, he'd asked a man how many languages he was acquainted with.

'Indeed, sir,' the man replied, 'I've enough ado in my ain.'

Burns remarked that behind there was one of his companions setting up a Gaelic Bible and another composing a Hebrew Grammar.

'These two,' the compositor told him, 'are the greatest dolts in the house.'

Burns apparently had been amused by the remark and said he'd make a note of it. That was so typical of Burns, Alexander thought. He was an observer – always fascinated by people and what they did or said. He had now become, of course, the most observed of observers.

There was a particular stool in the office which Burns always sat on while correcting his proof sheets. It came to be called Burns' Stool. One day, Sir John Dalrymple came to the office to correct proofs of his *Essay on the Properties of Coal Tar* and he settled on Burns' Stool. When Burns arrived, obviously looking for his favourite seat, he was quietly requested to step into the composing room for a moment. As soon as Burns had left the correcting room, the opportunity was taken to ask Sir John to give up his seat to the gentleman who'd just looked in, as it was his usual seat.

Sir John said, 'I will not give up my seat to yon impudent, staring fellow.'

It was then revealed to him that the 'impudent, staring fellow' was the poet, Robert Burns.

Sir John immediately left the stool, exclaiming, 'Good gracious! Give him all the seats in your house!'

Burns was then called in, took possession of his stool, and commenced the reading of his proofs.

Alexander felt all this adulation could not be good for Burns. It came from people of all levels of society and age groups. He had a regular correspondent of one of the Ayrshire gentry, an elderly widow – a Mrs Dunlop. Mrs Dunlop seemed to spend most of her time not only writing long letters to Burns, but to all her influential acquaintances, praising the poet and seeking whatever could be done for his benefit.

The whole business had got completely out of hand. Now it seemed all the Masonic lodges in the land wanted to honour Burns. And clubs like The Crochallan Fencibles, thanks to Willie Smellie, had roped him in. It was bound to affect Robert one way or another. He certainly was beginning to lose patience with some of the egotistical people who bombarded him with their poetry. He'd met a London business man called Symon Grey, who began pestering him with his verses. At first Burns had been polite and patient. Then Grey began posting large piles of his works to the poet. Robert was extremely busy but managed a hasty reply:

Symon Grey, you're dull today.

Unabashed, Grey immediately posted another bulky package of poems. Robert promptly returned them with another couplet:

Dulness with redoubled sway
Has seized the wits of Symon Grey.

These two rebuffs were not sufficient, however, to blunt Grey's vanity and yet another package of even more ornate poems arrived for Burns' 'immediate attention'.

Burns now responded with a verse-epistle which ended with the crushing quatrain,

Such damned bombast no time that's past
Will show, or time to come,
So, Symon dear, your song I'll tear,
And with it wipe my bum.

Alexander thought it a good example of how the poet's life in the capital city was beginning to strain his self control beyond endurance. He had advised Robert that a longer stay in the city would seriously affect his health, and even his work. Take the Crochallan Fencibles, for instance. It was a rule of the Club to subject candidates for admission to ridiculous and, Alexander felt, dangerous initiation ceremonies. Burns for instance admitted that he had been 'thrashed' in a style beyond all his experience but refused to say what particular form this hazing took. It hadn't done him any good, Alexander was sure. There was also their insistence on Burns adding to their collection of bawdy ballads. He eventually obliged with a few on the understanding that they would never be published.

Eventually, Burns took Alexander's advice but not exactly in the way he'd hoped. He had wanted Burns to return to his roots in Ayrshire. Burns himself had said that sooner or later it would be 'back to the plough'.

Now was the time, Alexander felt. Let him get back to where he belonged, in his coarse stockings and broad bonnet, working on the earth among the animals. He didn't belong in his now famous well-cut blue coat, buff-coloured waistcoat and buckskin breeches. Even his boots – for he still favoured knee-high boots – had acquired some sort of style. He had even worn the boots at the Duchess of Gordon's salon and had sported lace at his neck and cuffs. Alexander felt his mind twist into a sneer – quite the dandy!

No, let him go back to being the coarse peasant that underneath the new clothes he still was and always would be.

'All right,' Burns had said in the end. 'I believe it is time I left Edinburgh, Alexander. But not to go back to Ayrshire. At least not yet. I want to see something of my native country. I was thinking of embarking on a tour of the Borders. Then later, perhaps I could see something of the Highlands.'

Alexander reminded him of the health problems he suffered, especially the bouts of feverishness and pain.

'How can you ride on horseback for many miles every day, Robert, and in all weathers? And think of the hospitality that will be pressed on you everywhere you go and how your stomach cannot thole drink. I would feel much happier if I knew you were safely at home on the farm.'

Burns said, 'My dear friend, I am not a woman to be kept protected at home. I am a man and must face life like a man. But I know you mean well, and I appreciate your concern.'

Before he set off, he attended to some business, like arranging for a stone to be erected over the grave of the poet Fergusson. Burns had been shocked and outraged when he'd visited the grave and found it neglected and unmarked. He wrote to the bailies of the Canongate for permission to erect a headstone to 'my elder brother in misfortune and by far my elder brother in the muse.' Earlier he'd written something that Alexander suspected would get him into bother,

O Fergusson! thy glorious parts
Ill suited law's dry, musty arts!
My curse upon your whunstane hearts,
Ye E'nbrugh gentry!
The tythe o' what ye waste at cartes
Wad stow'd his pantry!

Robert had tried to persuade Alexander to accompany him on his Borders tour but Alexander was too busy at the hospital. And he was still working on his poetry with the plan of eventually publishing another book.

'Well, perhaps we can visit the Highlands together at a later date.'

'Perhaps,' Alexander said.

'I will write and tell you all that is happening on my travels. I will let you know when I'll be returning to Edinburgh.'

His Edinburgh friend Bob Ainslie ended up as his travel companion. Ainslie was a law student and fellow Mason whose family came from the Border country. No doubt en route both men, certainly Burns, would have romantic as well as other kinds of adventures, Alexander thought with some bitterness, while he was slaving away in the hospital and having only a few hours late into the evening to sit at his desk with a candle and his quill.

Although Burns still had feelings for Jean Armour, he'd recently confided, ' . . . to tell the truth among friends, I feel a miserable blank in my heart for want of her, and I don't think I shall ever meet with so delicious an armful again. She has her faults: and so have you and I; and so has everybody.'

So why didn't he go back to his country woman and be done with it? Surely now that Robert was so famous, the Armours would accept him. Hadn't old Armour dropped his criminal proceedings?

But Burns was still feeling hurt and bitter at being rejected by Jean and the Armours. Nothing would divert Robert from his Borders tour. 'I might never have the same chance again,' he said. 'What use am I to anyone as a loyal Scot if I don't know my own country?'

> Catch the moments as they fly
> And use them as ye ought, man!
> Believe me happiness is shy
> And comes not aye when sought, man!

'Anyway, Alexander,' he added, 'I've business to do. Books to deliver and book monies to collect en route from various subscribers.'

An approach by the musical printer, James Johnson, who wrote asking him if he'd help in creating lyrics, came too late to stop the tour. However, Robert had immediately written back to Johnson explaining they were on the point of leaving but he would be in touch again as soon as he returned.

He'd bought a mare for four pounds in the Grassmarket and called it Jenny Geddes. Jenny Geddes had been the woman who had hurled a foot stool at Bishop Lindsay in St Giles' Cathedral on 23 August 1637 when he was trying to introduce the Book of Common Prayer. She was enraged at the cleric for daring to 'say Mass in my lug'.

The artist Naysmith, with whom Robert had become friendly, had supplied a portrait of him for the first Edinburgh edition of his poems and Beugo had done engravings. Naysmith was such an admirer of Burns, he refused to take payment for the portrait.

Robert packed three dozen proof-prints of the Beugo engravings in his travel bag, ready to give away to admirers if asked for. So, Alexander thought, he now *expects* adulation from everyone, everywhere.

Alexander tried to appear jovial as he waved Burns off on his journey. But he experienced one of his now worryingly frequent surges of jealousy. Robert's heavy farmer's build was flattered on horseback. He looked tall and at ease. It was only when he walked that his years of hard labour on the farm showed in his solid, heavy tread. On horseback, he could have passed as one of the gentry.

Alexander managed a smile as he waved him off. He even wished him good luck. Of course, he told himself, he meant what he said. He would never wish Robert any harm. But Robert should have taken his advice. As a doctor, he knew that despite Robert's hard, powerful-looking appearance, he had serious underlying medical problems. He needed rest and warmth. He needed to take care, not strain his constitution and allow himself to be soaked by rain and battered by all the elements as he rode for hour after hour, day after day, through open countryside.

'Oh well,' Alexander thought, 'I've done my best.'

But long after Robert had left, he was still haunted by bitter thoughts of the unfairness of life. He was just as talented as Robert Burns. Indeed, more so because he was a clever doctor and surgeon as well as a poet. Yet what did his life amount to? He had no home of his own, no wife, not even a mistress. He would have captured some lady's heart by now, he was sure, but at every turn he was overshadowed by Burns. Even if Burns was not with him in person, his name would always come up in conversation and ladies especially would go into raptures of praise of him. Female society in Edinburgh seemed to think of nothing or nobody else. He experienced, just for a second, a black wish for something to happen to Burns that would prevent him ever returning. Immediately ashamed, he choked it off.

Robert was still the same generous-hearted loving friend of his Ayrshire days. And he, Alexander, was still the same friend who loved him in return. *Of course he was.* Nothing had changed. But in his heart of hearts, Alexander knew perfectly well that everything had changed completely.

18

Burns set off in great excitement, togged up in new travelling clothes.

'I'm so glad I've you for my travel companion,' he told Ainslie. 'I love Alexander like a brother, but he's a very serious fellow and he fusses around me like a mother hen. With you, I can talk nonsense, laugh at everything and nothing, and do foolish things without fear of a lecture.'

Ainslie laughed. 'That's because I'm as daft as you are, Rab.'

And so they set off in high spirits, their horses sometimes cantering at a leisurely pace, sometimes slowing to pick their way over rough terrain. Then coming to a decent path, they would spur the animals into an exhilarating gallop as they raced each other.

In Dumfries, they were given hospitality by Mr Burnside, a clergyman, and his wife, Anne. Robert raved about Anne afterwards.

'God forgive me, Ainslie, I almost broke the tenth commandment on her account. What simplicity, elegance, good sense, sweetness of disposition, good humour, kind hospitality – if I say one word more about her, I'll be directly in love with her.'

Robert rode the six miles out of Dumfries to meet and confer with his friend, Patrick Miller. Miller wanted him to lease a farm on an estate Miller had bought.

'I know he means well, Ainslie, but oh, something whispers to me that I'd be happier doing anything else but farming. He means no doubt to give me a bargain but more than likely, it would be the ruin of me.'

'Are you still thinking of Jamaica, then?'

Robert shrugged. 'I can't settle my mind. Farming is the only thing of which I know anything, and heaven knows I understand very little even of that. If I don't fix, I will go to Jamaica. Should I stay in an unsettled state, at home, I would only dissipate my small fortune and ruin what I intend shall compensate my little ones for the stigma I've brought on their names.'

As it was, Ainslie noticed that his friend was constantly dispatching five pounds notes to his brother, Gilbert, to help him.

He also penned very brief descriptions of the scenery on their journey but wrote six times as much about the people they met. To Robert, landscapes always came second to the people, especially the women.

They visited Ainslie's parents and Robert was particularly bowled over by Rachel, Ainslie's sister. They quickly became friends. There was no flirting from either side. Robert did not feel it right to have any sport with his best friend's sister.

But when they all attended church and the minister was bawling out a sermon about a text containing a severe denunciation of obstinate sinners, Miss Rachel, Robert noticed, was in great agitation at the minister's hell-fire preaching and was leafing through her Bible trying to find the text.

He gently took the Bible from her and wrote in the fly leaf:

> Fair maid you need not take the hint,
> Nor idle texts pursue;
> 'Twas guilty sinners that he meant,
> Not angels such as you.

After Ainslie's holiday time was up, he returned alone to

Edinburgh. Robert made for home and Mauchline. When he'd left Mauchline, he had been penniless and unknown. Now he returned a national celebrity. In Edinburgh and on the Borders tour, he had rubbed shoulders with the highest in the land. He had been lavishly entertained by the nobility and lionised by the literati. His tinder heart had been set alight by a whole series of attractive ladies, yet once home, his thoughts turned longingly to Jean Armour.

He went to her parents' house to see her and found himself as hopelessly in love with her as ever.

'But,' he told his friend, Gavin Hamilton, 'I'm absolutely disgusted by the Armours' servile, fawning, flattering attitude towards me. They practically threw Jean at me.'

Hamilton shook his head. 'Changed days, eh Robert?'

'Practically everybody's changed. Especially the servility of all the work-folk. Since I've returned home, their fawning attitude has nearly sickened me.'

Soon he was confined to the house with one of his lingering stomach complaints. To be so confined in such small, quiet surroundings – especially compared with his stay in the busy metropolis – lowered his spirits to zero. To divert himself and help keep his mind from dwelling on his misery, he wrote letters, especially a long, autobiographical letter to Dr Moore, a friend that Mrs Dunlop had introduced him to. And of course, he wrote to Mrs Dunlop, who had become his sort of mother-confessor.

After a couple of weeks, he felt physically much better but still restless and unhappy, despite discovering that his bonnie Jean was still as willing and as passionate as ever. He made love to her and held her in his arms and wished he could lie close to her like that forever. But urgent and exhausting book business called and he was forced to set off to Edinburgh again.

He also had a promise to his mother and sisters to keep. It meant making stops en route to purchase bolts of mode silk which he dispatched home to them. This was for the new

131

bonnets, cloaks and gowns that they were eagerly looking forward to having made.

In Edinburgh, he went straight to Alexander's lodgings and asked if Alexander would like to accompany him on a tour of the West Highlands where he had many books to deliver and money to collect for them. Alexander, as it happened, was due some time off and he was persuaded on this occasion to be his travelling companion. Not for the first time, Robert was sorely tempted to enquire about Susanna's whereabouts and her condition, but was too conscientious to break his solemn promise to the poor girl not to even mention her name to anyone.

He felt furious every time he thought about Neil Guthrie and what he must have done to Susanna to get her into such a state of terror. But the girl must be all right now, otherwise Alexander would have said something. Nevertheless he felt sad and disturbed at the thought of her.

It helped that despite Alexander's serious nature and the fact that he kept a conscientious doctor's eye on Robert, the journey was full of interest. It lifted Robert's spirits. Inveraray in Argyll was the most northern part of their journey. The Duke and Duchess of Argyll were subscribers to Robert's book, and from John Campbell, the fifth Duke of Argyll, Robert had a long-standing invitation to visit.

Robert and Alexander were soaking wet and travel-weary when they came to an inn where hopefully they could find rest and refreshment.

'No, no,' the innkeeper insisted – not knowing who they were – as he abruptly turned them away. 'I'm full up and far too busy with the overflow from the castle. His Grace is President of the Fishery Society and he's hosting members and officials before he leaves for the Hebrides first thing tomorrow morning.'

Robert had recently acquired a diamond-pointed stylus (a present from the Earl of Glencairn), such as was used by glass engravers, and he was so fatigued and angry, he scratched on one of the window panes of the inn before turning away,

Who'er he be that sojourns here,
I pity much his case.
Unless he comes to wait upon
The lord *their* god, 'His Grace'.

However, the next day, they met up with a merry party of
more hospitable Highland gentlemen. They stayed overnight
at the mansion of one of the gentlemen, and despite Alexander's
warnings about needing to rest in preparation for the next
day's journey, Robert danced and made merry after Alexander
had retired to bed, and the ladies left at three in the morning.
Next evening, they spent the night at Dumbarton where they
were given more Highland hospitality. Robert was also given
the Freedom of Dumbarton. Alexander had lost count of the
places where such honours had been conferred on Burns. It
was beginning to make him feel painfully depressed. He could
hardly bring himself to speak to Robert eventually.

And so they were riding soberly and quietly down the side
of Loch Lomond, when along came a Highlander at a gallop.

'I'm not going to be out-galloped by any Highlander,'
Burns suddenly announced, obviously pleased at the chance
of a bit of excitement.

'No, wait!' Alexander shouted in exasperation, as Burns
spurred his horse forward. 'Robert!' Alexander's voice rose to
a furious bawl. 'Don't be a fool!'

But the old mare, Jenny Geddes, strained forward and
despite the Highlander's good horse, began to pass him. Robert
shouted with excitement and delight. Then, unexpectedly, the
other horse wheeled to one side, throwing his Highland rider
and also Jenny Geddes and her rider to the ground.

Within moments Alexander reached the débâcle and helped
the two men to their feet. The Highlander quickly recovered
and rode off. Burns, however, was quite badly cut and bruised,
but he put up his hands and managed good-humouredly, 'All
right. All right. I'm a fool. I ought to listen to you.'

'Yes, you should, Robert,' Alexander growled as he examined

Robert's wounds. 'Fortunately, on this occasion, there are no bones broken. But you won't feel like riding for a while.'

However, once Alexander had patched him up, Robert felt fit enough by the next afternoon to continue on their journey, although in fact he was still in some pain.

In Paisley, they were spotted by an admirer of Burns' poetry, a Dr John Taylor. He pleaded with Burns to accompany him to his home. Both Alexander and Burns protested that they should be getting on with their journey. Burns, however, was eventually persuaded by the fact that Dr Taylor was particularly anxious for his young children to meet the poet. Burns had a fatherly fondness for children.

Once in Dr Taylor's house, his young family were summoned to meet the poet. Burns dandled one chubby little boy on his knee and said he would 'make an excellent subject for a poem'. This pleased the father enormously. The only thing that displeased him was that his eldest son, a tall, gangly lad, was so overawed by all the previous talk of 'the great man, Robert Burns', that he refused to appear.

Later, his father chastised him and said how the time would come that he'd bitterly regret not having had a sight of the great man to remember. The boy said, 'But I did see him, Father. I keeked at him through the doors.'

'Oh? And what did he look like then?'

'He was a big man, taller than me, with a brown complexion. He was broad-chested, erect and stood on sturdy legs hid in yellow top boots. He wore a blue coat and buckskin breeches. A very impressive figure, I thought.'

'Well done, lad.' His father was delighted. 'Well done. And I agree with you. I don't know why your mother insists he had a gloomy countenance and bearing.'

The young man smiled. 'I don't suppose you'll ever allow anyone to say a word against him, Father.'

'Indeed, I won't, lad. No, never. The man's a genius, and I'm proud to have had him in my home. I only wish he could have stayed longer but he said he had to return to Mossgiel.'

Alexander accompanied Robert as far as Tarbolton, because he felt it was time he paid a visit to his parents. He was shocked when he saw them. Admittedly his mother had never been a robust woman and his father was prone to the occasional attack of gout. But he had never before seen either of them in such a sad and worrying state. He soon discovered the reason. They showed him Susanna's note.

'We aye knew she was excitable an' reckless, an' had an awfu' imagination,' his mother said, 'but this time she seems tae have gone completely mad. Poor Neil has searched an' searched, aw tae no avail. We've aw been quite distracted.'

Alexander was silent and thoughtful for some time.

Eventually his father said, 'Have ye nothin' tae say aboot this, Alexander? D'ye no' care aboot what's happened?'

'Of course I care. I care about Susanna. What worries me, Father, is there may be some truth in what she's written.'

'Dinna be daft,' his mother cried out. 'Neil's been a good man tae yer sister.'

'How do you know that, Mother?'

His mother looked upset and harassed. 'He gave her everythin' any lassie could ever wish for. He aye behaved like a perfect gentleman.'

'In front of you and everyone else, no doubt. But it's what he might have been capable of in private that I'm wondering about now. I always thought there was a strange coldness about him. I should have enquired more deeply into that.'

His mother collapsed onto the settee. His father tottered over to sit beside her.

'Ye cannae believe, son . . . ' the old man quavered, 'ye cannae believe there's any truth in what the lassie said. Surely no'.'

'Why else would Susanna leave a luxurious home where to all appearances she enjoyed wealth and position – the things she always wanted in life? Knowing Susanna, she had to have a very, very good reason for giving all that up.'

'Och, ye surely remember what she could be like.' His

mother began to rally again. 'A right, reckless wee madam at times. No, she's just got it into her head that marriage disnae suit her. She was aye an innocent wee lassie as well.' Worry flickered over her face. 'Maybe Ah should have telt her what her duties were. Tae her man, Ah mean. Still, that's nae excuse for ravin' on like that.'

'What a time we've had,' her father said. 'And tryin' tae keep it quiet as well. We dinnae want tae cause a scandal. We've searched aw aroon here. Mysie an' John have been helpin' tae. We werenae fit tae travel tae Edinburgh tho'.'

His mother continued, 'We were waitin' till we had a try oorsels nearer at hand afore we sent word tae you, son. But noo that ye ken, ye'll dae yer best tae try in Edinburgh, won't ye? If we could just get her back tae her man, she'd be fine. Ah'm sure he's got a fright. Ah mean, whatever faults he might have, he's been that upset. He didnae want tae lose her. An' just tae make sure, we could have a word wi' him, couldn't we, Geordie? A discreet word o' warnin' that her faither an' me would be keepin' an eye on things noo tae make sure she wis aw right. You'll help tae find yer, won't ye, son?'

'Yes, of course.'

He had developed a blinding headache. God knows what kind of trouble Susanna could be in by now, what other kind of dreadful scandal. This could badly affect his career. It would surely ruin his reputation among the respectable quality, and bar him from every aristocratic family drawing room he'd acquired access to. One's family background was all-important to people like that.

He was glad to see his words of assurance had relaxed his parents and made them feel more hopeful and happier. But he felt anything but relaxed and happy. 'Damnation,' he kept thinking. He was concerned about Susanna and he'd do his best to find her. But why did fate keep tormenting him so?

He had always worked hard. He had devoted his life to helping people and to alleviating their suffering. He had never done anyone any harm. He had never over-indulged in drink

136

or fornication or any other vice. In what spare time he had from tending the sick, he laboured at producing excellent poetry. Nothing had turned out as he'd hoped and dreamed.

While a man like Robert Burns could idle around, pass the time with women, and enjoy life.

His mouth twisted. It reflected the hardening, the icy bitterness in his mind.

19

Susanna sat in a corner of the tavern, supping a bowl of watery porridge. As she did so, she was desperately trying to think of what she could do and where she could go next. At first, she did not hear the voice saying good morning. It was repeated and she looked up to see a woman smiling down at her. And what a woman! Susanna had never seen such a thick curly wig or such a high hat that was perched on top of it. A voluptuous frill of material frothed over her chest, making her bosom look enormous in comparison with her tiny waist. Her hands were hidden in an equally enormous fur muff.

'Margaret Burns,' the woman said, introducing herself. 'And you are?'

'Burns?' Susanna gasped. 'Are you related to the poet?'

'No, no. I only wish I was. May I join you?'

Susanna nodded. It was occurring to her that this was the kind of appearance in a woman that Neil would have hated. It made her warm to Margaret Burns.

'I was speaking to the landlord,' the woman said, ' and he tells me you arrived late last night looking for lodgings.'

'I don't think I'll be staying here another night,' Susanna said. 'It's not the kind of place I had in mind.'

'You're a married lady, I see.'

Susanna nodded again.

'Yet you are travelling alone and unprotected.'

'I did not wish to be with my husband.'

'Oh, I see.'

'I'm sure you can have no idea, madam.'

'I'm an experienced woman of the world, my dear. I know about men, believe me.'

'Do you know about madmen?' Susanna asked bitterly.

'All kinds, my dear. All kinds. And all of them have to be made to pay. It's the only way to deal with them, and to survive and remain free.'

'I don't quite understand. You mean punish them? Seek revenge? I just want never to see my husband again.'

'I can give you lodgings. But first you must give me your name. Any name you so choose. When I lived in Durham, I was called Matthews. When I came here, I took the Scottish name of Burns.'

'Anna.' Susanna hesitated. 'Anna McIntyre.' The housekeeper's name was the first that sprang to mind.

'Well, Anna McIntyre, would you like to take up my offer? I think we could get on fine, you and I.'

Susanna hesitated again, but then thought – why not? She couldn't stay where she was. Soon the place would be full of roistering drunken men again. And the room she'd slept in was neither clean nor comfortable. She'd already taken quite a liking to Margaret and could quite easily imagine getting on fine with her.

'Yes, all right, but first I must know what rent you would expect me to pay. I haven't much money and . . . '

'Och, don't worry about that,' Margaret interrupted. 'I've another lodger – Sally Sanderson. Money has never caused any problem. We'll work something out to suit you, never fear.'

Susanna felt light-headed with relief as she followed Margaret from the inn. She was taken to a flat in a nearby street that was as spacious as the one her grandparents had lived in. There she was installed in a bedroom which had a chest of drawers, a wardrobe, a bed and a small table and chair. The place looked clean and homely. Susanna was delighted. After

139

she'd unpacked her belongings and put them tidily away, she was called through to the kitchen where Margaret had made a pot of tea. They were sitting drinking it when a young girl arrived and was introduced as Sally Sanderson. She was dressed more in the style of a servant with a red, hooded cape, and she had a somewhat impudent look about her.

After a few minutes sitting chatting and drinking tea, however, she relaxed and even seemed to acquire a kind of vulnerability. Susanna guessed the hard, impudent look was some sort of superficial self defence. They had been talking about the terrible roads into Edinburgh – if they could be called roads, as some were no more than rutted paths. Then the awful condition of some of the inns en route.

Sally said, 'Talking about inns, one of the men I met last night – remember, the fat one – promised to come back tonight. That should save me going out. I'm sick of hanging about in this cold weather. It takes the heart out of me. If some of your men turn up and Susanna gets somebody, we could have another party – and to hell with the neighbours.'

Susanna stared at the girl in complete confusion.

'Sally,' Margaret said, 'away through to the room and tidy it up. There's still some bottles lying about from last night.'

'Oh, right,' Sally cheerfully agreed, and left the kitchen.

'You see, it's like I said,' Margaret explained to Susanna. 'We make them pay. We give them a good time – the men, I mean – but we make them pay.'

'You give parties and the guests pay?'

'That's right. But the good time has to include what all men want and enjoy above all else – sexual favours.'

Susanna was horrified. 'You mean . . . like what happens when you're married? You let them do that to you for money? I wouldn't let a man do that to me for anything. That's what I ran away from.'

'You as much as said your husband was a madman. I take it from that that he treated you cruelly – probably in an unnatural manner. We don't put up with anything like that here. No, no, it's all very jolly and friendly. You'll see.'

'No, I certainly will not!' Susanna could no longer hold her tea cup, she was trembling so much. 'I'll have to leave.' Tears filled her eyes. She had thought she'd found a safe refuge. Now she was tragically disappointed and afraid again – afraid of having to face the dark Edinburgh streets on her own.

'No, you don't.' Margaret patted Susanna's hand. 'You can stay here for as long as you like, and just pay your rent. Nobody will force you to do anything against your will.'

'Do you promise me?'

'I promise you.'

Susanna was still trembling but she took a deep breath and tried to relax. 'Then, if you don't mind, I'll go to my room.'

'We see to our own food,' Margaret said, 'so either you go out and eat in one of the taverns or you buy stuff at the market and cook for yourself in here.'

'Thank you. I think I'll go to the market and buy what I need.'

'Fine. Do you know where the markets are?'

'Yes, I've been to Edinburgh before and explored quite a bit. I used to come with my parents and then my brother. We visited our grandparents but sadly they're both dead now.'

'Right. I'll leave you be. But you must do the same for Sally and me. We get enough criticism and trouble from the neighbours. We don't want any from you.'

'I understand, and I appreciate your kindness. I really do.'

'Oh well, if we women don't stick together and help one another, who will? That's what I always say. And you'll come round to the idea of joining in, in time.'

'Never.'

Margaret smiled. 'We'll see.'

It took some initial courage for Susanna to venture out alone on to the city streets. Not because she was afraid of any of the vast crowds of Edinburgh inhabitants. She was only afraid of being found by her husband or anyone who knew her and could tell him where she was. However, she began to feel safer as she merged in with the crowds.

She even began to take an interest in her surroundings. Edinburgh was a place steeped in history, often very gory history. Here at the far end of the Cathedral was the Mercat or Market Cross. It was the main place of punishment. The fearsome beheading machine called the Maiden used to be here. It had been used in 1661 to cut off the head of the eighth Earl of Argyll. Then in 1685, it beheaded his son, the ninth Earl.

Before that, in 1650, the Marquis of Montrose, an enemy of the Argylls, met an even more terrible death. At the bottom of the Royal Mile, he was bound to the seat on the hangman's cart and drawn through silent crowds up the hill to the Tolbooth. Eventually he was hanged at the Mercat Cross. After his body was taken down, it was cut up and the pieces were distributed among the chief towns of Scotland. The head was stuck on the highest part of the Tolbooth. It remained there for eleven years until it was taken down and replaced by the head of the Earl of Argyll.

Alongside the wall of the Cathedral was a row of towering tenements called the Luckenbooths. The bottom floors consisted of shops. Then between the back of the Luckenbooths was a narrow alley packed with stables of merchants who hadn't any shops of their own. Susanna crushed around and managed to purchase from one or the other what she thought she'd need. Then, as she began to tire, her feelings of apprehension seeped back. She felt vulnerable and kept glancing around to check that no-one was following her. She began to imagine she caught glimpses of Neil's slim, elegant figure and his pale face and cold eyes. She began to run despite being hindered by the weight of her purchases. By the time she reached Margaret Burns' close, she was breathless and dishevelled.

'What happened to you?' Margaret asked. 'Has the devil been chasing you?'

'I thought I saw my husband.'

'You're that afraid of him?'

'Absolutely terrified,' Susanna assured her.

'Oh well, you're safe now.'

But was she? Susanna wondered. Men came here. What if one day, or one night . . . But no, she must get a grip of herself. She must not allow Neil to win, to ruin her life. She would be brave, she told herself firmly. And she would not allow her imagination to run away with her. She'd always had a terrible imagination.

Some things did not help though. It was unfortunate that Margaret had adopted the name Burns. It kept reminding Susanna of the poet and her foolish snobbishness.

Margaret and Sally often spoke of him, repeating stories they'd heard of him. 'He's the talk of the town,' Margaret kept saying. 'Oh, if only I could meet him. If only he'd come here.'

'Well, you never know your luck,' Sally said. 'And we can keep our eyes open for him and do our best. That includes you, Anna. You'll surely not turn your nose up at a genius – and a handsome one at that.'

'Actually, I have met him.'

'What?' The two women were all agog. 'When? Where? What's he like?'

Susanna hesitated. 'Well . . . I . . . I didn't know he was a poet. I mean at the time I thought he was just a ploughman. It was before he had his book published. But he had a disturbing attraction, I must admit.'

Margaret flushed with pleasure. 'The caddies said he's not often seen in the taverns but you'd be able to find out where he goes and then introduce us, Anna.'

'Oh no, I mean I wouldn't know.' Susanna became flustered. 'Anyway, I couldn't.'

'Why not?'

'Well . . . for one thing, I don't think he likes me.'

'Don't be daft! You're very pretty and I've heard he can't resist a pretty woman. He's always writing love poems about them.' She looked startled. 'He's written a poem about a woman called Anna. Was that you?'

'Oh no.' Susanna shook her head. 'I'm sure not.'

Margaret's eyes became wistful then. 'There was some gossip in a London journal linking my name romantically with his publisher's. Then it spread all over Edinburgh. Creech – that's the publisher's name – was absolutely furious and anything but gentlemanly in what he said about me. But Robert Burns wrote a poem in my defence. She sighed, remembering.

> Cease, ye prudes, your envious railings,
> Lovely Burns has charms – confess;
> True it is, she had one failing,
> Had ae woman ever less?

'Oh, I must meet him. You must find some way of introducing me, Anna. I've done you a favour. This is what I want in return.'

20

As soon as he returned to the capital city, Alexander sought
out one of the caddies. He could not, and would not, wander
about the dark and filthy wynds of the city, peering at women,
questioning tavern keepers. They would think he was a lecher.
Or a man looking for a whore. Nothing unusual in that. Only
it was unusual for him. He had an excellent reputation as a
doctor and a gentleman, someone who could be trusted and
who was above reproach. As indeed he was.

The reputation the caddies had was for being honest and
for knowing everything about everybody. He signalled to one
in the High Street to approach him, and the man came scurrying
across, his tousled hair and tattered clothes flapping around
him in the breeze.

Alexander said quietly, 'I need your help.'

'Aye, sir. Jist you say the word.'

'I am Doctor Wallace from the Infirmary.'

'Aye, Ah ken. A guid doctor, aye!'

'You too have a good reputation.'

'Thank ye, sir.'

'I'm hoping first of all, on this occasion, that you will be
discreet. I will pay you well but I do not want my name known
in this matter.'

'Ah understand, sir. Nae need tae worry yersel.'

'My sister has disappeared from her home in Ayrshire. I
believe she may have come to Edinburgh. I must find her. Can

you make enquiries? She is a pretty girl with dark, red-gold hair. Her name is Susanna.'

'Ah'll see what Ah can dae. Ah've already heard there's a new lassie wi' Margaret Burns. It may no' be yer Susanna bit ah'll speir aroon' tomorrow an' let ye ken for sure this time the day efter.'

'Very well.'

Alexander turned away in some consternation. Margaret Burns was a notorious woman of the town. Surely Susanna could not have sunk that low. Impossible! No, no, he knew Susanna could be reckless and foolish at times, but she was still a modest, well brought-up girl and she had never, he was sure, behaved with the slightest impropriety with any man in her young life. No, she would have found some reputable lodgings somewhere. But once what money she had ran out? What then? He shuddered to think.

He tried to put Susanna out of his head until he was due to see the caddie again. Meantime he was helped by the fact that he had been invited to attend a concert at St Cecilia's Hall where the music of Handel and Corelli was to be performed on violins by some gentlemen he knew. There were always large parties of ladies and gentlemen in the audience, and the last time he'd attended such a concert, one lady had caught his eye. He'd managed, with the help of Professor Purdie, to get an introduction. He discovered the lady was the daughter of a very wealthy businessman who had a large estate in Dumfriesshire and who, with his family, liked to enjoy a few weeks in the capital city every year. Alexander was delighted and immediately determined to pay court to the lady, who was known as Isobel McKenzie.

After the delightful diversions of the evening were over and he had returned to his lodgings, his worries returned a hundredfold. Here was his big chance. Mr and Mrs McKenzie had seemed taken with him and he was invited to take tea with them the following afternoon. They lived in the New Town in a very imposing terraced house with most elegant decor and furnishings in each room. He had shown interest in Mr McKenzie's business. He had complimented Mrs McKenzie on her excellent oatcakes and made several flattering and gallant remarks about Isobel's beauty and talent at playing the spinet. They had invited him to call again.

Now, through no fault of his own, he could be denied such a wonderful opportunity to court the beautiful Isobel by any scandal about his family coming to light. Apart from Isobel being an excellent catch, he had felt mightily attracted to her even before he knew who she was. In fact, as Burns would have said, he was directly in love with her. He felt excited as well as worried. Excited by the mere idea of courting Isobel and eventually – God willing – making her his wife. Worried lest Susanna would disgrace him and cause Isobel's father to ban him as a prospective suitor.

He hardly slept a wink that night and worked thoughtlessly, mechanically, all day until it was time for him to make his way to the point in the High Street where he'd arranged to see the caddie. He was early but within a few seconds, he caught sight of the ragged figure trotting towards him.

'Aye, there ye are, sir. Ah've found yer sister. At least there's a young lassie answerin' yer description moved in wi' Mistress Burns an' she calls hersel' Anna McIntyre. See that wynd over there? Doon there and third close on yer left.'

Alexander felt sick. He recognised the housekeeper's name. How could Susanna stoop so low? This was terrible. His mind in turmoil, he gave the caddie a generous amount of money.

'Thank ye, sir. Thank ye.' The caddie was so delighted he literally skipped away along the High Street.

What to do now? Alexander stood as if his silver-buckled shoes were stuck to the ground, as the hustle and bustle of the High Street elbowed around him and street cries reverberated in his head. They did not however drown out his anxieties. Should he go immediately to the harlot's house and drag Susanna away? What if she was with a man? How awful. How disgraceful. It would kill his mother and father if they found

147

out. He must think about the best and safest method of approaching the dilemma – for all concerned.

Back in his lodgings, he suffered another sleepless night and was so distressed, he almost sent an excuse to the McKenzies and did not turn up for his second visit. However, he couldn't risk losing the chance of paying court to Isobel. Eventually, hiding his distress as best he could, he called at the McKenzie house again. Mrs McKenzie suggested that 'the young people should take the air'. And so, with Isobel on his arm, he went parading around the New Town admiring, with her, the elegant new buildings.

'This is where I would like to live,' Alexander said, and meant it. 'One day, I hope to have a home of my own and it would be my dearest wish that it should be in a place like this, in one of these beautiful buildings.'

Isobel gave his arm a little squeeze. 'I understand how you feel. We used to lodge in the Old Town when we came up from Dumfriesshire, but I would never want to go back to live there again, even just for our yearly visit of a few weeks. Although,' she added, 'it can be fascinating and exciting to go to the Dancing Assemblies and the oyster cellars. There's not very much social life in the New Town yet.'

Before giving himself time to think, Alexander said, 'I'd be honoured to accompany you to the oyster cellars for an evening's entertainment.'

'And oysters?'

He smiled. 'And oysters.'

Then worry gnawed at him again. Like the taverns – in the wynds or in other cellars – the oyster cellars were always packed with all kinds of people. What if Margaret Burns, accompanied by Susanna and some low-class fellows, appeared? He still could hardly credit that his sister could be consorting with such people. She had always been so fussy about the company she kept.

Once having promised to take Isobel to the oyster cellars, however, he could not very well retract. To make matters worse, her father and mother decided to accompany them. 'Some magistrate friends of mine are going tomorrow,' Mr McKenzie said. 'We can make a grand party of it.'

Alexander suffered an immediate headache. Robert's publisher Creech was a magistrate. What if he turned up? He now could at least sympathise with Robert as far as a headache was concerned. Although his headaches, unlike those of his friend, were not accompanied with other aches and pains or depression. He was just acutely anxious in case Susanna might appear with Margaret Burns. It was well known that Creech had been hugely embarrassed and furious by an article in a London journal that said, 'Bailie Creech, of literary celebrity in Edinburgh, was about to lead the beautiful and accomplished Miss Burns to the Hymeneal altar.'

This and other squibs at his expense had come after Miss Burns had been brought before the magistrates after a complaint by a neighbour.

Creech had given a very severe decision. She was, he commanded, to be banished from the city, under the penalty, in case of return, of being drummed through the streets, besides confinement for six months in the house of correction.

Nothing daunted, Miss Burns had lodged an appeal with the Court of Session. At first it was refused. Then one of the private complainants acknowledged he'd been induced to sign the complaint and in fact he didn't know of any 'riot or disturbance' being committed in Miss Burns' house.

Creech, of course, was enraged at the outcome in Miss Burns' favour and hated the woman. Especially when the retraction he'd demanded that the newspaper make in no way cooled his fury. It said,

In a former number we noticed the intended marriage between Bailie Creech of Edinburgh and the beautiful Miss Burns of the same place. We have now the authority of that gentleman to say that the proposed marriage is not to take place, matters having been otherwise arranged, to the mutual satisfaction of both parties and their respective friends.

It would be absolutely disastrous if Creech joined the party at the oyster cellar. Alexander made what he hoped sounded a casual note of enquiry to Mr McKenzie. 'By the way, Mr Creech happens to be the one who published my poet friend's book. Do you know him?'

'Know him?' Alexander was taken aback at the roar. 'Know him? I would give my right arm to know him. You must arrange an introduction, Alexander. I would be obliged to you for ever after.'

For a moment, Alexander was confused. 'Mr Creech?'

'No, no, the poet Robert Burns, of course.'

'Oh . . . oh, yes.' He might have known, he thought bitterly. 'I believe he is on one of his tours at the moment. Up north, I think. But once he returns . . . '

Mrs McKenzie clapped her hands and rolled her eyes upwards as if in prayer. 'How wonderful! I can't wait to tell all of our friends. I must start planning the most prodigiously magnificent dinner and entertainment ever experienced in Edinburgh.'

Alexander groaned inside. It was always the same. The mere mention of Robert's name sent everyone – men and women alike – into raptures. Isobel was almost jumping up and down.

'Robert Burns! Robert Burns!' she was crying out, and clapping her hands with excitement.

His headache turned to thick black treacle inside not only his skull, but his heart. It churned heavily, darkly, sickeningly.

No-one noticed that there was anything in the slightest degree wrong. The room echoed with the delighted chatter and laughter of the McKenzie family. Alexander was not sure if the words 'Robert Burns! Robert Burns!' kept echoing in the room, or in his head. It didn't matter. He hated them just the same. He secretly vowed he'd do everything in his power to prevent the McKenzies – especially Isobel – from meeting Robert. But he had to be very careful in case it might negatively influence his case for Miss Isobel's hand. Yet he couldn't face the thought of introducing Robert to the family and then suffering once more the humiliation of being completely in the shade. Without apparently any effort, Robert would charm them with his looks, his presence, his erudition and witty conversation. He could be extremely witty – usually at the expense of someone else. Nobody, as a result, as far as he knew, had ever recorded any of Burns' conversations in journals, or anywhere else. They were so busy laughing, and listening to the conversations that went on so late, that everyone simply collapsed into bed afterwards.

It would be the same with the McKenzies. He hoped and prayed that Robert would keep away long enough from Edinburgh on this occasion until he established a formal engagement of marriage to Isobel. Or, even, had a marriage ceremony. The quicker he made sure of Isobel, the better.

Robert was a predator of single women. At least he was religious enough to adhere to the commandment, 'Thou shalt not commit adultery'.

Yes, Alexander thought desperately, his courtship of Isobel would have to be a very speedy one. Meantime he hit on an idea. He'd say that Burns wouldn't be back in Edinburgh for a couple of months. That way, they could return to their estate until he wrote to them and let them know an exact date. Or if they wished, he could bring Burns to their estate for a longer visit. They'd be sure to be delighted with that.

That's what he'd say. That's what he'd say.

21

Susanna discovered that Margaret Burns had originally come from a very respectable and wealthy family. Her father had been a successful merchant but he contracted a ruinous second marriage, resulting in Margaret being thrown destitute upon the world. This background solved what had been to Susanna the mystery of Margaret's superior education and personal demeanour. She had at one time been acquainted with the better class of society. She was also a beautiful woman with a handsome figure which was always decked out in the highest style of fashion. Susanna liked her. However, she still could not feel at ease with the way Margaret lived. Men came and went during the day. Most evenings were taken up with drinking parties. Locked in her bedroom trying to read by the light of a flickering candle, Susanna would hear the deep rumble of male laughter.

Margaret had tried to explain to Susanna that being with men needn't be so bad, indeed could be quite pleasant with the right person.

'You have been unfortunate, my dear,' she sympathised. 'So unfortunate. I can assure you that few men behave as your husband did to you. You were right when you described him as a madman. I feel so sorry for you.'

Susanna had felt better after confiding in Margaret and was grateful to her not only for her sympathy, but for not putting any pressure on her. She was allowed to retreat to her bedroom whenever she wanted and to stay there as long as she wished. During the day she sometimes took the air in a solitary walk, often early in the morning because then she thought she would be safer from being recognised. Although 'taking the air' in Edinburgh was far from being the same as taking the air in Tarbolton or the surrounding countryside. The wynds of Edinburgh were unlit and dark even during the daylight hours. Often the sewage that was flung out of windows at the sound of the ten o'clock bell was left for days, instead of being cleared up every morning by men employed for that purpose. The air was thick with the stench of a thousand chamber pots, and one had to be very careful where one put one's feet. Susanna would walk gingerly along until she reached the High Street. The obnoxious smell still clung in the air but at least the road was cleaner under foot.

There she could see, high up in front of the houses, painted signs in bright colours on a black background to indicate what each tradesman was selling. Here was a painting of a quarter loaf showing that inside that flat was a baker. Above was a periwig that advertised the trade of a barber. There was a picture of cheese, another of a firkin of butter. There was a vivid painting of a pair of stays, an equally colourful one of a petticoat and many other signs that all cluttered together to show where people could get the articles they wanted.

Here she could watch the City Guard doing their exercises. Or she could stroll along Fishmarket Close and stand watching the fishwives rapidly open shells and oyster-loving customers swallow alive the oysters in their own gravy.

Edinburgh had always enjoyed a good supply of salmon from the rivers Tay and Tweed, white fish from Newhaven and Musselburgh, also trout and eels from the Nor' Loch.

In the Lawnmarket, there was a prominent sign board which said, 'Cooked Nor' Loch Trout for Supper, and Eel Pies'. These delicacies were a favourite with Margaret and Sally, but Susanna's more delicate sensitivities prevented her from eating anything from the Loch. She knew, even if the others didn't, of the innumerable witches and other poor creatures who had been tortured and drowned there in the past.

Even if she'd told Margaret and Sally, they would probably just have laughed and continued to enjoy their suppers. Although they were kind and sympathetic to her, she could not believe that they had much sensitivity left in their natures, after not only allowing men physical intimacies, but accepting money and gifts from the men.

She suspected too that both Margaret and Sally believed that, in time, she would join them in their low style of life.

'But my dear,' Margaret said, 'the little money you have won't last forever and I cannot afford to keep you here rent-free. So then what will you do? What *can* you do?'

Susanna had no answer for that and, in fact, her money was fast running out. Her mind desperately sought for alternative ways to make a living but kept being hedged in either by pride or fear. Even if she could find work in a tavern, for instance, her pride would suffer agonies at having to serve drunken hordes every night. She would also be terrified in case Neil would suddenly appear and drag her back to imprison her in his mausoleum of a house.

Yet there were dangers even here in Margaret's house. The magistrates were hell-bent on persecuting her. They had tried everything to banish her from the city, so far without success. Margaret was a spirited woman who would not easily be defeated. But still, the day might come . . . Even now, the fight was beginning to tell on her. She had to apply rouge to her cheeks because they had become so pale. Susanna also observed that she did not fill her clothes. They had begun to hang loosely on her.

It occurred to Susanna, not for the first time, how helpless and vulnerable women could be if they did not have a protector or someone to support them. Sometimes she imagined that one day she might meet a nice gentleman who had just come to Margaret's house for company. Perhaps a gentleman who was a traveller, perhaps lonely, or a stranger in the city. Perhaps they would get talking and he would realise that she was a respectable girl – just a lodger in the house, a lonely stranger in the city like himself. And then a relationship would develop. He could become her protection and support. Then harsh reality would shatter her dreams. She was a married woman and nothing could come of any meeting she might have with any gentleman, no matter how nice.

She began, in desperation, to think of her brother. Surely Alexander would not allow her to be destitute – left penniless in the streets, reduced to joining the ragged army of men and women sleeping in closes and stairways.

No, she did not believe he would allow her to suffer in that way. After all, she had not been in the city for so very long. Hardly enough time for him to get the news from their parents and then to find where she was. But what if Alexander believed the best way was for her to return to her husband and to the mansion that most people would think of as luxurious? She shook with terror at the mere idea. She dare not risk such a thing. She clamped her arms across her chest and hugged herself and rocked herself to and fro. She'd kill herself first. At the same time she knew she would never have the courage to kill herself.

She didn't know what to do. In a way, it was like when she was living in the Guthrie house. She was reduced to the same frame of mind. Wondering and wondering, her mind going round and round in fearful circles, needing to escape from her problems and feel safe but not knowing how. Eventually, Margaret said, 'What about one gentleman to whom you could give your favours? No one else – just the one gentleman. Like a mistress, you know. You must have heard of mistresses. Even kings take mistresses, often more than one. It would be perfectly respectable.'

Susanna doubted this. Didn't believe it for a moment, in fact. Yet the thought kept returning to her mind until it became mixed up with her dreams and imaginings. She began to peep out of her window to view the men who visited the house. When it was dark, some of them arrived led by a caddie carrying a flaming torch to light the way. The flame sent shadows flickering around and making ghostly masks of the men's faces. But during the day they didn't look so frightening. Most of the men looked surprisingly respectable, in fact.

Margaret said that it didn't matter if Susanna was married or not. Men didn't marry their mistresses. Most of them who took a mistress were already married. Most of them were married to cold, unloving women and they were glad to turn to a warm-hearted girl who would give them a little happiness and pleasure every now and again. There were lots of perfectly respectable men who came to the house and others like it. Indeed, when the General Assembly of the Church of Scotland was held in Edinburgh, it was every brothel's busiest time.

Susanna should think about it, Margaret said. And she did think about it and she felt sick at the thought of it. At least, she sometimes did. At other times, the nice kindly gentleman of her longings and imaginings would take over and she'd dream of how safe and happy he could make her feel. Margaret said they would choose a nice kindly gentleman, it was the only way to solve her problem. Could she think of another way? She couldn't.

Unless of course her brother. She hadn't told Margaret about Alexander. He kept coming back into her mind despite the terror. She had always got on well with Alexander. Perhaps if she pleaded with him not to take her back to Neil . . . If he saw for himself how afraid she was of having anything to do with her husband, surely he would take pity on her and not force her to return to him.

One day, she plucked up courage to go to the Infirmary. She hung around outside for a time and then asked herself, 'What am I doing here? He will be too busy to see me here. He might not even be on duty.'

A few days later, she went to where he lodged with his professor friend. Or rather, she loitered outside in a state of nervous collapse trying to force her legs to carry her upstairs to his door.

Three times she went to his lodgings. On the third occasion, she was actually climbing the stairs when she heard Neil's smooth voice. It was only a superhuman effort that prevented her from fainting. He was saying, 'I'm sorry to have troubled you, sir. But I thought you would wish to offer your help once you knew that I'd be staying in the city for the next few weeks.'

Susanna stumbled breathlessly, and she prayed silently, back down the dark stairs and out on to the street. She never stopped running until she'd reached the safety of Margaret's house. She was glad to accept the glass of whisky that Margaret offered her.

Then, after she'd calmed down, she felt grateful in a way that she'd had the experience. At least she now knew that Neil was in the city and would be here for the next few weeks. If she had not known, she could have taken the air, innocently wandered about . . . Now she would not dare to put a foot outside the door.

'Have another whisky,' Margaret said.

And she did.

22

'You gave him short shrift,' Professor Purdie said.

Alexander nodded. 'Not a man I have a great liking for.'

'Mmm. A gentleman, a very polite gentleman, but I can understand your feelings. There's a cruel look about the man.'

'Indeed.' Alexander hesitated, wondering if he dared to confide in the professor. Professor Purdie, who was so assiduous in acquiring influential friends and patients? No, he decided not. But as he was thinking about his sister's problem, it suddenly occurred to him, with a rush of horror, that if *he* could find out where Susanna was, simply by asking a caddie, so could Neil Guthrie.

He wanted to go to Margaret Burns' house to warn Susanna, to hide her somewhere for safety, but at any moment the McKenzie carriage would be at the door to take him and the McKenzie family to the oyster cellar in the High Street. Indeed, he could already hear the clopping of the horses and the jingle of harness outside.

'I must go,' he told the professor. 'My friends are waiting.'

He called for a servant who lit the way downstairs in front of him with a lantern. The stairs were filthy and, as well as picking his way carefully with his elegant shoes so that he would not tread on any disgusting excrement, he had to roughly push aside some male and female vagrants.

In the carriage all was bright with lanterns and happy smiles.

'Ladies,' he said, settling himself beside Isobel. 'How beautiful you look.'

His heart swelled with love and pride as Isobel linked arms with him. How lovely she was in her gown of shot silk brocade with floral sprays in green, white and pink. Her powdered hair was elaborately dressed and decorated with plumes and gauze. Her mother looked very grand in her wide-panniered gown with its huge dangling cuffs. Her high powdered wig was also resplendent with plumes. Both ladies flapped energetically with fans in an effort to dispel the stinks of the street that wafted into the carriage.

The oyster cellar was entered through one of the laigh or low shops – dirty, squalid rooms below the street. It was here that the most fashionable people in town gathered by the light of guttering tallow candles and regaled themselves with raw oysters and porter arranged on huge dishes on a coarse table in the dingy room. It was here that there was much merriment and dancing and conversation in which both ladies and gentlemen took part without restraint. Many remarks and jokes that would have been suppressed as improper anywhere else were accepted here even by the most dignified and refined.

Alexander sought to banish Neil Guthrie from his thoughts. The man had just arrived in town. Surely he would take time to settle in to a tavern or other lodging first, and then wait until tomorrow and daylight before starting to make enquiries about Susanna. Neil Guthrie would not, could not, find his way about the myriad side streets and closes of Edinburgh in the dark.

'That will give me time to reach Susanna tomorrow and at least warn her,' he thought. Then he tried to relax and enjoy the company he was with. Some friends of the McKenzies had joined them. One was a bulky man with a grey powdered wig and bright, twinkling eyes. His lady was scraggy-necked but equally merry-eyed. The other couple, the man small and dainty with powdered thin hair and cunning eyes, was dressed in silk and had silver-buckled toes. His lady was enormously fat in a mulberry-coloured gown which revealed an alarming swell of bosom.

Soon they all had consumed a great many oysters and much porter and the room echoed with laughter and the noisy clatter of high-heeled shoes. Alexander danced with Isobel and talked with her and laughed with her, and Susanna and Neil Guthrie were completely forgotten. It was only hours later, when he was back in his lodgings and lying alone in bed, that his anxieties returned. Like it or not, he would have to visit the house of the harlot, Margaret Burns, and talk with Susanna. He didn't know what to do with her but at least they could discuss the problem and try to come to some kind of solution. Even if it was only a temporary one. He would explain to her that although, as her brother, he had a duty to her, she had also a duty to him. He had a reputation to uphold and protect, and although he would do all he could to protect her, at the same time she must keep his reputation and his safety in mind. Perhaps if he found her respectable lodgings in some country area where she was not known. Or somewhere in Glasgow even. Perhaps the latter would be the safest alternative. He tossed and turned in bed.

Then in the morning, he had to do a few hours' duty in the Infirmary. He had a couple of urgent operations to perform. Immediately afterwards, however, he made his way to where the harlot lived. He felt he was moving in a nightmare. Never in his life had he thought he would be doing such a thing. He had always been a prudent, fastidious, respectable man. All he had ever wanted in life was to be a good doctor, a respected poet. Then one day to be a faithful and loving husband and father.

He had been shocked enough about Robert Burns' loose attitude to women. Admittedly Robert never had anything to do with prostitutes but he, to use his own words, suffered from 'amorous madness, falling in and out of love very readily . . . '

Alexander had never been like that. He planned to wait for the right woman, the only woman who had all the necessary attributes for a lifelong partner. Now, at last, he had met her and he must not allow anything to spoil his plans.

He felt furtive and ashamed, and angry at Susanna for being the cause of getting him into such a situation. Immediately, of course, he chastised himself for having such an illogical notion. It wasn't Susanna's fault. It was that smooth-talking devil, Neil Guthrie.

Reaching the harlot's house, Alexander firmly grasped the 'risp' or rod of iron with the ring attached and rasped it up and down. Margaret Burns came to the door. He knew her by sight, having observed her several times in the street. He tried to remain cool and dignified.

'I believe my sister, Susanna, is living here. I wish to speak to her.'

Margaret Burns gave him an equally cool stare in return. She raised an eyebrow. 'I know of no-one here who has a brother, sir. You have had a wasted journey.'

'No, I have not, madam. I know my sister is here.'

'I must repeat, sir,' Margaret's voice turned to ice, 'I know of no-one here who fits your description. Now will you please leave.'

'I want to help her, you stupid woman.' Alexander was having a real struggle to keep his patience in check. To have extra difficulties like this added to his problems was not something he had been prepared for.

He saw the glint of anger flash in the harlot's eyes and realised she was about to bang the door in his face, when suddenly a timid voice came from somewhere in the shadows behind Margaret Burns.

'It's all right. He is my brother. Please let him come in.'

The door opened wider.

'You never mentioned any brother.'

'I know. I'm sorry.'

Alexander said, 'We urgently need to talk, Susanna.'

Margaret stepped inside. 'Come in. Come in.'

As soon as he put a foot in the lobby, Susanna rushed at

him and nearly knocked him over with her embrace. Untangling himself and tidying down his waistcoat and jacket, he repeated, 'We urgently need to talk.'

'Come through here.' Susanna led him into a surprisingly clean and respectable-looking bedroom with a chair and a small table beside the fireplace. On the table were several books.

Margaret came into the room carrying another chair. 'Here you are. Now, I'll leave you to your talk.' And she went out, closing the door behind her.

'Oh Alexander,' Susanna burst out. 'I'm so glad to see you. But I was afraid. You say you want to help me.' She hesitated. 'As long as you don't mean to force me back to Neil. I'd rather die. I'll do anything rather than go back to him.'

'I think you've proved that,' Alexander said, somewhat bitterly.

'It's not as it looks, sir.' For a moment, some of Susanna's old pride and pertness returned. 'I am only a respectable lodger here. I pay rent every week and keep myself to myself.'

Alexander sighed. 'I'm sorry, my dear. But I have been so worried. We all have, but before we discuss anything or anybody else, I must get you away from here. I have been thinking of different plans and have decided, if you agree, that perhaps lodgings in Glasgow might be the best and safest place. You would be too easily traced in a country area where everyone knows everyone else.'

'Oh yes, Glasgow would be excellent. Oh, thank you, Alexander. When can I go?'

'As soon as I can make some enquiries and arrange for time off from the Infirmary. I will tell the professor that a serious family emergency has arisen, which of course is perfectly true.'

'I'm so anxious in case Neil finds me here.'

'Tell Mistress Burns not to let him in. Not to let anyone in who is unknown to her until I return for you tomorrow.'

'I will pack my things immediately and be ready and waiting. Oh, Alexander, you don't know what this means to me. I will be forever obliged to you. You are the best of brothers, and always have been.'

Alexander put up a hand to ward off another attack of sisterly love.

'Just try to calm down, Susanna. And remember, I do not want anyone to know of my involvement in this. Warn that woman she has to forget she has ever seen me.'

'Margaret? Oh, we can trust her.'

'I sincerely hope so.'

'Oh, absolutely.'

He rose. 'Very well. I'll make what arrangements I can. We'll need a coach, for instance. More private than travelling on horseback. And I'll return here tomorrow, in the evening again.'

'I'll be ready.'

She saw him out, then skipped back to her room in uncontrollable joy and excitement.

Margaret sighed at the sight. 'Well, he's made you happy, all right. No regrets then about leaving your friend.'

Susanna immediately calmed down. 'Oh, Margaret, I'm so sorry. I mean, I'm glad and relieved to be saved from . . . I mean, I told you my husband's in the city and he could appear at any moment and drag me away. I'm relieved that my brother is saving me from that. But of course I'll miss you, my dear friend. You have been so kind to me. I'll never forget you.'

Margaret shrugged. 'I do my best.'

'I'm safe,' Susanna kept thinking. 'I'm safe. Thank God!'

23

Willie Nicol was a robust red-faced clumsy man and a classics master at the High School. He was well known by most people as a cantankerous Latin pedant, vain, touchy, irascible, and with an ungovernable temper. However, Robert saw redeeming features in the man and once he wrote of him, 'kind, honest-hearted Willie'. A bond between them of course was their Jacobite enthusiasms. In Robert's case, his feelings were more romantic and he believed that his ancestors had suffered for the cause of the Rebellion. Nicol spouted Jacobite views as he did everything else – with unbridled vehemence.

Robert was feeling cramped at his lodgings with his old friend, John Richmond. He had to share one uncomfortable mattress and one small table. There was little else in the room. And Mrs Carfrae, the landlady, who seemed to have taken a liking to Robert, was constantly distracting him and wearying him with her envious railings and complaints about the women upstairs. As a result, when Willie Nicol offered him lodgings in an attic room at his family home, he jumped at the chance.

He soon realised, however, that he didn't have much space or peace to write at the classics teacher's house either. As he said to Alexander, 'Willie and his wife are forever correcting homework and gabbling Latin so loud that I can't hear what my own soul is saying in my own skull.'

Robert decided to get out and announced to Willie that he was planning to set off on a tour of the Highlands. Willie offered to accompany him providing he was travelling by coach. Robert agreed, accepting the fact that Willie was not only fifteen years older than him and needed the extra comfort, but probably couldn't afford a horse. Despite the expense, Robert hired a post chaise and they set off. He was soon disenchanted with the idea of extra comfort travelling by coach along roads which were devilishly bad. However, he was eager to see more of his native land.

> Oh Scotia! my dear, my native soil!
> For whom my warmest wish to heaven is sent!

He and Willie set off from Edinburgh in high spirits. Previously Robert had written a journal at the end of each day of his travels. Now he wrote it in the coach but it had to be disjointed and with only brief fragments because of the way the coach jolted and jerked and swayed along the rutted Highland roads.

Even descriptions of people they met on the way were unusually short: 'Doig – a queerish fellow and something of a pedant . . . Bell, a joyous vacant fellow who sings a good song . . . Captain Forrester of the Castle, a merry swearing kind of man with a dash of sodger.'

Historic places were given even briefer mention, except the Druids' temple at Glenlyon. After describing it, Robert added, 'say prayers in it'.

He managed though to write long letters to his friends including Alexander, who began sourly to think that there couldn't be a castle Burns had not visited, a lord, an earl, a viscount, a duke left in the land he had not supped with.

Alexander took some perverse satisfaction, however, in learning that Nicol was proving a terrible thorn in Robert's side. He was forever taking the huff at the fuss being made of Robert by all the high and mighty and was continuously hurrying Robert on. At Blair Atholl, the Duke and Duchess of Atholl and their family apparently had been totally captivated by Robert. The ladies had even sent a servant to try to trick Robert's coach driver into loosening or pulling off a horse's shoe in order to secure a longer time in Robert's company but the ruse failed. The driver was incorruptible.

Evidently, Robert had written a letter in exasperation and anger about the Latin master's surly and diffident behaviour. It had been after a similar forced shortening of his visit to Castle Gordon and the Duke and Duchess there who had treated him, according to Robert, with the utmost hospitality and kindness.

Robert wrote of Nicol's behaviour, 'May that obstinate son of Latin prose be curst to Scotch-mile periods, and damned to seven-league paragraphs; while Declension and Conjugation, Gender, Number and Time, under the ragged banners of Dissonance and Disarrangement eternally rank against him in hostile array!!!!!!'

The driver, urged on by Willie, cracked the whip even more energetically over the horse to reach their next stop at Duff House. Still in a huff, Willie huddled in the library and left Robert to be guided by a boy from the local academy. When someone asked if he knew who Burns was, the boy said, 'Oh aye. We hae his book at home.'

He was then asked what his favourite Burns poem was and he answered, '"The Twa Dogs" and "Death and Doctor Hornbook", although I liked "The Cotter's Saturday Night" best because it made me greet when my faither read it tae my mither.'

Burns had not spoken up to that point, but then he put his hand on the boy's shoulder and said, 'Weel, my callant, I don't wonder at your greetin' . . . It made me greet mair than aince when I wis writin' it.'

He had obviously returned to his pure English mode of speech by the time he was being entertained by a large gathering of notables at Aberdeen because Bishop Skinner had written to his father about Burns saying, 'As to his general appearance, it is very much in his favour. He is a genteel looking young man of good address, and talks with as much propriety as if he had received an academic education . . . '

The Highland tour had lasted twenty-two days and covered about six hundred miles, and the most amazing thing to everyone was that, despite Willie's impatience and continued bad-tempered selfishness and chivvying, the friendship between him and Burns had survived.

Burns had reminded people who had remarked on this of Willie's vigorous talents, although admitting that they could be clouded at times by his coarseness of manners. 'In short,' he added, 'his mind is like his body, he has a confounded strong, in-kneed sort of soul.'

He also said that Willie's companionship had been like 'travelling with a loaded blunderbuss at full cock'.

Partly to get away from Willie's attic, Burns decided to make a short tour of Stirlingshire and to visit friends in Harvieston. The visit was especially to renew his acquaintance with Peggy Chalmers. He'd met her previously when she used to play the piano for his blind friend, Mr Blacklock. He had been captivated not only by her musical talent, but by her educated and lively conversation.

At Harvieston, he stayed for eight happy days. He wasn't on show. He was just enjoying the good company of good friends. He was a sociable man and in this situation he felt idyllically happy, so much so that he proposed marriage to Peggy. She refused him gently and kindly. He was immediately isolated in sadness.

He knew by this time, of course, that ladies of the gentry enjoyed his company, his poetry, his songs and his conversation, but at the same time kept him at arm's length. At least Peggy remained his affectionate friend and they kept up a correspondence with each other.

Back in Edinburgh, he moved from one attic to another. The rector of the High School, Willie Cruikshanks – like Burns, one of Nicol's few friends – offered Robert the use of the top floor of his house at the top end of Princes Street.

Robert was laid low with a cold at first but soon he was up again and enjoyed walks through the streets and over Arthur's Seat, but as usual it was the human side and not the countryside that impressed him most. Looking down from one hill at the smoking roofs of the cottages far below, he said that no-one could understand the pleasure to his mind the sight gave him, unless they had witnessed, like himself, the happiness and the worth they contained.

He decided he must settle matters with Mr Creech, 'which I'm afraid will be a tedious business.' It proved more than just tedious. It was a terrible struggle, in fact, to prise money due to him from his publisher. But he was not being singled out for this. Creech behaved in the same way with everyone.

Robert was pushed beyond endurance by having to constantly ask Creech to settle his accounts. One day, Alexander met him striding up Leith Walk brandishing a stick and looking and sounding extremely violent.

'What's the matter?' Alexander asked.

'I am going to smash that shite Creech.'

'Calm down.' Alexander blocked his path. 'You'll end up murdering the man and all that'll get you is hanged. What will your little ones do then?'

That stopped Robert. Whatever else he was or was not, and despite the fact that some of his little ones had been born out of wedlock, he always tried to be a good father to them.

It caused him much distress when he heard from John Richard, who had recently visited Mauchline, that Robert's daughter Jean, called after her mother, had died suddenly while he'd been on his Highland tour. The Armours had been looking after her. He suspected neglect by them and he was frustrated and angry as well as distressed. He mourned for the loss of the child and cursed the Armours. He couldn't bear to think of them, far less go and see them. He had not forgotten Jean's denial of their marriage, her desertion and rejection, her concurring with her father's destuction of the wedding certificate and fight to annul the marriage.

The last time he'd seen Jean, her flesh of course had been as weak and willing as ever. This had resulted in another pregnancy. He would face his own responsibility for that. But to travel to Mauchline and face Jean and the Armours now could mean he might say something hurtful he would later regret. He would see Jean and do what he could for her, but not right now.

He concentrated instead on his immediate surroundings and allowed the kind hospitality and friendship he was receiving at his lodgings with the Cruikshanks family to help soothe his troubled spirit. The Cruikshanks had a twelve-year-old daughter, Jeany. Burns called her 'Rose-bud'. She could play the harpsichord and Burns sat beside her every day as she played, concentrating so much on the music that he was unaware of anyone who spoke to him. He gave Jenny verses that he'd written and between them they adjusted the verses to music. The repeated trials and efforts to do this completely absorbed both the girl and poet. It was proof, Willie Cruikshanks said, of the easy relationship Burns had with children and young people. Robert promised Jenny that he'd write a song especially for her. He did and called it 'A Rose-bud, by my Early Walk'.

It was one of many songs he was to write. He also got in touch with James Johnson, who had earlier approached him.

'He has,' Robert told Alexander enthusiastically, 'not from mercenary veins, but from an honest Scotch enthusiasm, set about collecting all our native songs and setting them to music, particularly those that have never been set before. I'm assisting in collecting the old poetry, or sometimes, for a fine air to make a story when it has no words.' His dark eyes glowed with the strength of his emotion.

'I look on it as no small merit to this work that the names of many of the authors of our old Scotch songs, names almost forgotten, will be remembered.'

Before long, he was sole editor of the Museum project, as it was called, and when Johnson became pessimistic and low in spirits, Burns always reassured him. By his own energy and enthusiasm, he energised and enthused Johnson.

'You are a patriot for the music of your country,' Burns told Johnson, 'and I am certain posterity will look on themselves as highly indebted to your public spirit . . . Your work is a great one . . . To future ages your publication will be text-book and standard of Scottish song and music.'

Burns was writing more and more songs and now showing, everyone said, pure genius as a lyricist. But during this song-writing time, he told Alexander, 'I am hurried, puzzled, plagued and confounded with some disagreeable matters.'

These were his ongoing disputes with Creech about the money due to him. He had to constantly be there at Creech's office arguing, demanding. He desperately needed the money, for one thing to fulfil his obligations to Jean. He was being plagued by the Armours about Jean and the fact that she was pregnant again. He was also worried about whether or not he should take a lease on a farm offered to him. Alexander did not know any details about this and just told him he ought to go back to the farm with Gilbert and settle there, with his mother and his little daughter, Bess.

Then there was also, of course, the continuing correspondence about a place in the Excise. (He'd long since given up the idea of leaving the country.) He couldn't make up his mind whether to be a farmer or an excise man. He needed the money for future security and decided he'd have to be both (plus a poet as well, because he had to write and keep on writing). It was so like Robert. There were never any half measures with him. It was always everything at once and in the extreme.

Alexander said he was a fool not to take money from Johnson for all the work he had done and was still doing for him. After all, Johnson had offered to pay him. But, according to Robert, it was a labour of love 'for auld Scotland's sake', and he had told Johnson, 'As a remuneration, you may think my songs either above or below price; for they shall be absolutely one or the other. In honest enthusiasm with which I embark in your undertaking, to talk of money, wages, fee, hire etc., would be downright sodomy of the soul!'

Alexander secretly despised him for the amount of money he was needlessly throwing away. He did the same thing with yet another project offered to him by George Thomson, who wanted to match Scotch lyrics to arrangements by leading composers. He'd already engaged Haydn and Beethoven for this task.

'All I want,' Burns told Thomson, 'is a proof of each of the songs I compose or amend, I shall receive as a favour.'

Yet at the same time, he was worried about money. He had settled quite a sum by now on Gilbert, and on Jean Armour too. He was also getting worn out with having to keep knocking at Creech's door. He would have left Edinburgh, had it not been that he needed his money from Creech.

'Damn the man,' he kept telling Alexander. 'I'm tied to this city because of Creech.'

24

Alexander was harrassed beyond measure. He had heavy duties in the Infirmary. He had money worries. Money had had to be sent to his parents who were suffering financial difficulties. Now he had somehow to pay for a coach to transport Susanna to Glasgow. He'd also have to go with her to find her decent lodgings in the city, and pay for them of course. He was feeling at a very low ebb when Robert visited him one day.

'My dear friend,' Robert said. 'What ails you? Is there anything I can do to help?'

Alexander shook his head. Then, after a moment's hesitation, he blurted out, 'It's my sister.'

Burns was immediately on guard. 'Oh?'

'Her husband has been ill-treating her and she has left him. She is staying in most unsuitable lodgings in one of the wynds off the High Street. I must get her to Glasgow and safely settled in decent lodgings there.'

'You are a good brother, as well as a good friend, Alexander.'

Alexander sighed. 'It's not that I don't want to help her. It's just that I'm weighed down with so much at present. Professor Purdie and my other colleagues will be anything but happy, to say the least, if I take more time off just now.'

'Your poor sister must have suffered a great deal at the hands of Neil Guthrie to have come to this. Why not allow me to accompany her to Glasgow and see that she is safely settled? I know the city. I have visited it before. I could double this visit with business. There is a very good bookshop there. The owner, a Mr Smith, only takes five per cent commission. They're very decent sort of folk, the Glasgow booksellers, but oh, they're sare birkies in Edinburgh. I'll be glad of another visit to Glasgow, Alexander, and happy to be of help to you and your sister at the same time.'

Trust his clever friend to come up with an immediate solution, Alexander thought with some bitterness. And of course sell more of his precious books as well. He tried to quell the bitterness by telling himself that it was another example of Robert's generosity of spirit. It had to be admitted also that Robert's offer, in the circumstances, was extremely tempting.

'That is a most generous offer, Robert.'

Robert shrugged. 'As I say, I can sell more books while I'm there.'

Oh, you will indeed, Alexander thought.

'It would certainly be of great help to me.'

'Let us arrange it then.'

'I've promised to call for Susanna this evening. You can accompany me if you wish and we can discuss the matter with her. I doubt if she will have any objection to a change of companion. I will explain my difficulties and she will understand and be grateful for your help, I'm sure.'

Actually he was not sure. Susanna had never liked Burns. But in her present desperate circumstances, she would, he hoped, be able to overcome her previous distaste of the 'common ploughman'.

'Let us go now and see about a carriage,' Robert said. 'We can drive together to collect your sister and after you explain the situation to her, you can return to your duties and I'll proceed with her to Glasgow.'

'I will reimburse you for the expense of the carriage, Robert.'

'Think no more of it. I've told you, I need to see to business in Glasgow and I'll be glad to get away from Edinburgh and Creech for a time.'

Alexander was glad that Professor Purdie was not at home

to meet Robert. He would have made such a fuss and delayed any action by monopolising Robert's company for as long as possible. He could return from the Infirmary at any moment, however, and so they wasted no time in hurrying, side by side, away from the house.

Susanna was all packed and ready. By early evening, she had donned her cloak and was sitting on the bedroom chair, counting the minutes. Margaret and Sally were out, hoping to pick up some 'nice gentlemen' with whom to spend 'a pleasant evening'. They said they'd try to be back before she left. But they had said their goodbyes 'just in case'.

Susanna told Margaret – and meant it – that she'd be eternally grateful to her for taking her in and being so kind. She didn't go as far as saying, 'If you're ever in Glasgow, do visit me.' Kind and all as Margaret was, she was still a harlot and Susanna had no wish to be tarred by the same brush. Glasgow was to be her new life, her fresh start, and she must make a success of it. She knew success for her no longer meant dreams of marrying a wealthy man. For one thing, she couldn't forget she was already married and she would regret that marriage until the end of her life. She would have been more content to settle down even in a cottage if it was with a kindly, decent man. Tragically, it was too late for that now.

Sitting tensely, hands twisting together, she watched the candle send little orange flickers through the blackness. Her ears strained to hear her brother's footsteps on the stairs outside and then the racket of the rasp from the front door filling the house and galvanising her into a joyous rush to fling it open. Sitting, waiting, she blessed her brother a thousand times over. Dear Alexander, she had always known in her heart of hearts that he would not let her down.

Then, all at once, the grating, rasping sound reverberated through every room, scattering her thoughts. She grabbed her bag and stumbled through the dark hall. It was too dark to see the door handle and she had to grope for it. At last, her impatient fumblings succeeded. The door opened. The shadowy figure outside stopped her in her tracks. The immediate feeling of menace emanating from it told her it was not her brother. Before the smooth voice had finished murmuring 'My dear wife . . . ' she was fighting to shut the door. Neil's foot jammed it, and pushed it open. He caught her by the arm and forced her out on to the landing.

'Let go of me, Sir.' Her voice tightened with terror.

'This is no place for you. I'm taking you home.'

'I hate you,' she managed. 'I'm going nowhere with you.'

The dark stairwell echoed with the sniggering of some beggars who were squatting together around a candle. Neil's hand tightened painfully on her arm as he continued to drag her out on to the street. A carriage stood waiting, brightly glowing with lanterns, and the coachman sitting high in front, his whip at the ready. She was pushed roughly inside. Neil followed and shut the door. The coach started off but because of the crowds overflowing on to the road, and the horses and other coaches jostling to make a path, they only moved at a snail's pace.

Susanna continued to struggle and her struggles became wild when she spied Alexander and another man alighting from a carriage nearby. She screamed out Alexander's name and managed to throw herself against the door and burst it open.

'Alexander! Alexander!'

As both men came striding towards her to help her out of the coach, she recognised Robert Burns.

'Oh, thank God you're here. He was forcing me to go with him.'

'Not any more,' Burns said, lifting her bodily from the carriage. Neil, in sudden fury, made to jump from the coach to stop him. At the same time, the coachman, not realising what was happening and seeing an opportunity at last to whip the horses forward, made the coach jerk. Neil fell on to the road under the hooves of a galloping horse.

The rider dismounted, cursing the misfortune and insisting it was not his fault. The man had suddenly jumped in front of his horse before he could rein it back.

Alexander stepped forward then and explained that he was a doctor, he'd seen it was an accident, and he would attend to the victim. The rider was obviously relieved but before remounting and continuing on his way, he joined the little knot of people who had gathered to peer curiously at the unconscious man and to see what was going to happen next.

'Alexander, do you want to put him into our carriage?' Burns asked.

'Yes, I'll have to take him to the Infirmary.'

Susanna would far rather have left him lying in the road and rejoiced at the opportunity of escaping as fast as possible. She knew, however, that as a doctor, Alexander could not, and would not, do such a thing, not even to Neil Guthrie. As a result, she followed her brother's instructions, and travelled with him and Burns and the injured Neil to the Infirmary. Or at least he was supposed to be injured. She didn't trust him. He could just be acting. There certainly didn't appear to be any blood. It wasn't until she got a better look at him that she saw his wig had darkened with blood. Alexander ordered some men assistants to carry him into one of the rooms for examination. Susanna was instructed to sit and wait with Burns until Alexander came back.

When he did return some considerable time later, he was accompanied by Professor Purdie. Both men had very solemn faces.

Professor Purdie said, 'I'm so sorry, my dear Mrs Guthrie. Your brother and I did our best but the fractures were too serious.'

Susanna stared at the two men in disbelief.

'You don't mean . . . '

'Yes, Susanna,' Alexander said quietly, but avoiding her eyes, 'I'm afraid your dear husband has passed away.'

'Oh!' Susanna lowered her eyes and groped for a handkerchief.

Professor Purdie repeated, 'My dear Mrs Guthrie. I'm so sorry.'

It was taking all Susanna's will power to refrain from dancing, shouting hurrah!, cheering with joyous relief.

'Alexander,' she said, the quiet control in her voice matching his, 'what shall I do now? Where shall I go?' She turned to the professor. 'My husband and I were on our way to our estate in Ayrshire.'

'You must come home with your brother and me and stay for a few days until you recover. We will look after you, never fear.'

'There are still examinations to be made of the body – for teaching benefits,' Alexander said. 'Neil would have wished to help doctors and surgeons in this way. After that, we must make arrangements for the funeral in Tarbolton.'

He turned to Burns. 'You will, I hope, understand that this means a change to our previous plans, Robert.'

'Yes, of course,' Robert agreed. 'I'll leave you now.' He gave a slight bow in Susanna's direction. 'My condolences, Madam.'

With her lace-edged handkerchief pressed to the corner of her eye, Susanna nodded.

In the coach taking them to Professor Purdie's house, Susanna remained silent while her brother and Professor Purdie spoke in low respectful tones of medical matters. She was not listening. Her mind was racing ahead with all sorts of possibilities. She was free. *Really* free in every sense. Oh, the overwhelming relief! She thanked God. She vowed that never again would she forget to say her prayers and to repeat the words, 'Oh, thank you, God.'

There was the ordeal of maintaining appearances for the next few days, of course, and then the funeral, but if she could just keep proper, decent control of herself until after that, she would be all right.

This became even more difficult than she'd expected when a letter was delivered to Alexander from Robert Burns. The poet had sustained an injury which needed Alexander's attention. The coach in which he'd been returning to his lodgings had overturned on a corner and he was at present in great pain.

It was then the strange feelings that had been haunting Susanna recently suddenly resurfaced. It had been necessary to ignore them in order to survive the ordeal of keeping up a semblance of grief. Now she allowed herself to be aware of the thumping of her heart and the flutterings in her stomach when she thought of Robert Burns. He was not slim and pale and elegant in appearance like either Neil or Alexander. Nor did he speak with continuously smooth restraint. Strong emotion could fire his voice and burn in his eyes. His body was big and hard, his complexion brown and weatherbeaten. He wore no wig and his tied-back hair was long and as black as night. She experienced a longing to see him again.

She asked Alexander if she could accompany him on his visit to Burns. Her brother agreed and they set off to Burns' lodgings. Now, here was a man, she thought. A real man. Full of life and love and vitality despite his injury which prevented him from walking at the moment. She felt hot and flushed and joyous at the sight of him.

Alexander said after examining his friend, 'You've dislocated your knee cap, Robert. You'll have to stay in your room with your injured leg resting on a cushion on this chair. Do you hear me?'

'Yes, yes,' Robert sighed. 'It's just it's so unfortunate. I had such an important engagement . . . '

'Well, you'll just have to postpone it. The only way to return your leg to normal use is to rest it for at least a few days. More than likely for much longer. I'll come back and see you tomorrow and every day until you have totally recovered.'

Robert turned his dark glowing eyes on Susanna then. 'You are the luckiest of ladies to have such a brother and I am the luckiest of men.' He turned his gaze on Alexander again. 'My dear friend, how can I thank you for all your kindness to me?'

'Just do as I tell you,' Alexander said gruffly. It always made him feel uncomfortable and somewhat guilty when Robert showed such undisguised love and admiration for him. He knew in his heart of hearts that he did not deserve his friend's love or his admiration.

They stayed and chatted for some time. Susanna volunteered to make tea and felt honoured to be able to serve the poet with it. She had carried his book with her to Edinburgh and read it during her lonely evenings locked in the bedroom of the harlot's house. Read it over and over again. She spoke to him of her admiration of his poetry and the sentiments expressed.

'I especially admired and appreciated,' she told him enthusiastically, 'the one about the rights of women.' And, in an effort to impress him, she recited the first verse.

> While Europe's eye is fixed on mighty things,
> The fate of empires and the fall of Kings;
> While quacks of state must each produce his plan,
> And even children lisp the Rights of Man;
> Amid this mighty fuss just let me mention,
> The Rights of Women merit some attention . . .

Burns smiled somewhat ruefully. 'Alexander will tell you that it was not a very wise thing for me to write.'

'Why ever not?'

He shrugged. 'It expresses dangerous views in today's political climate. It has become almost a hanging crime to express admiration and agreement with the principles in Paine's book, *The Rights of Man*.' He smiled. 'No doubt the powers that be are even more afraid of women getting the rights they are properly due. But all I have done is claim and believe in three of the most harmless of rights, Protection, Decorum and Admiration.' He gave her a mischievous sideways glance. 'If necessary, that's what I'll argue anyway.'

'He keeps thinking of a career in the Excise for a long-term safe and secure income,' Alexander said. 'He's already undergone a course of training and instruction. I have warned him about the revolutionary things he keeps writing.'

It was Burns' turn to recite,

> Searching auld wives' barrels,
> Ochon the day!
> That clarty barm should stain my laurels;
> But – what'll ye say!
> These muvin' things ca'd wives and weans
> Wad muve the very heart o' stanes!

'I still maintain,' Alexander said, 'that you'd be far better to get back to farming.'

'Do you remember my friend, Patrick Miller?' Burns asked.

'Yes. Why?'

'He's offered me a seventy-six-year lease on a farm and three hundred pounds to cover the cost of building a farmhouse and making other general improvements.'

'Wonderful!' Alexander enthused. 'Where is it?'

'Ellisland, Dumfriesshire.'

25

Alexander tried not to think of Robert going to live in Dumfriesshire. He could not bear the idea of him living anywhere near Isobel McKenzie. He wrote telling the McKenzies of his sister's sudden bereavement and how he felt he had to give her the company and support she needed for some time after the funeral.

The McKenzies wrote back, as he hoped they would, and invited him to bring his sister to stay for a few weeks, or as long as they both wished, in their home in Dumfriesshire. This he promised he'd do immediately after the funeral. He determined that he would propose to Isobel without delay and be safely married to her before Robert fixed up with his Ellisland farm.

Damn the man, he kept thinking. Why had he to keep tormenting him like this? Of all the places in Scotland, he had to pick a farm in Dumfriesshire.

Before they left Edinburgh for Tarbolton, he and Susanna visited Burns every day. Alexander remembered a time when Susanna had thoroughly disliked Robert. Or so she'd said. Now, she could not hide how enamoured she was with him. Not that Robert paid her much attention, certainly not amorous attention. While Susanna had been making them a dish of tea and concocting some tasty dishes for Robert in the kitchen, he had confided to Alexander that he was madly in love (yet again!) with the most beautiful and intelligent lady in

Christendom, a Mrs Nancy MacElhose.

'Mrs?' Alexander had raised an eyebrow.

'Yes, alas. Nothing can come of it. Although she has left her husband. He is still in Jamaica. She has children to care for. She is also well connected in the town, and is very protective of her good name and reputation.'

'Oh dear.' A sarcastic note crept into Alexander's voice. 'She is faced with great difficulties then, poor woman.'

Susanna returned to the room then and the conversation was cut short. In subsequent conversations, however, Alexander learned that letters (a great many letters) were daily being exchanged between Burns and Mrs MacElhose, and he could just imagine how this frustrating situation would give Robert's muse free flow. Words, especially written words, and especially in letters, could completely carry him away. He used to, Alexander remembered, write passionate love letters for any young man to send to his sweetheart in Tarbolton and for miles around. He could just imagine what a torrent of emotion would be let loose and what ornate language there would be in such a plethora of letters. And what drama the pair would wallow in. Sometimes he thought Robert should have been an actor. The woman sounded as foolish and as sentimental as he was. They seemed well matched to play the love game and in so doing, to whip themselves into a paper passion. Apparently, they were writing six letters a day to each other, and they'd only met for a few minutes at an elderly spinster's tea party.

Mrs MacElhose was so prissy and fearful of her good reputation that she suggested that they use pseudonyms – classical names no less – Clarinda and Sylvander. This was obviously so that she could hide behind the pseudonym – let herself go as Clarinda but still imagine she was keeping her good name intact as the respectable Mrs MacElhose. (Daughter of a surgeon, niece of a Presbyterian minister, cousin to two Edinburgh judges.)

How ridiculous and hypocritical, Alexander thought. A love game it was and would continue as such, albeit a passionate one, a hot torrent of words. He could imagine the love poetry and songs (tragic, no doubt) that would come of all this, especially when it ended. As end it would. Burns always rushed for intimacy and this never worked with gentlewomen –even with those who had a high and even loving regard for him. It wasn't that he was brutish but simply that that was the way of men of his lowly station in life. Houghmagandy was the usually accepted thing. It hadn't got through to Robert, and Alexander felt sure it never would, especially when he was so highly sexed, that gentlewomen would never give way to such intimacies so quickly, and especially before marriage.

Meantime, of course, tied to his chair in his lodgings, Robert could not make any of his usual attempts at physical intimacy. He was certainly making up for it in the number of letters he was writing.

Alexander and Susanna had to take their leave of Robert to go to Tarbolton for Neil Guthrie's funeral. Robert thanked them both – especially Susanna – for all the kindness he'd received, and hoped he would meet with them both again soon.

It was just as well, Alexander thought later, that there never had been any shortage of money in the Guthrie family, because it was an expensive thing to die and even more so to be buried. Especially in this case, where there had been the added expense of the conveyance of the corpse from Edinburgh.

Then there was the usual winding sheet and the woollen stockings for the corpse's feet. There was the lyke-wake which meant everyone watching by the corpse all day and all night. The body was half-embalmed and laid out for view. The furniture was all covered in white linens and invitations had been sent out on folio gilt-edged sheets. People came from all over (mostly, Alexander guessed, in respect and in memory of old Guthrie rather than of Neil) and refreshments were served continuously. Indeed, it was a lavish feast with the minister saying blessings over the meat which he said 'improved the occasion'. The claret and ale and whisky went round and round the company with great rapidity until the mourners could not stand, but made hilarious staggering procession behind the coffin to the grave. It had been known that on such occasions, everyone had become so drunk that they had arrived at the graveside only to discover the corpse had been left behind.

Alexander remained sober enough to make sure this did not happen. Susanna had taken to her bed before the funeral, insisting that she was never going to set foot in Guthrie House ever again, not even for her husband's funeral. Her parents protested and pleaded and wheedled, all to no avail.

'I don't care what anybody thinks or how bad it looks,' Susanna cried. 'Tell them I'm prostrate, too ill with grief to attend. Tell them anything, I don't care. I'm not going.'

And that was that. Alexander had to see to everything and to suffer all the feasting and drunkenness of the funeral. English officers witnessing such an occasion had pronounced 'a Scots funeral to be merrier than an English wedding'.

Drinking, Alexander concluded, was *the* favourite vice of the century and brought no shame whatsoever. Quite the reverse. Certainly in Scotland, it was not thought of as a vice at all. The only good thing about it, if one could call it good, was that it resulted in plenty of work for physicians, surgeons and apothecaries.

Alexander was glad when the funeral was over, and doubly glad that it hadn't been a Highland funeral which could last for several days and where liquor was emptied in hogsheads.

Afterwards he asked Susanna if she wanted to accompany him to Dumfriesshire to visit his friends, the McKenzies, and she eagerly jumped at the chance.

'Will we break our journey in Edinburgh first?' she asked with shining eyes. 'It would be wonderful to see Robert again.'

'No, I was not planning to do that.'

'Oh, please, Alexander. Apart from anything else, he might need you.'

'There's nothing more I can do, Susanna. He needs a few

more weeks to completely rest his leg and to cure the swelling and bruising. That is all.'

'Oh, Alexander!' She pouted. 'Just to please me.'

He hesitated. He ought to see Professor Purdie and explain the further delay there would be before his return to duty in the Infirmary. He could also visit a printer and make enquiries about a new book of his poems.

'Oh, very well,' he said. 'Only for a couple of days.'

Susanna clapped her hands and skipped about the room in delight. 'Thank you, Alexander. You are the best of brothers, and I love you.'

'Tuts,' he muttered, turning away. 'Control yourself, Susanna. You are a young lady, not a child. And a widow lady, remember.'

'Oh, I'll act the solemn widow in front of others, never fear, but I'm surely entitled to some release in private. '

His thoughts turned to Isobel and his courting of her. He had written to her almost every day since they had last seen each other and had tried, as much as was in his nature, to make his sentiments of love and his honourable intentions clear to her. Her letters of reply were most encouraging. He would press his suit as forcibly as possible at their next meeting. By now, she must know of his urgent desire to make her his wife. He decided to confide in his family, and it gave him good feelings of happiness and content when his mother and father and Susanna were delighted and wished him well.

'We'll no' be able to travel tae yer weddin' tho', son,' his father said. 'Yer mother an' me arnae as fit as we used tae be. Especially yer mother. An' we'd love tae have met the lassie.'

'But I've no doubt Isobel and I will visit you after we are man and wife.'

Alexander decided that he would ask the McKenzies, in the circumstances, if there could be a quiet wedding. After all, Susanna and his family were supposed to be in mourning. He realised he was rather jumping the gun because he had not yet made a formal proposal and been formally accepted. But he was confident that all would be well. Love did not blind him as it did Robert. He had never been in love before. Robert was scarcely ever out of love. Alexander was a steady-natured, dependable and practical man. Robert was none of these things. Alexander knew that it was sensible for a man in his position (indeed any man) to find a wife with a good dowry, and he had found such a woman. Robert, for all his so-called genius and charisma, would be lucky if he ended up with a penniless country wench. Alexander expected that Robert was still thinking of Jean Armour as a wife and she could be the best choice for a farmer. The quicker this charade with Sylvander and Clarinda finished and he got back to farming with his ignorant but obviously fecund Jean, the better for all concerned. She could apparently read, and write a simple letter, but as far as he could discern, apart from Robert's book she had not read any book except the Bible. He would not be surprised in fact if she had not even read Robert's book. For all the fine, educated ladies he'd met, that was the best he could do.

Alexander tried to comfort himself with this fact and assure himself that Robert would prove no danger as far as Isobel was concerned. Yet he was not assured. He did not trust fate, and he did not trust Robert.

He cursed himself now for agreeing to take Susanna to visit Robert and to waste precious time in Edinburgh. He must get to Dumfriesshire before Robert was fixed up with any farm there. He guessed that a lot would depend on how long the love game with Mrs MacElhose would last. As long as Clarinda continued to keep Sylvander in an agony of frustration, Robert would hopefully stay in Edinburgh.

Alexander packed his bag in readiness to travel the next day, then settled down to spend a quiet evening working on some verses. He was pleased and proud of his new poems. He had worked harder than ever on this book. If there was any fairness in life at all, it would succeed. More than anything else, he wanted it to be admired by Isobel.

26

His Clarinda was adorable. She was such a beautiful little blonde with a shapely figure and dancing eyes. Her relatives were much less attractive to Robert. They infuriated him. Her second cousin, Senator of the College of Justice, Lord Dreghorn, had been cruelly neglectful of Nancy MacElhose. He had never helped her. On the contrary he had treated her with nothing but harshness and disapproval, despite the fact that she was living alone, and had no help from her irresponsible husband.

Of course, Lord Dreghorn and his equally vindictive cronies had already shown an obsessive hatred to other women – Edinburgh prostitutes. They had hounded these women and persecuted them unmercifully. Burns had become so infuriated with Dreghorn, he'd poured out his feelings in a pessimistic letter to his friend, Peter Hill.

'May woman curse them!' he'd written. 'May woman blast them. May woman damn them! May her lovely hand inexorably shut the Portal of Rapture to their most earnest prayers and fondest essays for entrance! And when many years, and much port and great business have delivered them over to Vulture Gouts, and Aspen Palsies, *then* may the dear, bewitching Charmer in derision throw open the blissful gate to tantalize their impotent desires which like ghosts haunt their bosoms when all their powers to give or receive enjoyment are forever asleep in the sepulchre of their fathers!!!'

The other relation of Nancy's that Burns hated was the Reverend John Kemp. Nancy, he knew, was in the habit of confiding in this cleric during little tête-à-têtes in his Tolbooth vestry where he solemnly advised and sermonised poor Nancy. Eventually, Nancy had written to Robert in some distress saying that he must cease to have any contact with her, and enclosing a letter from this man. Robert had immediately written back, 'I have no patience to read the Puritanic scrawl and damned sophistry. Ye heavens, thou God of nature, thou Redeemer of mankind! Ye look down with approving eyes on a passion inspired by the purest flame, and guarded by truth, delicacy and honour, but the half-inch soul of an unfeeling, cold-blooded, pitiful Presbyterian bigot cannot forgive anything above his dungeon bosom and foggy head.'

He wrote another letter at midnight, attacking 'your friend's haughty dictatorial letter', and adding 'Can I wish that I had never seen you? That we had never met? No, I never will! ... I esteem you, I love you, as a friend; I admire you, I love you as a woman, beyond anyone in all the circles of creation. I know I shall continue to esteem you, to love you, to pray for you, nay to pray for myself for your sake.'

He had been confined to his room for six weeks and he occupied himself with his reading, his correspondence with Nancy, and visits from some friends, including Mrs Dunlop. He told Mrs Dunlop that 'the miserable dunning and plaguing of Mr Creech has busied me until I'm good for nothing.' He also occupied himself with song-writing. If he had not, he felt he would have gone mad with the boredom and physical inactivity. As it was, depression was never far away.

He had turned to his Bible for consolation and, as he told a friend, he'd 'got through the five books of Moses and half way in Joshua. It's really a glorious book.'

At one point he received a letter from Nancy which said, 'When I meet you, I must chide you for writing in your romantic style. Do you remember that she who you address is a married woman? ... You have too much of that impetuosity which generally accompanies noble minds.' She also said, 'I entreat you not to mention our correspondence to anyone on earth. Though I have an innocent conscience, my situation is a delicate one.' For safety she had begun sending her letters with her maid, Jenny Clowe.

But eventually she wrote, asking, 'Do you think you could venture this length in a coach, without hurting yourself? I wish you could come tomorrow or Saturday. I long for conversation with you, and lameness of body won't hinder that. 'Tis really curious – so much *fun* passing between two persons who saw one another only *once*!'

It was after that meeting she'd accused him of irreligiosity. He was stung by this and had replied, 'If you have, on some suspicious evidence, from some lying oracle, learned that I despise or ridicule so sacredly-important a matter as real religion, you have, my dear Clarinda, much misconstrued your friend.'

Once Nancy discovered that he was an enemy of Calvinism, she began trying to convert him to her own narrow brand of Presbyterianism. But he stuck to his own sincerely held beliefs and told her, 'My creed is pretty nearly expressed in the last clause of Jamie Dean's grace, an honest weaver in Ayrshire – Lord, grant that we may lead a gude life! For a gude life maks a gude end: at least help weel!'

Nancy's letters were not the only ones he received. Much less welcome were the innumerable verse epistles by innumerable tyro poets asking (sometimes even demanding) his opinion and his help. He was pleased to praise and help anyone who showed even the slightest promise of talent, but so much he received was simply doggerel and bad doggerel at that.

He devoted some of his time to writing in connection with his Excise plans. He forced himself to draw on the influence of all the people in high places that he knew. To Graham of Fintry he wrote a long letter which included the passage, 'I now solicit your patronage – you know, I dare say, of an application I lately made to your Board, to be admitted an Officer of Excise. I have, according to form, been examined by a Superior, and today I give in his Certificate with a request for an Order for instructions.'

He had also written to Lord Glencairn. 'I wish to get into the Excise; I am told that your Lordship's interest will easily procure me the grant from the Commissioners.' He'd added by way of explanation, 'My brother's lease is but a wretched one, though I think he will probably weather out the remaining seven years of it. After what I have given and will give him as a small farming capital to keep the family together, I guess my remaining all will be about two hundred pounds. Instead of beggaring myself with a small, dear farm, I will put this into a banking house. Extraordinary distress, or helpless old age have often harrowed my soul with fears; and I have one or two claims on me in the name of father; I will stoop to anything that honesty warrants to have it in my power to leave them some better remembrance of me than the odium of illegitimacy.'

He enclosed a copy of 'Holy Willie's Prayer' and promised to call on his Lordship at the beginning of the following week 'as against then I hope to have settled my business with Mr Creech. His solid sense in inches you must tell. But meet his cunning by the Scottish ell.'

At the same time, he was thinking and worrying about the offer of the farm at Ellisland. He still had reservations about the state and worth of the land, despite the surprising fact that a worthy and intelligent farmer, John Tennent, a friend of his father's as well as his own, had viewed the area with him and thought the bargain practicable.

The business with Mr Creech, and all his other frustrations and misfortunes, had made him become thoroughly disenchanted with Edinburgh. He wrote to his friend Richard at Mauchline, 'As I hope to see you soon, I shall not trouble you with a long letter of Edinburgh news. Indeed, there is nothing worth mentioning to you; everything going on as usual – houses building, bucks strutting, ladies flaring, blackguards skulking, whores leering, etc., in the old way. I have not got, nor will for some time get the better of my bruised knee; but I have laid aside my crutches. A lame poet is unlucky; lame verse is an everyday circumstance. I saw Smith lately; hale and hearty as formerly. I have heard melancholy enough accounts of Jean; 'tis an unlucky affair.'

He was worried and upset to have heard that Jean, now nearly eight months pregnant, had left home after a quarrel with her parents and was at present on a visit to the Muirs of Tarbolton Mill. He vowed that as soon as his injury had healed and he was able to make some sort of financial settlement with Creech, he would return to Ayrshire and do what he could to help and comfort her.

Meantime he wrote a frosty letter to Creech, who replied with a promise on his honour that he should have the account settled on Monday. Now it was Tuesday and no word from the publisher. The only comfort in all his despair and frustration was an obliging and more-than-willing Jenny Clowe, Nancy's maid, who – because of the great number of letters being delivered to and fro – was very often in his company.

His business dealings with music publishers were developing in a much more satisfactory manner than those with Creech. The work on the second volume of the *Museum* was fast progressing. As well as editing it, forty of the songs in it had either been wholly written by him or revised and expanded by him. For the Preface, he wrote, 'Ignorance and Prejudice may perhaps affect to sneer at the simplicity of the poetry or music for some of these pieces; but their having been for ages the favourites of Nature's Judges – the Common People, was to the Editor a sufficient test of their merit. Materials for the third Volume are in great forwardness.'

He managed, despite the difficulties of his still painful knee, to attend a party in George Street in the New Town at the home of Dowager Lady Wallace, Mrs Dunlop's stepmother. This honour did nothing to cheer his worried spirits, and as he wrote to another friend that he loved dearly, Peggy Chalmers,

'God have mercy on me! a poor damned, incautious, duped, unfortunate fool! The sport, the miserable victim, of rebellious pride; agonizing sensibility, and bedlam passions!'

Later he wrote another letter to her saying, 'You will condemn me for the next step I have taken. I have entered into the Excise. I stay in the West for about three weeks, and then return to Edinburgh for six weeks instruction; afterwards, for I get employed instantly, I go *où il plaît à Dieu – et mon Roi*. I have chosen this, my dear friend, after mature deliberation. The question is not at what door of fortune's palace shall we enter in, but what doors does she open to us?'

His knee took a turn for the worse and his worries increased. He feared that it 'for some time will scarcely stand the fatigue of my Excise instructions.'

As for the farm, it was in such a run-down condition that it would not be possible for him to take the lease for some time yet.

Meantime he wrote to Captain Richard Brown, saying he would arrive in Glasgow on Monday evening and planned to put up for the night at the Black Bull Inn in Argyle Street, where the Edinburgh coach terminated. He said he hoped that Richard could meet him there, adding, 'I am harried as if hauled by fifty devils, else I would come to Greenock.' But he would, he said, keep all day Tuesday free in the hope that Richard could manage. Richard did not even wait for Tuesday, and was waiting in Glasgow on the Monday to meet the coach.

Robert's younger brother, William, was also there to meet Robert off the coach. Robert was delighted and the three of them had a happy evening together. Robert still managed that evening, however, to write to Nancy. But he could not write every day after that, as Nancy had asked him to. From Glasgow he travelled to Paisley where he had promised to call on 'My worthy, wise friend Mr Pattison', who 'did not allow me a moment's respite . . . '

He met many others on his travels en route home. When he managed to write to Nancy again, he tried to reassure her:

'My dearest Clarinda, you are ever present with me; and these hours that drawl by among the fools and rascals of this world, are only supportable in the idea that they are the forerunners of that happy hour that ushers me to the Mistress of my Soul.'

At last he reached Mauchline and visited Jean at the Mill. There he managed to arrange for her to move back to Mauchline but not to her parents' house. Instead he found her an upstairs room and kitchen in the home of his old friend, Doctor John MacKenzie. By doing this, he felt sure that Jean would have the best and immediate medical attention when her time came. He also managed a reconciliation between Jean and her mother, and arranged for Mrs Armour to look after Jean during her confinement.

He was so busy, he again had to neglect his promise of writing to Clarinda every day. He had also to apologise to his friend, Willie Cruikshanks, for not writing sooner, complaining that 'I have fought my way severely through the savage hospitality of this country – to send every guest drunk to bed if they can.'

He wrote in similar terms to Clarinda: ' . . . yesterday, I dined at a friend's at some distance; the savage hospitality of this country spent me the most part of the night over the nauseous potion in the bowl. This day – sick – headache – low spirits – miserable – fasting, except for a draught of water or small beer now eight o'clock at night – only able to crawl ten minutes walk into Mauchline, to wait the post in the pleasurable hope of hearing from the Mistress of my Soul.'

In reply, she lectured him for not writing as often as he'd promised (although he'd in fact written twice as many letters as she had), and also attacked his friend Pattison: 'In the name of wonder how could you spend ten hours with such a despicable character?'

Towards the end of her long, angry lecture, however, she said, 'Love and cherish your friend Mr Ainslie. He is your friend indeed.'

Robert had then to leave Mossgiel again to call at Galston

and Newmilns, where he had to collect sums of money owing to him for the Edinburgh Edition. He wrote to his friend Robert Muir, 'and I shall set off so early as to dispatch my business and reach Glasgow by night.' In Glasgow he had more book business to attend to. Muir had been seriously ill and Robert told him that he hoped that 'the spring will renew your shattered form', but he could see that Muir was dying.

In an attempt to comfort and console his friend, he wrote, ' . . . an honest man has nothing to fear. If we lie down in the grave, the whole man a piece of broken machinery, to moulder with the clods of the valley – be it so; at least there is an end to pain, care, woes and wants; if that part of us called Mind, does survive the apparent destruction of the man – away with old-wife prejudices and tales! Every age and every nation has had a different set of stories, and as the many are always weak, of consequence they have often, perhaps always been deceived; a man, conscious of having acted an honest part among his fellow creatures; even granting that he may have been the sport, at times, of passions and instincts; he goes to a great unknown Being who could have no other end in giving him existence but to make his happy; who gave him those passions and instincts, and well knows their force . . . It becomes a man of sense to think for himself; particularly in a case where all men are equally interested and where indeed all men are equally in the dark.'

Not long after trying to comfort his friend, Robert was in desperate need of comfort himself. He received the news that Jean had given birth to twin girls and both had died.

He cursed not only the injury that prevented him from immediately going to her, but also his insecure financial position. He had to get his affairs in order so that he had a decent home and some security to offer her.

27

Susanna was plunged into one of her quandaries. She had fallen deeply in love with Robert Burns but her traumatic experiences with Neil Guthrie were still vivid in her mind, with all the pain and fear that had accompanied them. She could not bring herself to imagine physical intimacy with Robert, or any man, ever again.

She was relieved when she learned from Alexander about the poet's 'paper passion', as he called it, with the Edinburgh woman. In a way, it was her protection. It made her feel safer to adore Robert, to look at his black hair and brows, his expressive eyes and mouth, and to allow her heart to melt at the sight of him. She gazed at him leaning back on one chair with his injured leg resting up on another. She dashed eagerly about making him dishes of tea and tasty meals and arranging and rearranging the cushion under his knee.

She was glad when he paid little more than friendly or brotherly affection towards her. Yet oh how she loved him and admired him and longed to be his sweetheart and stay close to him forever.

Alexander had warned her before they'd arrived in Edinburgh. 'Remember, Susanna, you are supposed to be in mourning. At least try to act the part and behave with some decorum.'

She managed to do so with everybody else, but Robert knew her true circumstances. There was no need to look mournful with him. Even if there had been the need, how could she sit silently with bowed head and downcast eyes when in the company of genius? She felt honoured to be in the same room as him. Doubly so when he entertained her by reading one of his poems or encouraging her to join in singing one of his songs.

> Green grow the rashes, o;
> Green grow the rashes, o;
> The sweetest hours that I e'er spent,
> Were spent among the lassies, o . . .

> He made her laugh at the way he recited
> I'm o'er young, I'm o'er young,
> I'm o'er young to marry yet;
> I'm o'er young, 'twad be a sin
> To tak me frae my mammy yet . . .

Alexander did not seem even amused, far less join in the singing or the laughter. He was such a solemn fellow. She told him so and he gave her a sullen, warning stare.

'It would fit you better, madam, to show some solemnity. You seem to forget you have come straight from your husband's burial.'

She flushed and lowered her eyes. She wanted to burst into a torrent of words of explanation to Robert, but it was impossible to talk in any detail of the gross obscenities and indecencies she had suffered. She had never even been able to speak of them to her brother.

Robert sighed. 'Don't chastise the girl. It's my fault. It's been a selfish indulgence on my part to take the opportunity to laugh and sing. I was feeling so low in spirits before you came. Anyway, we both know, Alexander, that Susanna's marriage was not a happy one and Neil Guthrie was cruel to her. It's not surprising she doesn't mourn for the loss of such a man.'

'At least I'm glad I have been the means of cheering you a little,' Susanna said, tossing a defiant glance in Alexander's direction.

He was the best of brothers, yet in some ways such a strange fellow. He had depths in him that she could neither understand nor reach.

While they were chatting to Robert, Susanna – to her delight – discovered that he was planning to take up the lease of a farm in Dumfriesshire. That meant, once Alexander was married, she could be connected to the McKenzie family and no doubt could often go for weeks at a time to stay on the Dumfriesshire estate, as she was about to do now. The McKenzies and Robert would be neighbours. All sorts of possibilities and opportunities opened up before her.

She could see Robert often – every day perhaps. They could become close. The idea quickly became a heady mixture of joy and terror. She tried to tell herself that she was being ridiculous. The cause of her terror was dead and gone. Robert was not Neil. Robert was a loving and gentle human being, who would not purposely hurt anyone, not even an animal. Not even a mouse. She had been most moved by his poem, 'On Seeing a Wounded Hare Limp by Me – which a fellow had just shot at'.

> Inhuman man! curse on thy barb'rous art,
> And blasted be thy murdrous-aiming eye!
> May never pity soothe thee with a sigh,
> Nor never pleasure glad thy cruel heart! . . .

She had nothing to fear from Robert Burns. She knew that perfectly well. Her mind kept repeating the words and totally believing them. It was her soul and her weak flesh that quailed. There was neither reason nor logic in her fear. She knew that. Yet her fear would not go away.

Time! That's what she needed, she told herself. After all, Neil was hardly cold in his grave. She hadn't had time to get used to the idea that he was dead, that she was actually, truly free of him, that she was safe.

'I must give myself time,' she thought. 'I will be all right, once I can relax for a time in Dumfriesshire.'

She plied Robert with eager questions – when would he be going, did he know that he could be neighbours with the McKenzies, and that Alexander was going to marry Isobel McKenzie? She caught Alexander's eye and was so taken aback by the fury in it, her voice died in her throat. Why on earth he should appear so enraged at her for talking about Dumfriesshire and his marriage, she could not for the life of her understand. He'd never indicated that there was to be any secrecy attached to his plans. One would have thought he would have been more than happy to have her speak of them, or to speak of them himself, and share the good news with his friend.

Robert was enthusiastic in his congratulations. He sounded a bit wistful too. 'Remember how we used to talk and plan about marrying a good woman and settling down with our own fireside, Alexander?'

To make a happy fireside clime to weans and wife
That is the true pattern, and sublime of human life.

'You are a lucky man, Alexander.'

Susanna never failed to be amazed at how poetry came so spontaneously to Robert's lips. Alexander had once remarked, rather dismissively, she'd thought at the time, how Burns had spouted at the Crochallan Fencibles Club what he'd called 'An Address to the Haggis'. Since then, to Alexander's disgust, it was now always recited at every Crochallan dinner as if it was a kind of holy writ. Susanna had asked Robert about that and he'd laughed and said,

'Oh that? I just made it up on the spot as a bit of fun.'

And he'd recited the poem with mock seriousness and great panache. Then he'd laughed again. 'It was just a bit of nonsense.'

Still Alexander didn't laugh. He looked so colourless, compared with Robert, with his white powdered hair and pale, lean face. He seemed restless, as if already half way from the house. What was the matter with the man?, Susanna thought in exasperation. Then it occurred to her that probably Alexander was impatient to hurry on his way to be with his lady love. She sighed. Well, she could understand that. She was being selfish, keeping him in Edinburgh. Nevertheless, she could not tear herself away. She kept chatting to Robert until Alexander said,

'Susanna, you're tiring Robert. He needs to rest. Come, it's time we left him in peace.'

Robert protested that, far from being tired, he was enjoying their visit and was mighty glad of their company. But Alexander was already on his feet and handing Susanna her cloak.

Susanna said, 'We'll see you again tomorrow, Robert.' Then to Alexander, 'We can stay another day, can't we?'

'It depends on the rest of the business that I have to do and how long it takes. We'd better not make any promises.' He smiled at Robert. 'Continue to rest for a few weeks yet, Robert, and we'll see you on our way back.'

'Do you think you'll be a married man by then?'

'I hope so.'

'Then you must bring your new bride to meet me and I'll write a poem for her.'

Alexander gave a slight bow. 'Goodbye, Robert.'

'Is there something wrong?' Robert asked.

'Of course not.'

'Then shake my hand.'

Alexander went forward then and took Robert's proffered hand. 'It's just that I have rather a lot on my mind at the moment.'

Robert pumped Alexander's hand up and down in both of his. 'It's good of you to make time for me, my dear friend, and I do appreciate it.'

Susanna shyly put out her hand and Robert took it, and raised it to his lips.

'My dear friend,' he said gently. She could have fainted with pleasure and gratitude but managed to smile and walk from the room along with her brother. Once outside, she asked him,

'Are we going to stay for another day, Alexander? I do hope we are.'

'We will leave first thing tomorrow morning.'

'Must we?' She could not hide the intensity of her disappointment. 'Oh, Alexander, you said . . . '

'Never mind what I said. Listen to what I'm saying now. We leave tomorrow. Apart from anything else, it will save you making any more of a fool of yourself than you've done already.'

Susanna could not believe that he was being so hurtful towards her. She had never before heard such a nasty tone in his voice.

'What do you mean? I was only trying to be kind and helpful.'

'You know perfectly well what I mean. You are a fool with men. I would have thought you should have learned your lesson by now.'

'But, you know as well as I do, that Robert is nothing like Neil.'

'Oh yes, Robert is charming, isn't he? But don't you remember how charming Neil was? You were always telling me how charming Neil was.'

'But . . . but Robert loves and respects women. Neil despised them. He hid that fact well at first, I'll give you that. But think of the tender love poems and songs Robert has written, Alexander. They come from his heart and as he says in one of his poems,

> The heart aye's the part aye,
> That makes us right or wrang.

'Don't you dare quote his poetry to me!'

200

Susanna stared at her brother in astonishment. His pale face was flushed, his mouth contorted.

'What on earth's the matter with you?'

She could see he was now struggling for control. Eventually he said in his usual calm, self-contained doctor's voice, 'Nothing, my dear. I'm perfectly all right. Just a bit of a headache. Don't worry. It'll pass.'

He even managed to smile.

28

Alexander could have killed Susanna. Almost the first thing she said when they arrived at the McKenzie estate was, 'Did you know that you and Robert Burns are going to be neighbours?'

Isobel was astonished, ecstatic. 'No!'

'Yes, he's taking the lease of a farm at Ellisland.'

'Mother, did you hear that? Robert Burns is coming to live in Dumfriesshire.'

'Yes, it's wonderful news, dear. Absolutely wonderful. Robert Burns as our neighbour!'

There it was again. Robert Burns. Robert Burns. Would he never hear the end of it? Without even the man being here in person, he was completely overshadowing him. Alexander felt sick with anger. It was only with the greatest difficulty that he clung to a polite, smiling front. How could he prise Isobel away from her excited chatter with Susanna?

He had planned quiet walks in the beautiful countryside, romantic strolls along the banks of the Nith with the gentle lapping of the water and the fragrant breeze refreshing them. He'd dreamt of relaxed evenings in the library or drawing room, alone with Isobel. In his mind's eye, he saw himself broach the subject of the future and her quiet pleasure in hearing of his plans. He heard himself propose to her and felt the warm glow of her acceptance. Then the sharing of this happy news with her parents. The congratulations. The toasts to their health. All the talk of when the wedding would take place. The women, no doubt, would chat about what they'd wear.

Now all the attention and the talk was of Robert Burns. Robert Burns. How he'd grown to hate the very name. There were still times, of course, when he was in Robert's company and experienced the warmth of the man's friendship and trust. Then he felt ashamed and made every effort to control his negative feelings. He'd tell himself that it wasn't really Robert's fault that there was such a hysterical fuss about him. Robert was still exactly the same young man he'd known in Ayrshire. He had not changed at all.

He'd tell himself that Robert couldn't help having such a facility for rhyme. He obviously had been born with it. Despite bouts of ill health, despite hard physical labour, his continuing energy for spontaneity in writing and especially for creating poetry and song was amazing.

Alexander had seen him at a dinner in Selkirk get up and say a grace that he'd composed on the spot.

> Some hae meat and cannae eat,
> And some wad eat that want it;
> But we hae meat, and we can eat,
> And sae the Lord be thanket.

It *must* be something he'd been born with. He'd once scribbled a verse on the back of a bank note at the time when he was thinking about emigration:

> Wae worth thy power, thou cursed leaf!
> Fell source of a' my woe and grief;
> For lack o' thee I've lost my lass,
> For lack o' thee I scrimp my glass;
> I see the children of affliction,
> Unaided through thy curs'd restriction;
> I've seen th' oppressor's cruel smile,

Amid his hapless victim's spoil,
And for thy potence vainly wisht,
To crush the villain in the dust!
For lack o' thee, I leave this much loved shore,
Never perhaps to greet old Scotland more.

Scribbled spontaneously on the back of a bank note! Alexander groaned to himself. There was no stopping the creative flow – no circumstances could divert it. Only death itself, Alexander suspected, would silence the man.

Unexpectedly, he experienced a tiny lift of hope and desire. For just a moment he understood how the seed of murder could take root. Hastily he crushed it. What was he thinking? He was a doctor, dedicated to saving life. He was a man of conscience.

Burns could not even help his good looks or his charm, any more than his muse. But no, he *could* help the way he behaved, especially towards women. That was something he purposely planned and indulged in because, for one thing, it fed his muse. He knew it, and Burns knew it. He'd once said, 'The joy of my heart is to study men, their manners and their ways.' Like a cannibal, he fed on people, especially women. And he enjoyed doing it. He revelled in his social life and all the people he met socially, especially women. He was a people predator, especially with women.

Alexander's soul caved in with anxiety at the thought of Burns meeting and charming and stealing Isobel from him. His mind darted desperately about.

What could he do?

He had not been born with the vivid good looks of Burns. He gazed at his reflection and despaired of his pale, thin face and rather long nose. He had not the easy charm and ready wit of Burns. He did not possess that cruel edge that enabled Burns to write his wicked satires.

What could he do?

And all the time the voices in the McKenzie drawing room echoed in his head.

'Robert Burns. Robert Burns.'

He tried to divert the conversation. He tried to bring up the subject of plans for Isobel and himself. He even tried to play on Susanna's supposed grief and mourning. He suggested a walk by the river and his heart lifted when Isobel agreed. Then Susanna joined them despite his cold look of disapproval.

She had the cheek to ask him later, 'What's the matter with you?'

She was always asking him that now.

'What do you think?' he hissed angrily. 'I wanted to get Isobel on her own so that I could make a formal proposal and talk about our future. You are unbelievably selfish and thoughtless, Susanna. I wish now I'd never brought you here.'

'Oh, Alexander, I'm so sorry. You are right. I have been selfish and thoughtless. I'll be more careful in future. I promise. It was just Isobel and I were wrapped up in our conversation about Robert.'

'I know,' Alexander managed in a low voice. 'Oh, I know. I'm heartily sick of hearing about the man!'

'But . . . but . . . I thought he was your friend. I thought you were as much taken up with admiration of him as we all are.'

Alexander took a deep breath before speaking again.

'Yes, I am. Of course I am. But you do go to such extremes in everything, Susanna, and today I was so looking forward to speaking to Isobel about other things.'

'I'm sorry, Alexander. I really am. It won't happen again. At least, I won't be the one to introduce Robert's name into the conversation. I cannot see how I can stop everyone else.'

Nor could he. It was something he would have to suffer yet again. And again. And again . . .

'But surely,' Susanna said tentatively, 'you didn't need to rush your proposal right away today. You have plenty of time.'

Plenty of time he had not.

The only thing he could think of was to make it clear to the McKenzies that Robert would be weeks confined to his room because of his injury and then he had to go home to his family in Ayrshire to settle things. It would be some months before he came to Dumfriesshire. So it would be better not to get so excited about the poet and put all thoughts of an inevitable meeting with him out of their minds at present.

'But never fear,' he added, 'I will arrange a meeting when the time comes.'

It worked to some degree. The excitement and talk eventually settled down and was directed into other channels. Alexander managed his quiet walk alone with Isobel and made his proposal.

To his surprise and chagrin, she did not immediately accept. She would think about it, she told him kindly. They hadn't, after all, known each other for very long. At least to get to know each other personally, rather than first by correspondence. She had given him quite a different impression in her letters, he felt sure. He had made his feelings and his intentions perfectly clear in his letters and she had warmly responded.

This change of attitude – for he was sure it was a change of attitude – could only be explained by the news of Burns coming to Dumfriesshire and her intense desire to meet him. She preferred even the idea of Burns to him. She would be completely swept off her feet by him when they did meet.

He couldn't bear it. He couldn't allow it to happen. He sank into a secret black cauldron of emotion.

Susanna said, 'What on earth's wrong with you?'

'Will you stop asking me that, Susanna? You are driving me mad with your silly nagging.'

Susanna looked astonished and upset but she fell silent. She took to watching him, though, casting curious glances in his direction.

Eventually, she said sympathetically, 'Isobel must have refused you! Oh, I am sorry, Alexander. And I can't understand it. You are a good man and you love her. And I thought she had such a high regard for you too.'

'She has not refused me.' Alexander pushed the words out. 'She just needs a little time to think about my proposal. I was rushing things too much, just as you suspected. Everything is going to be all right,' he added, as much to reassure himself as his sister.

'Yes, of course.' Susanna looked relieved. She even laughed. 'And you accuse me of being a rash and hasty extremist. It must be a family failing.'

He favoured her with a cold, calm smile. 'Indeed. Indeed. We both need to acquire some patience, it seems.'

But he felt far from patient. He felt murderous when the conversation about Burns and the plans to entertain him still went on and on. They planned to invite everyone for miles around, it seemed. Only Isobel tried to suggest that it would be so much nicer to have him to themselves for as much time as possible – rather than share him with all the gentry of Dumfriesshire.

Alexander could see it all even now. He knew exactly what was in her mind. He was going to lose her to Burns. He did not stand a chance. He was going to lose the only woman he had ever loved. He was going to lose the chance of one day being the owner of this huge house with its many glistening chandeliers, beautiful furnishings and original paintings, worth in themselves a fortune. He was going to lose the chance of one day living at ease as the inheritor of this huge estate.

All because of that aimless failure in life, Robert Burns. He might have some talent as a poet and song writer. But he was a farmer born and bred. Always had been, like his father before him. And he was a failure as a farmer. Every farm he'd had so far had failed, and no doubt he'd fail at Ellisland. He was also stupid and careless with money. Not a penny had he bothered to take from his song publisher. And he'd blithely spent most of what he earned from his books on holidaying all over Scotland, fornicating wherever he could in the process.

He'd come here, enjoy being fêted and entertained, and have Isobel immediately eating out of his hand. There would be no question of *him* taking his time and not rushing things. He believed in always going for intimacy with a woman as quickly as possible. Hadn't he admitted that?

Something had to be done. Alexander was not going to lose Isobel. He was not going to give up his chance of a good life here. Not for anyone. But certainly not for an irreligious profligate like Robert Burns.

No, something had to be done.

29

Susanna knew she was being reckless and unwise. As usual. But oh, she didn't care. She couldn't help it. She lied to Alexander and to everyone. She said she felt she ought to pay a visit to Tarbolton and see her poor parents who had not been in good health for some time. Isobel pressed her to return as soon as possible.

'Already you have become my dearest friend, Susanna. I shall miss you.'

'Thank you, Isobel.' Susanna embraced the girl. 'I will, of course, be very happy to return.'

Alexander helped her into the coach. A family of father and mother and daughter were also travelling that day and Susanna was thankful when the daughter sat next to her and not the big, scarlet-faced, sweating father. She couldn't bear a man's body to be next to hers. She was still far from conquering her terror and revulsion of any close contact with any man. Burns lightly kissing her hand had been a tentative, indeed delightful step in her so longed-for release from past terrors. They *were* past. She knew that. Her brain told her that her ordeal was definitely over. It was over and done with. She was free.

Only she didn't *feel* that it was over. She didn't *feel* free. At least not of her terror of any intimate contact with men. Even with Robert Burns. Yet, oh how she longed for intimacy with him.

She wanted him for his gentle, loving, yet manly personality, for his glossy raven hair, his dark hypnotic eyes, his unique and wonderful talent. But most of all, she longed to be loved by him, to lie in his arms and be gentled by him.

She had to, she must, overcome her foolish, illogical terrors.

'I'm perfectly all right now,' she kept repeating to herself in time to the thundering of the horses' hooves. 'I've nothing to be afraid of. Nothing at all. Nothing at all. Nothing at all . . . '

She was not going to Tarbolton as Alexander believed. She was carrying on to Edinburgh and was staying in the city at an inn as near as possible to Robert's lodgings so that she could visit him every day. She wanted to be with him all day, every day, but she knew he needed time on his own to write his many business letters and, no doubt – her mind darkened with jealousy at the thought – letters to his 'paper passion'.

But a paper passion, she thought recklessly, surely could not compete with the vibrant, real-life passion she could and would offer Robert. Her heart thumped against her rib cage so strongly and noisily at the daring thought, she feared one of the other occupants of the coach might become aware of it. But the coach was rattling and thumping over the stony road and the horses were straining along at what seemed a desperate and alarming pace. Everyone was concentrating on the dangerous swaying of the vehicle. The young woman clutched at her wide-brimmed hat and began to whimper.

The older woman asked her husband, 'Are we nearly there, Edward?'

'Yes, yes,' he replied. 'Just hold on.'

There had been no conversation with Susanna on the journey. She had discouraged any attempts by keeping her head turned away as if all the time preferring to concentrate on observing the passing countryside.

She was relieved when at last the journey was over and she was in the capital city with its noisy pell-mell of people, the pungent smells, and the shadows enveloping the streets from the high tenements. She couldn't help remembering Margaret Burns and Sally and felt ashamed that she could never bring herself to meet up with them again. They had done her no harm. Indeed, they had been extremely kind, but they were from a different world. She could not bear to step back into that world again. She wished them well and if she accidentally came across them, she would greet them kindly before passing on.

Now she wasted no time, after obtaining a respectable room, in calling on Robert. He was sitting alone and exactly as she remembered him from her last visit. The man in substance was even more vibrantly, shockingly attractive than the man she remembered.

'Alone?' he said.

She began fussing about making tea, producing the cake and biscuits she'd brought from the MacKenzies – supposedly for her mother and father.

'Alexander is totally carried away with his Isobel. He has proposed to her and she tells him she needs a little time before giving him her answer. He is waiting in much anxiety.' She laughed nervously. 'He accused me of taking up too much of Isobel's time and attention. Attention away from him and his proposal, and eventual discussion of their future plans. Anyway, I have been banished to Edinburgh and then to visit my parents for a time.'

'Not banished, surely!'

She shrugged. 'Well, not in so many words. But I know he was pleased and relieved when I left. Oh, but at the same time wishing me well,' she hastily added. 'He is the best of brothers. But we have been worried about you, as well as our parents, and Alexander hopes my visits will put our minds at rest. How are you, Robert?'

'Oh, much better. Worries of one kind or another still torment me. But I am cheered by the thought of having such good friends who are so concerned about me.'

He was smiling at her but was it her fevered imagination, or did she see in his dark, observant eyes a recognition of the real reason for her visit? He was aware, of course, that from a lady's point of view, it was not at all proper to visit a gentleman alone in his lodgings.

She no longer cared about propriety and the social niceties. All she cared about was him. She wanted to touch him, caress him, hold him. He was not slim and elegant with lean calves and long, silver-buckled feet like Alexander and Alexander's other male friends and acquaintances. He was broad-shouldered and solid looking.

And oh, those black, smouldering eyes. Had there ever been such eyes in any man before? She ached to touch him. All she needed to do was walk across the room and touch him, and he would know. It would be an invitation and he would know.

She trembled on the verge, and could have wept broken-heartedly when the terror, like a huge wave, came crashing over her once again, drowning all passion. She couldn't do it. She made an excuse to go and fetch plates from the kitchen for the cakes and biscuits. There, she leaned against the kitchen table for support and she hated herself. How stupid she was! How *stupid*!

Yet again she tried to tell herself, to repeat over and over, 'I'm perfectly all right now. I've nothing to be afraid of. Nothing at all. Nothing at all. Nothing at all . . . '

But it was no use. Neil Guthrie had ruined her life. She suddenly realised that if she could not show her passionate love for Robert Burns by any physical contact, she would never be able to do so with any man.

She hoped Neil Guthrie would burn forever in hell. Her face hardened, her body stiffened. She returned to the room and acted the calm hostess, pouring out tea, encouraging Robert to try the delicious baking from the wonderfully talented cook the McKenzies were fortunate to have found. She encouraged Robert to tell her all his news. At least it would stop her stupid chatter. She listened to him and watched the way his expression could change. He could suddenly become animated and gladdened by something, then – just as quickly – saddened by something else.

She sat opposite him, a neat-waisted, straight-backed little figure in plum velvet with a demure ruffle of lace at cuffs and bosom, and one long curl placed prettily over the front of her left shoulder. She laughed when she should at his amusing anecdotes and made sympathetic murmurs when he confided his serious worries. She even listened calmly when he spoke in praise of Nancy MacElhose.

And all the time she was thinking, 'Oh Robert, Robert . . . '

And wishing with all her heart that she could undo the damage that Neil Guthrie had done to her.

Afterwards, in the shadows of her room at the inn, she wept over her inadequacy. He had enjoyed her company, he said. He valued her friendship, he said. He had been a perfect gentleman and she loved him all the more for not sparking off her terrors by anything other than gentlemanly conduct. He had not even kissed her hand when she left him. There was only a slight bow, and a smile, and gentle words of appreciation for her care and attention.

But oh, his eyes – his eyes seemed to say so much more. Or was it her longing for him that made her imagine he wanted her too?

30

Burns' sudden decision to marry Jean Armour, especially at the height of his apparent passion for Nancy MacElhose, astonished, puzzled, and even angered the few people who heard of it at the time. He tried to explain.

To Mrs Dunlop he wrote, 'In housewife matters, of aptness to learn and activity to execute she is eminently mistress; and during my absence in Nithsdale, she is regularly and constantly apprentice to my mother and sisters in their dairy and other rural business. In short, I can easily *fancy* a more agreeable companion for my journey of life, but, upon my honour, I have never *seen* the individual instance . . . Circumstanced as I am, I could never have got a female partner for life who could have entered into my favourite studies, relished my favourite authors, and without entailing on me at the same time, expensive living, fantastic caprice, apish affectation, with all the other blessed, boarding-school acquirements which (pardonnez-moi, Madam!) are sometimes to be found among females of the upper ranks, but almost universally pervade the misses of the would-be gentry.'

To Peggy Chalmers he wrote of Jean, 'I have got the handsomest figure, the sweetest temper, the soundest constitution and the kindest heart in the country . . . although she scarcely ever in her life, except the scriptures of the old and new testament, and the psalms of David in metre, spent five minutes together in either prose or verse.'

But he added a sentence about her singing voice, describing it with a phrase from Milton as '. . . the finest wood wild' he had ever heard.

Nancy MacElhose said of his marriage that it was a 'perfidious treachery' and a 'fatal mistake'.

Someone else said of his marriage to Jean that although her good singing voice might '. . . rise to B natural all day long, she would still be a peasant to her lettered lord, an object of pity rather than equal affection . . .'

Another friend believed Robert had always had to have two women, one for his body and one for his mind. He'd tried often enough but could never get both in the same person.

The wedding ceremony was a very quiet affair. It had not been until much later that Robert had managed to write to other friends, apart from Nancy MacElhose and Mrs Dunlop, to tell them of the marriage. First of all, he'd been laid low with the 'fashionable influenza'. This had stirred up his all too frequent feverish symptoms, as well as the aches and pains and palpitations that had plagued him for years. There had been a time during one of his tours that these symptoms had been so bad that a servant of the family with whom he was staying had to remain up all night to watch over him.

As soon as he was better of the influenza, but still feeling weak, he had once more to see about the Excise. His little surplus of money regularly went to help support his brother Gilbert and the rest of his family in Ayrshire. And if that support was withdrawn, Gilbert would be ruined.

He wrote to an influential friend asking if he could be instructed in his Excise duties nearer home, rather than in Edinburgh at the moment, and he explained his present situation and state of health. This was duly arranged. He then met with much more difficulty and problems. He had to try to explain some of his political indiscretions from the past, like his verses about 'the idiot race' and others.

He was reminded that he was, after all, having to swear allegiance to his King. It was his first glimpse of the greatest and most painful and difficult problem he had as an Excise officer – the need to curb his democratic pen and tongue. It was something he did not always manage to do successfully.

The business with Ellisland had also to be settled and, for a long time, he had to live alone in a draughty, smoke-filled hovel until the farmhouse home for his wife and children could be built. Jean stayed with his mother and brother and sisters while he tried to work the fields and also supervise the building work. He now found himself to be a part-time farmer, a part-time poet, and a part-time Excise man. He had to gallop for about two hundred miles every week 'to inspect dirty ponds and yeasty barrels'. As a result, he was finding no time as yet to write to friends and bring them up to date with his changed circumstances. The songs he composed were hummed to himself while jogging the long miles on his excise duties. He didn't even have time to contact Alexander who, no doubt, would be married himself by now and back to doctoring in Edinburgh.

At last the house at Ellisland was ready. Jean and two girl relations, who worked as servants, arrived. The usual superstitious procedure was performed. A family bible and a bowl of salt had to be placed one on top of the other and carried into the new house. This was to bring good luck to everyone who tenanted the farm. Burns, with his wife on his arm, followed the bearer of the bible and salt, and so entered upon the possession of his home.

He did not have much time and certainly not much leisure to enjoy his new house and the company of his family. Apart from the usual hard work on the farm, although he was now helped by two farm labourers, his Excise duties were extremely varied. Duty had to be levied on the '. . . making of soap, paper, pasteboard, millboard and scaleboard respectively; and upon printing, painting and storing of paper; or dying of silks, calicoes, linen and stuff respectively; and upon tanning, tarving, or dressing of hides and skins, and pieces of hides and skins, and upon making of vellum and parchment respectively; and upon silver-plate and manufacture of silver respectively; and on the Inland Duties upon coffee, tea and chocolate respectively; and upon making malt, and making and importing rum, cyder and perry respectively; and duties upon glass . . . and upon every coach, Berlin, Landau, Chanat, Calesh, Chaise-marine, Chaise, Chair and Caravan, or by what name so ever such wheel carriages now are or hereafter may be called or known . . .'

Duty was mostly charged during manufacture, and this entailed Burns having to make visits day and night. Then there was a huge amount of paperwork, and of course distances travelled on horseback in all weathers. He had sometimes to be on the saddle four, or on occasions five days a week. Often he arrived back at Ellisland exhausted after riding for thirty or forty miles. Then he would have to write his excise book reports.

He became so overworked, exhausted and depressed at this period, he wrote to his dear friend, Peggy Chalmers, '. . . when I think of you – when I think I have met with you, and have lived more of real life with you in eight days, than I can do with almost any body I meet with in eight years – when I think of the improbability of meeting you in this world again – I could sit down and cry like a child.'

In the same letter, he conceded that he may not have married Jean 'in consequence of the attachment of romance', but went on to say that he had no cause to repent it.

Again it was observed that there were always two Robert Burns's. The one who was a tenant farmer, intent on making 'a happy fireside clime'. And the other man, the poet – eager, indeed desperate, to broaden his intellectual horizons and not be spiritually destroyed by the grindingly hard physical conditions of his life.

He wrote to Mrs Dunlop and enclosed some verses of a song he'd composed.

> Should auld acquaintance be forgot,
> And never brought to mind?

Should auld acquaintance be forgot,
And auld lang syne?

For auld lang syne, my jo,
For auld lang syne,
We'll tak' a cup o' kindness yet,
For auld lang syne.

He also managed to pen another song, this time about the love between a man and his wife, and their growing old together.

John Anderson my jo, John.
When we were first acquent;
Your locks were like the raven,
Your bonnie brow was brent;
But now your brow is beld, John,
Your locks are like the snaw;
But blessings on your frosty pow,
John Anderson my jo!

John Anderson my jo, John,
We clam the hill thegither;
And mony a canty day, John,
We had wi' ane anither;
Now we maun totter down, John,
And hand in hand we'll go;
And sleep the gither at the foot,
John Anderson my jo!

His spirits were eventually raised by meeting his neighbours – Captain Robert Riddell and his family who lived at Friars Carse. Robert Riddell, at thirty-three, was four years older than Burns and was himself devoted to music, coin-collecting, and other antiquarian pursuits. Riddell had built a 'Hermitage' in the grounds of his mansion because he'd discovered the area had been the site of an old monastic retreat. The two men quickly became good friends and Riddell gave Burns a key to the Hermitage, where he composed some verses.

Very rashly – for a man with an Excise commission – Burns wrote an open letter to an English newspaper addressed to William Pitt, criticising the government's unfair treatment of the Scottish distillers. He wanted it to be anonymous but the paper printed his name. He sent a copy to Mrs Dunlop 'for your sole amusement; it is dangerous ground to tread on.' He also enclosed the lyrics of *Afton Water.*

> Flow gently, sweet Afton, among thy green braes,
> Flow gently, I'll sing thee a song in thy praise;
> My Mary's asleep by thy murmuring stream,
> Flow gently, sweet Afton, disturb not her dream.

He received not a very pleasant letter from her in which she upbraided him for something else she accused him of writing.

'I heard a man say lately he had seen a poem of yours so grossly indelicate he was ashamed to read it alone on the braeside.' She went on to say that she hoped this was 'one of the follies long cast to air and polished off by mine, if not by better company.'

Burns was annoyed. It could have been one of the bawdy ballads he'd collected by various authors and not originated by him at all. It could have been, on the other hand, one of his that he'd been persuaded to pen for the entertainment of the Crochallan Fencible Club. Either way he was annoyed.

'I am very sorry that you should be informed of my supposed guilt in composing, in some midnight frolic, a stanza or two perhaps not quite proper for a clergyman's reading to a company of ladies. That I am the author of the verses alluded to in your letter is what I much doubt. You may guess that the convivial hours of *men* have their mysteries of wit and mirth; and I hold it a piece of contemptible baseness to detail the sallies of thoughtless merriment or the orgies of accidental intoxication, to the ear of cool Sobriety or female Delicacy.'

He was seriously worried about who the man was who had tried to undermine his long standing and treasured friendship with Mrs Dunlop. He couldn't bear the high regard she had always had for him to be tarnished. He knew he had enemies who were jealous of him, but for someone to try to undermine one of his most valued friendships made him feel very uneasy and apprehensive.

31

She knew. Alexander had done his best to keep the fact of Burns' presence in Dumfriesshire from Isobel, and he had done so successfully for a time. That was while Burns had been living in isolation in some hovel or other while a farmhouse was being built. Now, however, he was installed in the farmhouse with his wife and young family. And Isobel knew.

Alexander had by now received two long letters from Burns bringing him up to date with the news of his marriage, and the conditions at Ellisland. He was of course suffering the usual difficulties with the land. He'd written that after a shower had fallen on a field of new-sown and new-rolled barley, it looked like a new paved street! 'Soil,' he said, 'there never was such soil; but I see how it has been – God has riddled the whole creation, and flung the riddings on Ellisland.'

At one point, in one of his moods, he'd written, 'My nerves are in a damnable state. I feel that horrid hypochondria pervading every atom of both body and soul. This farm has undone my enjoyment of myself. It is a ruinous affair on all hands. But let it go to hell! I'll fight it out and be off with it.'

He'd also written about how he'd been caught and scolded by his wife for singing a bawdy ballad to himself. Alexander noticed that to Burns, it seemed to afford some sort of release at the most difficult times of his life to turn to coarseness like that. It was, Alexander supposed, part of this fighting, go-to-hell kind of attitude.

All the apparent difficulties and work, of course, did not stop Burns having a social life and adding to his seemingly endless list of friends, especially women friends. Only, women usually became more than just friends. This time, he'd made friends of neighbours called Riddell – Captain Robert Riddell and his wife Elizabeth, and their daughter-in-law, Maria. Maria's husband was away from home a great deal and it was what Burns had written about Maria that tormented Alexander. He could recognise the usual signs of Burns falling in love. He raved on about how wonderful this woman was, how beautiful, how talented, how intelligent, etc. The fact that she was married did not, on this occasion, seem to matter.

Alexander had always believed that Burns would and did draw the line at having any physical intimacy with a married woman. But here, all Alexander's suspicions were aroused. And, if married women were not safe against this callous, unprincipled predator, then Isobel was not safe. He had at last succeeded in winning her hand in marriage, helped to some degree, he knew, by her parents. They were eager to enjoy retirement in their house in Edinburgh and have him give up his doctoring and run the Dumfriesshire estate.

He shared their eagerness. There was nothing he would enjoy more than being safely installed as lord of the manor, and of such a large estate.

Isobel was a dutiful daughter and eventually agreed to the match. All had been going well. It was a quiet, contented life they were building together.

Then suddenly Isobel flared into life. She and Susanna, who had been living with them, heard that Burns was now in the area. Oh, the excitement that was immediately engendered.

Robert Burns. Robert Burns. The house reverberated with his name.

The last time Alexander had felt so angry was when he'd learned that Susanna had visited Burns in Edinburgh on her own. After all his warning! How stupidly indiscreet of her. What would people think? Especially as she was still supposed to be in mourning?

'But I was only thinking of his welfare,' she protested. 'I took him some food and reading and writing material.'

She lied. At least about only thinking of his welfare. She was thinking of herself and her obsession with Burns. She just wanted to be with 'the great man', as she called him, and to worship at his altar.

As they all did. Stupid women! Isobel would be the same. Even enlightening them of some of Burns' many faults did nothing to dampen their enthusiasm and admiration. He obviously was not as clever as one of Burns' so-called friends – one of the Ainslies. Ainslie, Alexander long ago had found out, had spied on Burns at every turn and passed on information about him in a detrimental way to people that Burns loved – or imagined he loved – like Nancy MacElhose. He had particularly insinuated himself in with her. Ainslie was a despicable character and acted in the way he did for no reason except that he was a despicable character.

'But I have a reason,' Alexander told himself, 'a very good reason to clip Burns' wings in whatever way I can.' He had already convinced himself that his marriage, his whole way of life, was at stake.

But no matter what he did, Burns always won. Take writing, for example. Alexander had published his second book of poems, on which he'd laboured long and conscientiously. This time the book had been reviewed. It was damned forever with the words 'uninspired and pedestrian'.

Burns on the other hand kept bringing out yet another book, yet another edition, to nothing but praise.

One important part of Alexander's life – his writing life – had been ruined. He wasn't going to allow more heartache and humiliation to lay his life to waste. Hatred burned in him.

Isobel and Susanna were pressurising him into arranging a meeting with their hero.

'Go and see him, Alexander,' Isobel pleaded. 'Persuade him to come and visit us.'

Susanna said, 'I will come with you, Alexander. Robert and I are good friends. He will agree to be Isobel's guest if I ask him. We can suggest a date that gives your mother- and father-in-law time to come from Edinburgh. They would not want to miss such an occasion.'

Robert Burns. Robert Burns.

'All right, I'll go,' he growled, beaten down eventually, 'but you don't need to accompany me, Susanna.'

'Oh yes, I do. I do. He would come to please me. I know it!'

Already she was running for her cloak and bonnet. And so they set off in the carriage, Alexander sitting silent and still, Susanna fidgeting endlessly with her dress, her cloak, her hair, her bonnet. Once at Ellisland, Susanna burst into the farmhouse and greeted Burns with such delight and in front of his wife, that Alexander was ashamed of her. And of course Burns greeted her with equal pleasure. His wife didn't seem to mind. She had always been an unexceptional, plump girl and now she was an unexceptional, plump matron. It was taken for granted, he knew, that she was never included in any invitations or outings organised by the Riddells or any other of the local gentry. Nor, he was sure, would she have wanted to be included. She was obviously perfectly content in the part of a farmer's wife and happy and grateful to be the wife of such an exceptional man.

Susanna chattered away to Burns while his wife made them a cup of tea. She never joined them, did not even sit down, but cheerfully busied herself with the children and other housewifely duties.

Burns of course was persuaded to visit the McKenzies and a date was set. A message was immediately posted to Mr and Mrs McKenzie. Then endless talk began between Isobel and Susanna. What the dinner menu would consist of. What they would wear. How they must ask Burns to read some of their favourite poems.

'He's such a good reader. He gives such a wonderful performance. Just like a professional actor.'

Robert Burns. Robert Burns.

And there he was with his raven black hair and brows, and glossy dark eyes. There he was in his well cut blue coat and fawn breeches and waistcoat and lace at his neck and cuffs. Not forgetting his polished, knee-high boots.

Oh, how all the ladies twittered and fawned around him. Especially Isobel.

Oh, how Alexander hated him. Yet he still could feel ashamed of his hatred. Especially when Robert congratulated him on having such a lovely wife and a lovely home and on how well he was running the estate. Already he had made a name in the district, according to Robert. Word had got around that he was a good and fair employer. That was perfectly true, of course. He was as good and conscientious an employer of workers on the estate as he'd been a good and conscientious doctor to his patients.

But what would anything matter if he lost Isobel? The problem was that Robert had a warm and loving nature that was hard to resist. *He* even found it hard to resist. Nevertheless, he did not trust him. At least not with women.

He remembered how, while carrying on a passionate correspondence with Nancy MacElhose, Robert was every now and again having sexual gratification with Nancy's maid. Alexander could hardly credit it. The maid – Jenny Clowe, her name was – would deliver a letter from her mistress and when the mood was on him, or probably when he was so frustrated with not being able to possess Mrs MacElhose, he had houghmagandy with the messenger.

Who could trust a man like that? A man like that was capable of anything.

What a ridiculous fuss Mrs McKenzie and Isobel made of Burns at that first dinner party. Even Mr McKenzie joined in the singing of praises.

Robert Burns. Robert Burns.

It made Alexander sick. The worst of it was they were already planning and discussing other meetings, other social occasions. There would be no end to it. There was no use trying to console himself with the fact that Burns wouldn't, couldn't, have all that much time for socialising when he had to do so much work, especially for the Excise.

Burns had always shown an amazing amount of energy. He kept burning himself out, of course, hitting rock bottom, but then, miraculously, gaining another surge of high spirits.

He had even started a country library system with Riddell. They called it the Monkland Friendly Society. Captain Riddell had been elected President of the Society and his name guaranteed a good patronage but it was obvious to everyone that it was Burns who did all the work.

Burns was treasurer, librarian and censor. He made up the rules. He encouraged ordinary people in the country to read, saying that those who did were likely to be 'a superior being to their neighbour, who, perhaps, stalks beside a team, very little removed except in shape from the brutes he drives'.

And all the time he was continuing to write poetry and songs. He was supplying songs for two very different editors, James Johnson and George Thomson. How and when he did this, while coping with such a workload, Alexander could not imagine. He'd even composed what even he had to admit to himself was a masterpiece. Admitting this was like plunging a dagger into his own heart.

He read the long poem, 'Tam o' Shanter', only because Burns gave it to him to read while he was in his company. Despite his reluctance even to look at it, the words leapt exultantly from the page. He could feel the rhythm of Tam's horse in the words as they galloped along. Even the first verse had a hypnotic rhythm to it.

> When chapman billies leave the street,
> And drouthy neebors, neebors meet,
> As market-days are wearing late,
> An' folks begin to tak the gate;

While we sit bousing at the nappy,
An' getting fou and unco happy
We think na on the lang Scots miles,
The mosses, waters, slaps and styles,
That lie between us and our hame,
Where sits our sultry, sullen dame,
Gathering her brows like gathering storm,
Nursing her wrath to keep it warm.

Of course, the McKenzies insisted Burns read the poem on his next visit. After he finished, there was complete silence for a moment or two — the kind of stunned hush in a theatre before riotous applause breaks out.

Oh, how Burns was applauded. They said he should write for the theatre and he said he was thinking about it. How could he possibly do it? All sorts of powerful emotions and confusions were churning inside Alexander.

Mrs Burns had said in connection with the writing of 'Tam o' Shanter' that one day, one of the farm servants had rushed into the house saying that the master had gone mad. He was marching up and down a hillock, shouting and laughing to himself. She had told the man just to leave him be as it was the best thing to do when he was like that. Eventually, it began to rain so hard that she had to go out and find Burns and bring him back herself. She found him sheltered under a tree with a piece of paper and pencil in his hand and still talking and laughing to himself.

He had been composing verses of 'Tam o' Shanter' and that night he'd read the whole poem to the assembled family and servants. The children had become so frightened by the reading that they'd hidden under the table.

Mrs Burns was insisting that he'd written it all on the one day and Alexander believed her. Although Burns said, 'All my poetry has the affect of easy composition, but is the result of laborious correction.' 'Tam o' Shanter' seemed to have leapt white hot from the mind of Burns. It brimmed with his miraculous energy.

It made Alexander despair. Nothing could be done to stop such a man. Unless he burned himself out for good. The thought gave Alexander a glimmer of hope.

32

Kate Watson was a poor widow woman who on local gala days kept a shebeen. Robert went to her door and everyone expected the seizure of the contraband barrels Kate had inside. Instead, Robert gave a nod and a gesture with his forefinger. It brought Kate to the door.

Burns said to her, 'Kate, are ye mad? Dinna ye know that the supervisor and I will be in upon you in the course of forty minutes? Goodbye t'ye at present.'

This friendly hint was immediately and gratefully acted on. It saved the widow a fine of several pounds. The annual revenue loss only amounted to five shillings. Kate was not the only poor person to whom Robert showed mercy during his early morning house visits on the day of a gala or fair.

Nevertheless he was an energetic and conscientious officer, and when dealing with real smugglers and serious offenders, he was as enthusiastic and even more efficient than most other excisemen. He explained his method to Alexander and the McKenzies: 'I recorded every defaulter; but at the court, I myself begged off every poor body that was unable to pay, which seeming candour gave me so much implicit credit with the Hon. Bench that with his compliments, they gave me such ample vengeance on the rest that my decree is double the amount of any division in the district.'

The detecting officer was given not only half of all fines imposed, but half the produce of seizures as well. As a result,

Robert was able to add a considerable amount to his basic salary. He had to do a great deal of riding in a wide area, however, and it was hard and fatiguing. As a result, Robert started trying to obtain a position in his own locality. All seemed to be going fairly smoothly until he had a terrible blow.

The Earl of Glencairn had gone to Portugal for the sake of his health but his condition had worsened there. He decided to return home but died before the ship reached England. Robert was grief-stricken, absolutely heartbroken. He wrote a long poem, 'Lament for James, Earl of Glencairn', which ended with,

> The bridegroom may forget the bride,
> Was made his wedded wife yestreen;
> The monarch may forget the crown
> That on his head an hour has been;
> The mother may forget the child
> That smiles sae sweetly on her knee;
> But I'll remember thee, Glencairn,
> And a' that thou hast done for me.

He wrote immediately to ask when the Earl's remains would be interred, 'so that I may cross the country and steal among the crowd, to pay a tear to the last sight of my ever-revered benefactor'.

Robert bought a grey tail coat and black gloves in readiness but he was snubbed by the Earl's relations and not even invited to the requiem service held in Ayrshire. They did not even acknowledge the beautiful Lament he sent to them. Normally any kind of snub, especially one delivered by his so-called superiors, made him angry and retaliate with savage satire. But on this occasion, he was only grief-stricken and heartbroken at the loss of his dearest and most loved friend.

His low spirits affected his health and he was laid low with nervous symptoms of headaches, depression and palpitations.

He wasn't able even to write up his excise books. He couldn't raise his head, far less ride over ten parishes. Thankfully, when he recovered, he was given a transfer to Dumfries Third Division.

For a time, Robert rode between the farm at Ellisland and Dumfries every day. If the weather was very bad – and it often was very bad – he stayed overnight at the Globe Tavern in Dumfries. There he became familiar with Anna Parks. Anna Parks was a relative of the owner of the Globe and she worked there as a barmaid. She was a friendly girl, to say the least, and was very taken with the handsome poet who, lonely without his wife and family, easily succumbed to her charms.

The result of this familiarity was Anna Parks' pregnancy. Mrs Burns and Anna Parks both gave birth within little more than a week of each other. Afterwards, Anna gave her baby up to Robert, and Jean looked after the little girl, along with her own. Anna Parks disappeared from the local scene after that, and it was said she later married a soldier. A friend asked Jean if she wasn't angry at Robert for this behaviour but she just replied, 'Oor Robin should hae had twa wives.'

Robert had also been writing letters in support of a male friend who was in trouble. Indeed, he went to quite extraordinary lengths in his efforts to help his friend, who was James Clarke, the principal schoolmaster in Moffat. The patronage of the school was in the hands of the lords of the magistrates and town council of Edinburgh. Robert not only drafted a letter for Clarke to send to the Lord Provost of Edinburgh, but wrote himself to many influential people he knew in attempts to prevent Clarke from losing his job. He told one friend that Clarke was 'suffering severely under the persecution of one or two malicious but powerful individuals of his employers'. Robert had never lifted a finger against his own children and always believed in teaching by getting them interested in any subject. His letter to a friend about Clarke was therefore uncharacteristically robust.

'He is accused of harshness to some perverse dunces that were placed under his care' he wrote. 'God help the teacher,

231

a man of genius and sensibility, for such is my friend Clarke, when the blockhead father presents him his booby son, and insists on having the rays of science lighted up in a fellow's head whose skull is impervious and inaccessible to any other way than a positive fracture with a cudgel!'

Robert, while the dispute was going on and despite the fact that he could little afford it, gave his friend the loan of quite a large sum of money.

Ultimately everything was settled in the schoolmaster's favour and Robert sent him a note saying, 'Bravo! Clarke. In spite of Hopeton and his myridons thou camest off victorious!'

His delight at this was soon swamped by the news that Mrs Nancy MacElhose was leaving for Jamaica to rejoin her husband and try for a reconciliation. All his romantic dreams came back to him in a torrent of emotion that poured out in a hasty scrawl on a card in the Sanquar Post Office. He immediately posted the card as a parting gift.

> Ae fond kiss and then we sever!
> Ae fareweel, and then forever!
> Deep in heart-wrung tears I'll pledge thee,
> Warring sighs and groans I'll wage thee.
>
> Who shall say that fortune grieves him,
> While the Star of Hope she leaves him?
> Me, nae cheerful twinkle lights me,
> Dark despair around benights me.
>
> I'll ne'er blame my partial fancy;
> Naething could resist my Nancy!
> But to see her was to love her,
> Love but her and love forever.
> Had we never lov'd sae kindly,
> Had we never lov'd sae blindly,
> Never met or never parted,
> We had ne'er been brokenhearted . . .

His general health was not good and he was finding his life harder and harder to cope with. He never seemed to get a minute's peace. He was a sociable man but the number of visitors coming to his farm from every part of Scotland, eager to meet the Bard, was becoming exhausting. He had recently been listed for promotion to Supervisor and so he decided he must give up Ellisland and farming for good. He would move permanently to Dumfries. He'd had more than enough of the rigours of farming and the move would also cut down the amount of riding he had to do, too often in terrible weather, that increased his aches and pains and feverish symptoms. It would also stop him having to spend so many nights away from home.

The crops and farming effects were auctioned off and a crowd came to fight for what they regarded as a bit of Poet Burns. Robert told Alexander in disgust that he'd never seen such drunkenness. Folk were lying about and decanting, causing even the dogs to get so drunk they couldn't stand.

He remained sober throughout, just as he'd done at the Riddell household when there had been a competition for 'The Whistle'. This whistle was of historical significance and was always awarded to the person who could match everyone drink for drink and be the last person able to blow it after everyone else had become unconscious.

Riddell had invited two neighbouring land owners to take part in the competition for the trophy. After the dinner, Robert was elected to sit at a separate small table and watch that there was fair play. Two bottles had been placed in front of him but he asked the servant to bring him pen and paper and while the marathon drinking spree was going on with Riddell and his wealthy neighbours, Robert composed a song. Eventually, after the other men were carried to bed, he walked home.

Once the farm was handed over, Robert packed everything, including his wife and family, into a cart and they set off for Dumfries trailing Jean's milk cow on a rope behind them. The family with them consisted of Robert and Jean, and their sons

– Robert aged four, Francis aged two, William aged eight months – as well as Elizabeth Parks, Anna Parks' daughter by Robert.

Dumfries was a densely packed, bustling place that crammed along the ridge of the bend of the river Nith. It had a hospital, a poor house, several boarding schools for young ladies, a weekly newspaper, two libraries and branches of three Scottish banks. There were horse and cattle fairs, and mail coaches to and from London, Edinburgh and Portpatrick.

It was a low-lying town and surrounded by undrained marshland which caused the place often to have a pall of cloud hanging low over it. It was humid and oppressive in the summer months and very dank and chilly every winter.

When the river was in spate, it burst its banks and caused distressing flooding. The High Street ran parallel to the river and off it were about a dozen vennels or lanes at right angles. Robert and his family settled in the middle floor of a tenement in the Wee Vennel. It was more often known, however, as the Stinking Vennel because of the rubbish and raw sewage which flooded down its gutters and into the river. The only place Robert found to get some peace to write or study was in a middle room no larger than a bed closet.

The town had a busy social life, helped by three large inns, several taverns, a coffee house and seventy-five smaller premises licensed to sell spirits, not to mention illegal drinking dens. Here nevertheless was a focal point for people with moderate income who enjoyed polite society. The Assembly Rooms were a regular meeting place for well-to-do residents, and a glittering addition to the social scene was provided by the officers of the Fencible infantry and cavalry regiments stationed in the town.

In the flat above the Burns family was George Haugh, the local blacksmith. The flat below was the office of the Distributor of Stamps for Dumfries and Galloway. He was a man called John Syme and soon became one of Robert's closest friends.

Robert's friendship with the Riddells continued and he

helped Maria to get some of her prose work published. She had written an account of her stay in the West Indies. Robert gave her an introduction to the printer, Willie Smellie, when she went to Edinburgh to visit her husband's relatives.

He wrote, 'Mrs Riddell, who takes this letter to town with her, is a character that, even in your own way as a Naturalist and Philosopher, would be an acquisition to your acquaintance . . . To be impartial, however, the lady has one unlucky failing, a failing you will easily discover, as she seems rather pleased with indulging in it – where she dislikes or despises, she is apt to make no more a secret of it than where she esteems and respects . . . '

His family now settled in the Wee Vennel, Robert took up new duties in the Port Division. He was immediately plunged into a dangerous job of leading a company of dragoons to capture a French smuggling vessel. He succeeded in bringing the ship and its crew into Dumfries harbour. His courage and success in doing this would have merited much praise from his superiors. However, the next day at the public auction of the ship's effects, Robert bought the ship's four guns and dispatched them, at his own expense, to the rebels of the French Convention. This, for a servant of the Crown, was not – to say the least – a wise thing to do. But Burns was finding it more and more difficult to curb his democratic beliefs and feelings. He'd managed to express them in various ways. He'd written songs, 'A Parcel of Rogues in a Nation' and 'Scots, Wha Hae'. The last verse of 'Scots, Wha Hae' was a rousing,

> Lay the proud usurpers low!
> Tyrants, fall in every foe!
> Liberty's in every blow!
> Let us do, or die!

Robert could have been in serious trouble, especially in connection with the guns. He escaped dismissal or being officially censured because an influential friend reminded the

Excise Commissioner that both he and Burns were Royal Arch Masons. Instead of dismissal, Robert was severely reprimanded and warned about his future conduct. He was also told that he should be obedient and not think. Robert tried to defend his right to think, and his democratic beliefs. He wrote to the Excise Commissioner of his 'independent British mind, oppression might bend but could not subdue'.

'Have not I, to me', he said, 'a more precious stake in my country's welfare than the richest Dukedom in it? I have a large family of children, and the probability of more. I have three sons whom, I see already, have brought with them into the world souls ill-qualified to inhabit the bodies of slaves. Can I look tamely on, and see any machinations to wrest from the birthright of my boys, the little independent Britons in whose veins runs my own blood? No! I will not! Should my heart stream around my attempt to defend it!

'Does any man tell me, that my feeble efforts can be of no service; and that it does not belong to my humble station to meddle with the concerns of a People? I tell him that it is on such individuals as I, that for the hand of support and the eye of intelligence, a nation has to rest. The uninformed mob may swell the nation's bulk; and the titled, tinsel courtly throng may be its feathered ornament, but the number of those who are elevated enough in life, to reason and reflect; yet low enough to keep clear of the venal contagion of a Court; these are a nation's strength.'

He survived the cannonade and subsequent political indiscretions, but none of them came anywhere near making him suffer the different kind of anguish that was yet to come.

33

Alexander told himself that he'd be doing his friend a favour. Robert himself admitted that he was getting absolutely exhausted with not only so many strangers coming to his door, but also the local gentry inviting him to join them in one social occasion or another. Coming home in the evening after riding for many miles, aching in every bone, he wanted and needed to relax with his family.

Isobel was one of the worst offenders – indeed *the* worst – in putting social pressures on Robert. Apart from anything else, it wasn't decent for a married woman to be seeking another man's company so much, or raving about him so much. The Riddells were nearly as bad. Isobel and Susanna had become friends with the Riddells and were included in their social evenings. Robert was always their honoured guest, of course. When Isobel had her soirées, the Riddells cam – more to have yet another opportunity to be in the company of Scotland's Bard, as he was so often referred to now.

The Riddells were the most influential family in the area. If, somehow, they could take a different view of Burns, if they for some reason ostracised him, then all the local gentry would follow suit.

As a result, Robert would have the peace he needed. Even Isobel, for all her admiration of the man, was, he knew, very conscious of what was required by etiquette and society, especially the upper realms of the rural society she was proud to be part of. There were unwritten rules and invisible barriers over which one did not step. Isobel was carried away by Robert because she believed he was not only a genius, but a *gentleman*.

Alexander thought of a plan. They were all going to the Riddells for supper. There were other friends of the Riddells there including a party of officers. During supper, Alexander could see that the young officers at the table were feeling put out by Burns' sparkling conversation and by how he was entertaining the ladies and taking up all their attention. Alexander knew that they would be more than willing to take Burns down a peg or two. After the supper, the ladies retired to the drawing room and left the men to their 'toasts' and 'healths'.

Sometimes Robert retired with the ladies to avoid the heavy and prolonged drinking. It played so much havoc with his digestive system and nervous headaches. On this occasion, Alexander persuaded him to stay with the men, most of whom were wearing the King's uniform. All of them, especially Alexander, kept diverting Robert with stories of people they'd met while abroad. Robert was particularly intrigued with French people and the state of the nation there. At the same time, Burns' glass kept being refilled. Alexander knew of course that it took very little to make Burns drunk. Soon he became very drunk and fired up to a degree of reckless abandonment.

Alexander proposed 'a rag'. They were all to re-enact the 'Rape of the Sabine Women'. Each of the men would be a Roman and each was allotted a woman. Robert, who had become very enthusiastic about the theatre and any kind of acting, had no problem agreeing to the supposed play acting. They were all going to dash into the drawing room together, pounce on the woman allocated to each 'Roman' and kiss her.

As planned, they burst open the drawing room door. But all the men held back in the shadows of the other room while Robert rushed in, grabbed Maria Riddell and kissed her passionately. The shocked silence in the room made Robert suddenly realise that he was alone. All the ladies, especially Maria, were horrified and affronted. Robert realised that he had been the victim of a trick.

When the men entered the room, they pretended to be shocked at the animal behaviour of a common gauger. So at the root of it, it was a question of class. A gauger in liquor had insulted and affronted a lady of the 'quality' and in front of other members of the gentry. Class, after all, was class. Such behaviour was unforgivable.

Burns was ordered from the house. Speechless with shame, he left alone and in disgrace to travel back to Dumfries. He was near to tears in the acuteness of his anguish. Next day he wrote a long letter. Although it began the words, 'To the men of the company I make no apology . . . insisted on my drinking more than I chose . . . no right to blame me . . . ', it went on: 'But to you, madam, I have much to apologise for. Your good opinion I valued as one of the greatest acquisitions I had made on earth, and I was truly a beast to forfeit it. To all the ladies I present my humblest contritions for my conduct, and my petition for their gracious pardon . . . an intoxicated man is the vilest of beasts . . . it is not in my nature to be brutal to any one . . . to be rude to a woman, when in my senses, was impossible with me.'

His letter did nothing to reverse the situation. Maria and the rest of the Riddells ignored him, snubbed him. Not only the Riddells; all the local gentry did the same. Even Isobel McKenzie passed him in the street.

Susanna was the only one who came to speak to him and try to give him comfort. She said she agreed it was a stupid and cruel trick. She had heard the men sniggering behind the door and knew it had been their plan to humiliate him.

She was sure that Alexander was sorry for any part he had played in what had happened. Alexander had not contacted him in person, but had written apologising for any part he might have unwittingly taken during the evening. He said he had been so drunk, he could not remember. Now he had loyalty to his wife to consider and they had decided to go to Edinburgh to visit her parents. Robert said he knew who would be to blame.

It would be the young officers – snobbish, epauletted puppies – trying to put the ploughman gauger in his place.

He did not care about them. They were not worth thinking about. But he cared very deeply about losing the friendship of Maria and Elizabeth, and Elizabeth's husband, his dear friend Robert Riddell.

And of course, Alexander. He knew that Alexander would have to consider his wife but he was grateful when eventually Alexander came to see him on his own.

'Isobel, alas,' Alexander said, 'refuses to have anything more to do with you, Robert.'

Every apology to the Riddells was ignored and Robert continued to be passed on the street with only an icy glance, especially by Maria and Elizabeth. Robert's anguish and regret turned to hurt and anger, then to nastiness and a desire to wound. But he was deeply touched by Susanna's loyalty. She visited him as often as she could and he tried to show his gratitude for her continuing and devoted friendship by reading his poems to her. He knew this pleased her greatly.

He tried to concentrate on his song writing. He wrote 'The Deil's awa' wi' th'Exciseman', among others. Also, he composed love songs, 'Bonie Wee Thing' and 'Wilt Thou be my Dearie?'. However, he was finding himself once more on dangerous ground with the Excise authorities. He was aware of their watching presence. They were now suspicious about his *The Rights of Women*. They suspected it mirrored *The Rights of Man* by Thomas Paine. Paine's book had been banned. It was a dangerous business to own a copy, as Robert did. He was also aware that he had enemies in and around Dumfries. Someone kept spreading rumours about him. One rumour being spread was that he'd remained seated in the theatre with his hat on when 'God Save the King' was sung, while everyone else stood up with their heads uncovered.

Robert tried to keep silent. But for a man with such a democratic tongue it was painfully frustrating. He had at least to try, for the sake of providing some substance for his wife and children. For their sakes as much as his own, he struggled to avoid the fate of Paine and Thomas Muir. Paine had been tried, in absentia, in London and outlawed from England forever. Muir, an enthusiastic follower of Paine, had been sentenced to fourteen years' penal servitude in Botany Bay.

Robert was accused of being too pro-France. He certainly disliked the Tory administration of William Pitt and had nothing but contempt for the reigning royals, the House of Hanover, but he had complete loyalty to his country and his people. He could not deny, however, like Fox and the Whig party Fox led, his complete opposition to war: 'War I deprecate, ruin and misery to thousands are in the blast that announces the destructive demon.'

He was an anti-militarist who yearned for the brotherhood of man. In this most dangerous political climate, he was going to publish more dangerous verses but his friends kept him back and persuaded him to give his copy of Paine's *The Rights of Man* and other radical books to a neighbour, George Haugh the blacksmith, to hide in his house.

Susanna also pleaded with him to be more careful. She even offered to take away his 'dangerous books', as she called them, and hide them herself. He smiled at her childish eagerness. He thanked her and explained that he could not get her involved and risk causing her any trouble. Despite his friends' entreaties, he still managed to go ahead and express his dearly held beliefs in song.

> Is there, for honest poverty
> That hings his head, and a' that?
> The coward-slave, we pass him by —
> We dare be poor for a' that!
>
> For a' that and a' that,
> Our toils obscure, and a' that,
> The rank is but the guinea's stamp —
> The man's the gowd for a' that.   (gold)

What tho' on hamely fare we dine –
Wear hoddin grey, and a' that?
Gie fools their skills and knaves their wine –
A man's a man for a' that;
For a' that and a' that,
Their tinsel show, and a' that;
The honest man, though e'er sae poor,
Is king o' men for a' that.

Ye see yon birkie ca'ed a lord,   (conceited fellow)
Wha struts, and stares, and a' that;
Tho' hundreds worship at his word,
He's but a coof for a' that;   (fool)
His ribband, star, and a' that.
The man of independent mind,
He looks and laughs at a' that.

A prince can mak' a belted knight,
A marquis, duke and a' that;
But an honest man's aboon his might,
Guide faith he mauna fa' that! (may not lay claim to)
For a' that and a' that;
Their dignities and a' that;
The pith o' sense, and pride o' worth,
Are higher rank than a' that.

Then let us pray that come it may,
As come it will for a' that,
That sense and worth, o'er a' the earth,
May bear the gree and a' that;   (come off best)
For a' that, and a' that,
It's comin' yet for a' that,
That man to man, the warld o'er,
Shall brothers be for a' that!

He had also been writing letters and poems (often under a pseudonym) for a London newspaper and the paper then offered him a post in London as a reporter and general contributor at a good salary. He felt he had to decline.

'Your offer is indeed truly generous', he wrote, 'and most sincerely do I thank you for it; but in my present situation, I find that I dare not accept it. You well know my political sentiments; and were I an insular individual, unconnected with a wife and family of children, with the most fervid enthusiasm I would have volunteered my services: I then could and would have despised all consequences that might have ensued.'

He said he would write an occasional piece if he could do it in a way that would be safe from the spies with which his correspondence was now beset.

Troubles and worries of one kind and another came fast and furious. He was deeply upset on hearing of Robert Riddell's death and immediately composed a sonnet for the *Dumfries Journal* which he said was 'a small heart-felt tribute to the memory of the man I loved'. His rheumatic pains increased with a terrible fever. He was in agony from head to toe. A local man he'd become friendly with and who shared his political views was a doctor – William Maxwell – and he came to attend to him. Maxwell had seen something of the Revolution in France and had once joined the National Guard there. Previously Robert had told Mrs Dunlop, 'Maxwell is my most intimate friend . . . on account of his politics is rather shunned by some high aristocrats, though his family and fortune entitle him to the first circles.'

Robert admired Maxwell enormously and was grateful to him for his many visits while the fever and rheumatic pains were at their worst, and especially grateful that he did not expect immediate payment for his medical services. Robert's Excise pay had dropped severely and he was acutely worried about how to keep feeding his family.

Then, while he was still suffering from his illness, Elizabeth, his much loved and only daughter by his wife died while at Mauchline. He was distraught. He was not even able to travel to the child's funeral. He still had not recovered from this blow when he wrote some months later to Mrs Dunlop, 'I am so poorly today as to be scarce able to hold my pen, and so deplorably stupid as to be totally unable to hold it to any purpose. I know you are pretty deep read in medical matters but I fear you have nothing in the *Materia Medica* which can heal a diseased spirit.'

Because he'd had to run into debt with his landlord, he'd added wearily, 'I think that the poet's old companion, Poverty, is to be my attendant to my grave.'

Jean soon presented him with another chil – a son that he called James Glencairn. He explained that the name was 'in grateful memory of my lamented patron – I shall make all my children's names altars of gratitude'.

He was grateful also to be given – albeit temporarily – the post of Supervisor because of the illness of the normal superior, Findlater. It meant a welcome, though not very large rise in his salary. Because of the war, things were very bad for the Excise with no French imports. Everybody was affected financially. He also thought the offer of the post might mean his political indiscretion had been forgiven and forgotten.

He had to work hard for a few extra pounds. There were long days in the saddle, sometimes starting at five o'clock with a fourteen-hour day. The monotonous creaking of leather saddle and stirrups as the sturdy pony plodded on endlessly almost sent him to sleep. Only the raw chaffing of his inner thighs and the cramping of his muscles kept him from dropping off. He had to stand up on the stirrups to ease the stiffness in his spine and buttocks, before slumping back into the saddle.

On Christmas Eve, he had to ride forty miles and visit twenty traders through hard frosts and heavy snowfalls. He tried to keep his spirits up and use sheer willpower to keep going. What strengthened his will more than anything was the fact that he desperately needed the money. What would happen after Findlater returned, he dared not think.

He worried that the powers in the Excise were just using him at the moment because they knew he was the only officer who could do the job as well as, if not better than, Findlater. The spies and the enemies would still be there, ready to pounce on any excuse to ruin him.

The world situation was no better. The Revolution in France had been taken over by men of property who were now moving to protect their ambitious plans. They did not want the Revolution to go any further towards democracy. Jacobins were guillotined. The dreams of liberty, equality and fraternity were being killed. This was the France that was now threatening to invade Britain.

With his usual and remarkable method of walking a dangerous political tightrope, he expressed his rebel streak and put his message across in the poems and songs about the world brotherhood of man. At the same time, as a fop to the establishment and for the sake of his family's welfare, he joined the Dumfries Volunteers. He even wrote a song for them, 'Does Haughty Gaul Invasion Threat'.

He knew his every utterance was being carefully scrutinised. Well, let's see what they make of that, he thought.

34

Robert wrote to his old friend, Mrs Dunlop, 'May life to you be a positive blessing while it lasts, for your own sake; and may it yet be greatly prolonged, is my wish for my own sake and for the sake of the rest of your friends! What a transient business is life! Very lately I was a boy; but t'other day I was a young man; and I already begin to feel the rigid fibre and stiffening joints of old age coming fast o'er my frame . . . '

He then went on at some length about his democratic views and in the process also made derogatory remarks about the French royal family. After that, he never heard from Mrs Dunlop again. He could not fathom how he had offended the old woman. Mrs Dunlop had warned him more than once, of course, not to express his political opinions to her because she could not agree with them. Four of her sons and one of her grandsons were army officers. One of her daughters had been married to a Frenchman and another married a Royalist refugee. But for years now, he had always been frank with her, and she with him. Now, even when he wrote telling her of his illness and the death of his little daughter, he was met with stony silence. He was deeply distressed. This loss, on top of the many other worries and troubles he was suffering, was very hard to bear.

To add to his financial worries, he had an extra, rather large expense. As a member of the Dumfries Volunteers, he had to have his uniform made by a tailor who was himself a member of the corps. The uniforms had all to be paid for by the members – white kerseymer breeches and waistcoat, short blue coat faced with red and a round hat surrounded by bearskin, similar to the helmets of the Horseguards.

All the Volunteers had to turn out in the park several times a week for drill and target practice. Soon, Robert became as quick with his musket as with his pen. His song, 'Does Haughty Gaul Invasion Threat', became a great favourite and not just locally, despite its last line in which behind Burns the patriot, Burns the democrat could still be glimpsed:

> But while we sing God Save The King
> We'll ne'er forget The People!

Robert was unable to attend the inaugural march through Dumfries because of a severe attack of toothache, but he did manage to keep up the drills in the park. In private to his friend Syme (also a Volunteer), he called the Dumfries Royal Volunteers the 'awkward squad'.

But Syme said, 'Well you've surprised us, Robert, with your dexterity in handling arms.' Syme told another friend, 'Burns and I are one and indivisible, but what with his occupation and mine, we meet only by starts – or at least occasionally – and we drink as many cups of tea as bottles of wine together. We are two of the best privates in the Dumfries Royal Volunteers. But not to flatter myself nor him, I would say that hang me if I should know how to be happy were he not in the way of making me so at times.'

One light appeared on Robert's otherwise bleak horizon and he suspected his dear little Susanna had had something to do with it. Maria Riddell wrote to him enclosing some poetry she had penned and asking for his opinion. He was thankful that at last she had forgiven him and that this was a first step in renewing their friendship. Maria invited him to accompany her on the King's birthday celebration but he was so exhausted with the constant pain in his joints he was suffering, he had to refuse her invitation.

'I am in such miserable health', he wrote. 'Rackt as I am with rheumatisms, I meet every face with a greeting like that of Balate of Balaam – "Come curse me Jacob; and come defy me Israel." So, say I, come curse me that east-wind; and come defy me the north!'

He was struggling as defiantly as he could but as well as the pain, his financial worries kept increasing, partly because of a move from the Wee Vennel to bigger accommodation to house his growing family. The new house was in the Millbrae Vennel. It was a substantial, two-storey dwelling house with a comfortable parlour in which they could entertain guests, although now he had little, if any, strength left for entertaining. He concentrated as much as he was able on the education and religious instruction of his children. He read the Bible to them every night as his father had done before him. He would leave his children, however, to decide for themselves when they were older what their views on religion would be.

He never ceased worrying about Jean and the children and the poverty he might leave them in. His Excise income had now been halved. In desperation, he wrote to his old friend, the schoolteacher James Clarke. In addition to helping Clarke a few years before, he had also loaned him money that Clarke was still paying back in instalments. In acute embarrassment, he asked if Clarke could send him an advance of a guinea from the next payment due. Clarke did so immediately.

Some time later, Robert was forced to write again. Delicacy forbade him from sounding as if he was only calling in a debt. Instead he made excuses and apologies as if he were asking a favour: 'My dear Clarke,

'Still, still the victim of affliction, were you to see the emaciated figure who now holds the pen to you, you would not know your old friend. Whether I shall ever get about again, is only known to HIM, the Great Unknown, whose creature I am. Alas, Clarke, I begin to fear the worst! As to my individual self, I am tranquil; I would despise myself if I were not; but Burns' poor widow! and half a dozen of his dear little ones, helpless orphans, there I am weak as a woman's tear – Enough of this! 'tis half my disease! –

'I duly received your last, enclosing the note. – It came extremely in time, and I was much obliged to your punctuality. – Again I must request you to do me the same kindness. – Be so very good as *by return of post* to inclose me another note. – I trust you can do it without much inconvenience, and it will seriously oblige me . . . '

He was also forced to write to Thomson, his musical publisher, saying, 'After all my boasted independence, curst necessity compels me to implore you to send five pounds . . . For God's sake, send me that sum, and send it by return of post . . . '

Thomson, only too aware of the hundreds of songs Robert had given him without any payment in return, sent the five pounds at once. Indeed, Robert was still struggling to write and supply songs for Thomson, like 'Fairest Maid on Devon Banks'. And

> O, my luve's like a red, red rose,
> That's newly sprung in June:
> O, my luve's like the melodie
> That's sweetly play'd in tune.

This song made Susanna weep. But she was weeping at the sight of him as much as the sound of the song.

'I'm sorry, it's so beautiful,' she sobbed.

His Bonnie Jean held Susanna close and comforted her as he would like to have done. He doubted, however, if he would have the strength any more.

His friend and doctor, Maxwell, tried potion after potion in an effort to help him, all to no effect. Eventually, he advised Robert to 'take the waters'. By that, he meant that Robert should travel to Brow, a hamlet on the shores of the Solway, drink the water from the well, ride daily and walk every day up to his armpits in the waters of the Solway. Robert had his doubts about all this as a cure. He was even more doubtful that he would have the strength to either go riding or to plunge into the water every day. However, he decided to take Maxwell's word for it and to try his very best to carry out his friend's advice.

Brow was almost ten miles from Dumfries and so, at the beginning of July, Robert rode painfully out of the town and headed for the decayed and dismal hamlet of Brow. The place was used as a staging post by the cattle drovers taking their herds south to England. There were only a few run-down cottages and a very rough and ready inn where Robert lodged in a bedroom at the back.

It took all his spirit and manliness to struggle every day to the shore and force himself, despite his pain and the palpitations of his heart, to submerge himself in the icy water. Soon after he arrived, he heard that Maria Riddell had gone to nearby Lochmaben for her own health's sake. She invited him to dine with her and sent her carriage to fetch him.

She wrote of this meeting, 'I was struck by his appearance on entering the room. The stamp of death was imprinted on his features. He seemed already touching the brink of eternity. His first salutation was: "Well, madam, have you any commands for the other world?" I replied, that it seemed a doubtful case which of us should be the soonest, and that I hoped he would yet live to write my epitaph. He looked in my face with an air of great kindness, and expressed his concern at seeing me look so ill, with his accustomed sensibility. At table he ate little or nothing, and he complained of having entirely lost the tone of his stomach. We had a long and serious conversation about his present situation, and the approaching termination of all his earthly prospects. He spoke of his death without any of the ostentation of philosophy, but with firmness as well as feeling, as an event likely to happen very soon, and which gave him concern chiefly from leaving his four children so young and unprotected, and his wife in so interesting a situation – in hourly expectation on the lying-in of a fifth. He mentioned, with seeming pride and satisfaction, the promising genius of his eldest son, and the flattering remarks of approbation he had received from his teachers, and dwelt particularly on his hopes of that boy's future conduct and merit. His anxiety for his family seemed to hang heavy upon him, and the more perhaps from the reflection that he had not done them all the justice he was so well qualified to do.

'Passing from this subject, he shewed great concern about the care of his literary fame, and particularly the publication of his posthumous works. He said he was well aware that his death would occasion some noise, and that every scrap of writing would be revived against him to the injury of his future reputation: that letters and verses written with unguarded and improper freedom, and which he earnestly wished to have buried in oblivion, would be handed about by idle vanity or malevolence when no dread of his resentment would restrain them or prevent the censures of shrill-tongued malice or the insidious sarcasms of envy from pouring forth all their venom to blast his fame.

'He lamented that he had written many epigrams on persons against whom he entertained no enmity, and whose characters he should be sorry to wound; and many indifferent poetical pieces which he feared would now, with all their imperfections on their head, be thrust upon the world. On this account, he deeply regretted having deferred to put his papers in a state of arrangement, as he was now quite incapable of the exertion . . . The conversation was kept up with great evenness and animation on his side. I had seldom seen his mind greater or more collected. There was frequently a considerable degree of vivacity in his sallies, and they would probably have had a greater share, had not the concern and dejection I could not disguise damped the spirit of pleasantry he seemed not unwilling to indulge.

'We parted about sunset on the evening of that day; the next day I saw him again, and we parted to meet no more!'

Robert wrote to his friend Alexander Cunningham, from

whom he'd just received a very comforting letter, 'Alas! my friend, I fear the voice of the Bard will soon be heard among you no more! For these eight or ten months I have been ailing, sometimes bedfast & sometimes not; but these last three months I have been tortured with an excruciating rheumatism, which has reduced me to nearly the last stage. – You actually would not know me if you saw me. – Pale emaciated, & so feeble as occasionally to need help from my chair – my spirits fled! fled! – but I can no more on the subject – '

He promised to send his friend some songs after he returned to Dumfries, then continued: 'Apropos to being at home, Mrs Burns threatens in a week or two, to add one more to my Paternal charge, which, if the right gender, I intend shall be introduced to the world by the respectable designation of Alexander Cunningham Burns. My last was James Glencairn, so you can have no objection to the company of Nobility.'

By this time, Robert had lost his appetite and all he could swallow was a little thin porridge laced with port. His landlord did not have any port, and when Robert's bottle ran out, he had to struggle to the nearest inn a mile distant. Arriving there, Robert put the empty bottle on the counter and asked if the innkeeper, John Burney, had any port for sale. Robert added, in painful embarrassment, that he had no cash to pay for it but he offered his Armorial seal, the recent gift from George Thomson by way of payment for some of his songs. Robert began unfastening the seal from his watch fob but the landlady stamped on the floor in distress and indignation and her husband took Robert in his arms, gave him the port and led him gently to the door with tears in his eyes.

A few days after that, Robert was well enough to visit the manse of Ruthwell and have a cup of tea with the minister's wife, her daughters and a friend of theirs. It was a lovely sunny afternoon. The friend later described the visit: 'His altered appearance excited much silent sympathy; and the evening being beautiful, and the sun shining brightly through the casement, Miss Craig was afraid the light might be too much for him, and rose with the view of letting down the window-blinds. Burns immediately guessed what she meant; and, regarding the young lady with a look of great benignity, said: "Thank you, my dear, for your kind attention: but oh, let him shine: he will not shine long for me!"'

While he was at Brow, Robert managed to write a few letters. One was a final despairing plea for reconciliation with Mrs Dunlop. He was heartbroken when it was ignored. Well aware of and bitterly resenting the malicious slanders which were circulating about him and no doubt would increase after he was gone, he wrote to another friend, 'Some of our folks about the Excise Office, Edinburgh, had and perhaps still have concerns and prejudices against me as being a drunken, dissipated character. – I might be all this, you know, and yet be an honest fellow, but you know that. – I am an honest fellow and nothing of this.'

Another letter was to his cousin James, who on hearing of Robert's circumstances, had earlier written offering financial assistance. Robert wrote, 'When you offered me money assistance – little did I think I would want it so soon . . . A rascal of a haberdasher to whom I owe a considerable bill taking it into his head that I am dying, has commenced a process against me and will infallibly put my emaciated body into jail. – Will you be so good as to accommodate me, and that by return of post, with ten pound. – O James! did you know that the pride of my heart, you would feel double for me! Alas! I am not used to beg!'

The haberdasher's bill for a few pounds had only been a run-of-the-mill letter sent out to every customer reminding them of outstanding payments due. By this time, however, Robert was in such a feverish and weakened state, he had become confused and reverted to the horrors of penury that had been his father's fate and had blighted his childhood.

He was in torment too with the fear of what might happen to his own children. He had an urgent need to get back to them and his bonnie Jean, who was in the last stages of her latest pregnancy. He wrote to her to tell her he was returning to Dumfries: 'My dearest love . . . '

Oh, how he loved and needed her.

35

It was a sickness of the heart and mind. Alexander knew it. It had taken such root in him, it reached to his very soul. He struggled to control it but it was always there – even when Burns was taken ill, even when he had moved to Brow, even when he saw the man was dying, he could not completely banish the blackness in himself. He could not capture again the light of love he had once felt for his friend.

For a time, Alexander had thought things had changed. Isobel stopped speaking to Burns. She held herself aloof. She even passed him on the street. But Susanna kept trying to make excuses for him, kept insisting that nothing was the poet's fault. It was the foolish and spiteful young officers who had played a malicious trick on Burns who were to blame. Isobel began to soften. He could see it. Then they learned that Maria Riddell had contacted Burns and reawakened their friendship.

Susanna determined to visit him and Alexander felt he had to accompany her. They even visited him in Brow. He could see that Burns had become very fond of Susanna but he guessed, as with Ainsley's sister, that Burns would never flirt with his friend's sister. However, Burns had given Susanna a poem, which she had allowed no-one to see. So precious was it to her, she carried it about with her and was often seen reading it over to herself. She must have it well off by heart by now. But she was a strange girl at times. He couldn't make out whether she liked the poem, or it distressed her.

Then Isobel started talking of going with them to visit Burns. Alexander forbade it, saying that she would be too distressed at the sight of him. Susanna agreed with this.

'Oh, Isobel, it would break your heart. It breaks my heart to look at him in his present state. If he improves a little, I shall let you know and we will go together. Alexander is right – knowing you to be a lady of such sensitivity, he realises, as I do, that you would be too upset.'

'Susanna,' Alexander explained, 'has gone through such trauma when she witnessed her husband's suffering. It has prepared her to some extent but you, my dear, have had no experience of illness.'

Susanna said, 'I'm trying to persuade Alexander to overrule Maxwell, Robert's doctor, and do something to help the poet. Maxwell is doing him no good whatsoever. Quite the reverse, I think.'

Alexander sighed. 'Maxwell is Robert's friend, Susanna. Robert has total faith in him and I'm sure the good doctor is doing his very best.'

Of this Alexander had no doubt. He also knew that Maxwell's best was not good enough. He knew that despite exercise and cold water bathing being the generally accepted treatment used by every medical man for miles around, it was not good enough. He believed that rest and warmth would have been a far more successful treatment for Robert's rheumatic fever and what, he felt sure, was a serious heart condition resulting from the fever – unlike Maxwell, who had diagnosed it as 'flying gout'.

However, he, Doctor Alexander Wallace, had too often been pooh-poohed and disbelieved for his 'fancy modern notions'. Patients in Ayrshire had deserted him in droves in preference for his father's old-fashioned methods. They would do so again if he tried. Burns would prefer to continue putting his trust in his much-loved friend, Maxwell. Sometimes, sitting by the bedside, he caught Burns staring at him with large, sad eyes and he wondered with a little spurt of panic if there was reproach in that stare, if Burns could see what was in his mind and heart and soul.

He would quickly take Burns' hand in his, and smile at him, and ask him if there was anything he could do for him. Burns would smile in return and shake his head.

Susanna would sit at the bedside and she and Burns would smile at each other, almost as if they shared a secret. Or there was some unspoken understanding between them that he was not privy to. Alexander suspected that Susanna did not want to share Burns with Isobel, and that was why she had persuaded his wife to stay away. But he knew that Isobel would come sooner or later. He tried not to think of that. He could not bear to see her smile at Burns and look at him with a tenderness and love that she had never shown to him.

But Burns would die and that would be an end of it. He tried not to think of that either. It made him feel emotionally confused, sad and agonisingly guilty. He should have told Burns what he thought of the daily painful, courageous walk into the icy waters of the Solway. He should have taken his friend in his arms and physically stopped him. He should wrapped him in a warm blanket and led him back to warmth and safety.

But such thoughts were unbearable now. He told himself instead that he could not have gone against another doctor's advice. It would have been unethical to interfere in the treatment of another doctor's patient. Anyway, Robert would not have allowed it. The doctor in question was one of his most admired and closest friends.

No, he'd done what he could by visiting Robert as often as possible, and being there to try to support him by his company and loyal friendship. He had also tried to help and advise Jean who was in the last stages of her pregnancy. He advised her to rest. He told her she needed to get someone in to nurse Robert. She had taken his advice and now a neighbour's daughter came in regularly. A young woman called Jessie Lewars. At Burns' request she sang all his songs to him and her sweet singing voice seemed to soothe him.

One day, with hardly enough strength to lift a pen, Robert wrote a poem for her.

> O wert thou in the cauld blast
> On yonder lea, on yonder lea,
> My plaidie to the angry airt,
> I'd shelter thee, I'd shelter thee.
> Or did misfortune's bitter storms
> Around thee blaw, around thee blaw;
> Thy bield should be my bosom,
> To share it a', to share it a'.
>
> Or were I in the wildest waste,
> Sae black and bare, sae black and bare,
> That desert were a paradise,
> If thou wert there, if thou wert there;
> Or were I monarch o' the globe,
> Wi' thee to reign, wi' thee to reign;
> The brightest jewel in my crown
> Wad be my queen, wad be my queen.

The facility with which he'd thought of such a beautiful poem, of any poem at all in such impossibly difficult circumstances, forced Alexander to admit to himself that the man must be a born genius.

Every time he and Susanna went to see Burns now, they had to crush through crowds that had gathered in the street outside his door. Word had spread around that he was dying and Dumfries had become like a town besieged. The last time they'd gone, Burns' friend Syme and another fellow Volunteer, John Gibson, were at the bedside with tears in their eyes. Burns managed with some of his old, wry humour, 'Don't let the awkward squad fire over me, John.'

When Doctor Maxwell arrived, Burns said, 'What has brought you here? I am but a poor crow, and not worth picking. I haven't feathers enough to carry me to my grave.' He pointed to his pistols. 'Take these, Maxwell. I couldn't leave them in better hands.' Alexander knew that this was meant to serve as payment for the doctor's bills and Maxwell knew it too.

Maxwell sent Burns' children across the road to Jessie Lewars' home so that the poet could have peace and quiet. Jean was ordered to the next room and to bed. After a time, Syme and Gibson became so overcome by emotion that they had to leave. Half way through the night, Maxwell also left, promising to return first thing in the morning.

Alexander could see that Burns was not liable to last until his doctor friend returned and so he and Susanna sat on. At close on five o'clock in the morning, Alexander whispered to Susanna, 'I'll go and tell Jean to get up and come through so that she can say goodbye.'

Susanna looked round at him with large, tragic eyes, then turned back to the bed and leaned forward to take Robert in her arms and lay her cheek against his. When Alexander came back he saw the poet had lost his fight for life. Susanna was still lying against him, arms around him, her tears wetting his face.

Alexander pulled her away and led her outside. She was weeping helplessly, her beautiful poem echoing in her mind, the loving tenderness of it melting away all her fears.

> Lang hae we parted been,
> Lassie, my dearie;
> Now we are met again,
> Lassie, lie near me.
>
> A' that I hae endur'd,
> Lassie, my dearie,
> Here in thy arms is cur'd –
> Lassie, lie near me.

Alexander was beyond weeping. He had suddenly realised that although Robert Burns the man had gone, his words would live on with everyone, forever.

> And for auld lang syne, my jo,
> For auld lang syne,
> We'll tak a cup o' kindness yet,
> For auld lang syne . . .